THE CHILDREN OF VENUS

"All things must come to a balance or be consumed by the other, this rule is true on all planes of existence."

—Persephone, Overseer of Earth

Copyright © 2022 Hayley Nuttall

The Children of Venus
First edition ISBN: 979-8-9864688-0-8
E-book edition ISBN: 979-8-9864688-1-5

All rights reserved
Published by Cleere House Press LLC
www.hbnuttallwriting.com
First edition: August 2022
Published in the United States of America
Cover design 2022 by Hayley Nuttall

THE CHILDREN OF VENUS

H.B. NUTTALL

Dedication

To my dad, who taught me to the look and wonder at the stars.

To my baby sister, in which this book wouldn't exist without her.

To my little sister, who always believed in me.

To my husband, who showed me that there is more to reality than the physical dimensions we mere humans perceive.

Table of Contents

Part I: Descensu

Space is cold.
Space is infinite.
And it is far from empty.

It's within the infinite cold the mind wanders to non-existent corners. It folds and envelopes time, tearing light from gravity and creating giants that stop the heart upon sites never to be seen.

It is beautiful—*it is deadly*.

Chapter 1: The Space Archeologist

Marshall Wilson quit his job.

He signed the ruinous termination paperwork, severing himself from the university.

What would his colleagues think? Would his students care about his disappearance? It didn't matter; this wasn't the first time he'd left a job impulsively.

The university's human resources manager trembled as she handed him the paperwork already approved and notarized.

He read them over. She pretended to organize loose documents. All the while she kept peeking over his shoulder, giving uneasy looks at the person who stood in his shadow, observing his actions.

Wilson signed the final page and handed them over.

"A wise decision Dr. Wilson," the heavy voice behind him said, "at SIC, we take care of our own."

He swallowed the bitter bile taste in his mouth. He didn't want to think of how the Space Intelligence Corporation persuaded him to go this far, to leave his stable university career for them. He never imagined his day would end like this.

It certainly didn't begin that way.

*   *   *

Wilson awoke that morning thinking about the hospice again.

Fifteen years, he thought. It's been fifteen years today.

He tried to avoid it. But the visions still followed him in his isolated commute to the university. He could still smell the room's artificial cotton scent and hear soft Chopin playing; *her* favorite. He squeezed the steering wheel, remembering the feel of her weak grip within his hand.

Marshall, the memory of her parched lips barely parted as they spoke, only a whisper of her voice escaping. *Don't let me—*

His fingers combed through his prematurely graying hair as he pushed the memory to the back of his mind. It didn't help that his beaten-down car's air conditioning broke again in the Florida sauna. By the time he parked in his usual spot outside the humanities building, his hair was greased and his collared shirt had blotched armpit stains.

He did his routine check in the rear-view mirror.

Good, he thought. *At least I didn't forget to shave again.*

And that was when he saw them.

Peering into the mirror he looked at the building behind him. Waiting at the entrance were two people: one woman and one man. Both had hair slicked back and wore the recognizable SIC uniforms: white corporate suits with gold stitching on the shoulder that formed the famous comet insignia. A gold ball shooting from a tail that molded the words *Space Intelligence Corporation*.

SIC recruiters.

It wasn't unusual to see them around the campus recruiting and offering internships to prospective students. But it was unusual for them to be anywhere in proximity to the humanities building, a place with the least amount of foot traffic.

Wilson grabbed his antique briefcase and left the car. As he approached the building, he felt that uncomfortable prickle on the back of his neck. The SIC recruiters watched him from behind gold sunglasses.

They're scanning me, he thought distastefully, imagining the augmented reality tech cleverly hidden within their opaque glasses. He didn't like it when people hid their faces; made it hard to read them. Even in his lecture hall, he had students remove things that covered their faces, including any AR tech required by other professors. Old-fashioned? *No*, he told himself. *Cautious*.

He gave a polite nod as he passed them to enter the building. They ignored the nod, though their heads continued to follow him as he went through the double glass doors.

* * *

The dim lecture hall lights flickered from lack of maintenance. The smell of hidden mold overpowered Wilson's senses but soon faded as familiarity desensitized them. A handful of university students trying to fill a humanities credit sat with grim expressions. They yawned as he lectured, some playing silent games on handheld viewing pads.

"We often make a critical mistake when evaluating our ancient ancestors," he said to the stoic crowd. Behind him, a screen projected images of Hellenistic people and buildings. "Because we are graced with innovative technology, we view ourselves far superior. Take a good look. Are we so dependent on our technology that we're rendered helpless without it?"

Offended expressions filled the room as students leaned in to whisper, murmurs echoing.

"Take Socrates for instance," Wilson continued. "He looked down on students reading as opposed to memorizing. He believed if his students read too much, they'd rely on information being written down for them, and therefore not think for themselves. One could argue that's the same today."

Wilson paused.

They entered; the SIC recruiters.

They stood in the doorway, gold sunglasses still hiding their faces.

"Let me ask," he shook off their gaze, "how much do *you* actually know?" He held up his viewing pad. "If I took away all your assistance to solve a simple math equation, could you do it? In the early days of space exploration, the astronauts of the infamous Apollo 13 mission relied on their minds to solve advanced physics equations. At most, they used an abacus, but it was their intellectual prowess that returned them to Earth."

The SIC pair nodded to one another. The woman even lowered her glasses slightly.

"Well, our hour is up," Wilson said, using the control panel on his podium to turn off the screen behind him. The students followed by logging out of their viewing pads and packing them away. "I expect you all to have your essays submitted by Friday. With the end of the semester coming, I won't be able to grant an extension. See you then."

Students filed out of the hall, wary eyes on the recruiters. As the room emptied, the SIC pair came forward.

"A very good lecture Dr. Wilson," the female recruiter said. Her voice was low and professional, just like all the others that visited the campus. "I especially like how you tied space exploration into a seemingly unrelated topic. We like that."

Wilson packed his briefcase. "Of course you would."

He made a move to leave, but the recruiters blocked his path.

"I have office hours I need to attend to." Wilson made a move to push them aside.

"You have no office hours that students are interested in," the male recruiter said with a heavy voice.

"Shouldn't you be recruiting in the STEM buildings?" Wilson said, irritated.

"Shouldn't you still be working for NASA?" the woman asked. "Space archeologist?"

NASA. *Space archeologist.* It was no secret he once worked for NASA, but only a select few knew his previous passion. His former occupation was long-discredited, and he regretfully distanced himself from it to get this university job.

"All right," he set the briefcase down. "I'm listening."

"There aren't many in your field nowadays," the male recruiter tilted his head. "Could make one invaluable. It'd be nice for you to use that skill set again, wouldn't it?" He paused. "You lost more than a job when you left NASA."

The hospice vision flashed once more across his mind. *Fifteen years.*

Wilson swallowed his breath.

"We can send you where NASA wouldn't," the male recruiter continued.

Wilson thought about it. SIC was always testing new space transports. A routine launch to orbit Earth was more than he could've ever hoped for when he worked for NASA. But did they need a space archeologist for this?

"How do I know you'd follow through?" He made sure not to hide the skepticism in his voice.

"Don't worry doctor," the female recruiter took off her sunglasses, dark eyes intent on Wilson. "You'll see, at SIC we're loyal. We take care of our own."

From there it all blurred together; canceling classes, entering the self-driving SIC vehicle, and arriving at one of their office hubs.

They made him wait in a room void of everything—no windows, no visible vents—the seemingly still air somehow kept cold. The entire ceiling was one light, reflecting off the only furniture present: a chrome table and two chairs.

Wilson sat and checked his watch.

Close to noon. Why keep him waiting? Was it an intimidation trick? He'd come this far, didn't he? Why wait now?

The door finally opened. A woman entered.

"I'm not going to pretend I want you here," she said. She didn't wear a sleek SIC uniform like the recruiters. Instead, she wore informal military apparel, her dark hair, almost black, tied back loosely from her long thin face. "But a job's a job, right?"

Her eyes avoided him, looking through a file she held.

"Um, I guess?" Wilson said.

She looked up from the file, thin lips hard and straight, thick brows furrowed.

"You guess?" She slammed the file onto the table.

"Wow," Wilson leaned back, "are you always this flattering?"

She stared him down, her piercing blue, hooded eyes demanding submission.

"I'm Captain Marie Cocteau," she said, straightening her broad shoulders. "You may call me Captain Cocteau or just captain. I don't care which as long as you address me properly."

"Why does it matter?" Wilson said. "I don't work for you or SIC."

"Well that's good," her harsh grin bared teeth. "Technically, neither do I. "

Wilson crossed his arms. Who was this woman that commanded respect? "Then why are you in a SIC facility?"

Cocteau pulled up a chair, placing its back against the table edge. She swung her leg over the seat and leaned into the backrest informally. "For the same reason you are."

Wilson shook his head. "I don't know why I'm here."

"Really?" Cocteau didn't sound convinced. "How much did the recruiters tell you?"

"Enough to get me in this room."

Silence.

Cocteau was abnormally still.

"Interesting name," Wilson said, trying to break the tension. "French?"

He couldn't tell if she was offended or annoyed.

"If you're asking about the name, yes," Cocteau said. "But me? I'm an American mutt. Though I can't say the same for all our comrades."

"Comrades?" He didn't think anyone could use such an ancient term. He didn't mind.

"You see," she leaned close. "SIC is putting together a mission, a small team with me in the lead. And you're—" she looked at him with a distasteful grin, "—the last one they apparently need."

"Where are we going?"

"Can't tell you," Cocteau inched her file forward. "Here's the deal. You say yes, I show you what's in the folder. The moment you open it, you are bound by confidentiality and officially contracted to the job."

He heard of SIC doing this before; keeping their new project under wraps, not even letting the crew know what they were in for.

"*You* want me for the mission?" By her expression, he didn't believe her like he did the recruiters.

"No," Cocteau said with a hard tone. "SIC wants you for this mission. I don't need another inexperienced lop-head blowing himself up or launching himself into the unknown because he doesn't actually know a damn thing about space. The truth is, I couldn't care less if you decided to show up today. But I don't have a say in this. I'm only here to extend the invitation and persuade you to join my team."

"Well, your methods of persuasion are astounding," Wilson said, not entirely thrilled. If he agreed to this job, he'd be forced to work with this woman, who was about as charming as a hungry Doberman. "I bet you're just a pillar of delight with all your associates."

She almost cracked a smile. "Glad we're off to a good start. So we have a yes?"

"I still don't feel entirely comfortable saying yes to an employer who's already made it clear she thinks I'm an incompetent invalid, just to name one." Wilson scratched his head. "Not to mention you don't work for SIC, which begs the question why the military is interested. Seriously, what do you think?"

"I'm only here out of safety protocol," Cocteau shrugged. "Standard procedure, for the little thing SIC is doing. But I promise you this," she pointed to the ceiling, "you'll get the whole story up there."

"In the ceiling?" He tried to be sarcastic. He didn't want to be a guinea pig for some new space vehicle that malfunctioned before it even left the atmosphere.

She raised her eyebrows. "Aren't you supposed to be some kind of genius, even for a space archeologist?"

She pointed up again and knocked him on the side of the head with her free hand.

"Hey!" He battered her away. "Who do you think you are—"

"Up *there!*" She emphasized.

It dawned on him.

Up *there*. . .

"You mean?" He took a deep breath. This mission was more than a routine orbit launch. It was further, well beyond Earth into the dark abyss. Fantastical images of the cosmos filled his vision as he thought of NASAs broken promises.

And he thought of the hospice again, and *her* final whispers— *You will see me again*. . .

Cocteau nodded with a half-smile. "Yeah, way out there."

Wilson ripped the folder open and began reading its contents.

"Not supposed to tell you where the mission is and I didn't," Cocteau said. "But a little bird told me you wouldn't say no if you had an inkling of where it would be."

Wilson flipped through data sheets filled with meaningless numbers and written reports. He came across photos of a planet, and screenshots of a desolate, molten surface.

"What is SIC doing on Venus?"

"Well, I'll guess you'll find out," Cocteau smirked, "now that you're a member of SIC. Welcome aboard Marshall Wilson, you're a space archeologist again."

Chapter 2: Up There

"A space archeologist?" the old man laughed. "That's one I've never heard of!"

A bald man in his seventies sat next to Wilson, laughing hysterically.

Wilson rolled his eyes. He sat in a SIC transport atop one of the many transportation hubs scattered around the state. He was strapped with all manner of buckles and safety gear wrapped around his head.

The rest of the passenger cabin was lined with rows upon rows of seats like his, all bolted to fiberglass floors, surrounded by geometric chrome designs smoothed into the walls. The smell of rancid oil stung through an artificial flowery scent as SIC employees wiped cleansers over long metal grab rails that jutted out of the floor and ceiling.

"Tell me," the bald man wiped his watery eyes, "what does a space archeologist do exactly?"

"Same thing as a regular archeologist," Wilson said. "Except in space."

"And what might that be?"

"Well," Wilson took a breath. "I study artifacts, structures, and interpret various objects for information about past civilization."

"From space?" The bald man's eyes widened. "You're crazy."

Wilson shifted his head uneasily. "Maybe I am."

No one took his occupation seriously. They didn't actually understand what he did. Studying excavation sites from orbit allowed him to see things you can't on ground level, though it was the probes that entered orbit, never him.

As SIC developed new tech for space travel, people began asking about possibilities of intelligent life in the beyond and what that looked like. Who better to study evidence of possible civilization than those who already did on Earth? The archeologist occupation evolved. At the height of its popularity, space archeologists sent probes to other worlds to do as they did on Earth. None were successful.

If they wanted to keep you, they would've found another position, a memory rang in his head, the voice of a now distant friend. *You know they were just looking for a reason.*

Wilson felt that twinge of anger from years before. How his superiors would churn if they saw him now, employed by SIC.

No use ruminating, he thought. *I do enough of that already.* Instead, he turned his thoughts to three days ago.

He was walking along the beach, Cape Canaveral. It was sunny enough, even though weather predictions said rain. He kicked a crumpled beer can out of his path. The cracking of waves splattered cold droplets on his face, as the wind whipped his hair violently away from his face. He pulled his jet black jacket around him tightly, the ocean air filling his nose and mouth with the taste of salt.

One question stuck to his mind. Should he go?

The once white sand beach was stained, like blood on white silk. Black blotches, surrounded by litter covered the beachside, leftover from drunken midnight gang raves. The beach technically closed at sundown, but no one cared enough to patrol it. At least not anymore. Broken glass made it sparkle a sickly amber, a constant reminder of what was.

Wilson stopped, squinting his eyes across the beach and putting his hand across his forehead to block the sun. He could see the old launch site from here.

"To think," Wilson said to himself. "People used to come from everywhere to see this."

And he had been one of them once before he joined NASA. Sitting on the beach, in the blistering sun, with humidity so thick he could drink the air. But that was how he liked it, and how *she* liked it. Watching her—with her hair flying back just like the ocean waves as they felt the ground rumble from the shuttle launch.

Then SIC happened and NASA stopped launching shuttles. Wilson stopped going to the beach, and stopped watching *her* hair. . . *her smile. . . her eyes. . .*

Too painful. A chill in the air came from behind. He turned as a line of dark clouds approached. He estimated another ten minutes before the storm hit.

He stood, staring at the abandoned launch site in the distance.

"They want me to go," Wilson said to no one in particular. "SIC wants me to go to space. To another world. To Venus. "

He could hear the storm approaching, rain dumping down on the beach, washing away the stains.

His mind was made up, nothing holding him back. "I'll go."

And now he was packed into a SIC transport, waiting to launch.

The bald man coughed.

Wilson loosened his straps and leaned forward. "Are you well enough to travel outside the atmosphere?"

The man waved him off. "Ah, it's nothing. Just my age showing. You know I'm retired."

"That's nice." Wilson leaned back, not wanting to have this conversation.

"Retired," the man said proudly. "And now I'm going to be a SIC member. Honorary, of course."

"Yeah," Wilson said, closing his eyes. "And how much did you have to pay to be honorary."

"Humph," the man sneered. "Well, if you're going to be like that."

"Like what?" A stern voice said. Captain Cocteau was on board. Wilson opened his eyes to see her, dressed down in black and white camo, fists on her hips.

"Is he bothering you?" Cocteau gestured at Wilson, giving him a warning look.

"Lady, he's being a pain-in-the-ass," the man emphasized each word.

Cocteau cracked a smile. "Let me know if he continues being one." She turned to a group of people boarding from the outside platform, carrying hot, moist air with them.

"Alright people, let's get strapped in," Cocteau clapped her hands. "We've got a schedule to keep."

"We're in no hurry dear," a hunched woman with a frail voice said.

Cocteau looked like someone had drowned a puppy at being referred to as 'dear.'

"Please excuse my mother," another woman with a bun said, putting her arm over the hunched one.

Then Wilson realized it. The man next to him, everyone entering the transport; no one was a day under sixty.

"Um, Cocteau?" Wilson watched SIC employees strap the aged passengers in. "What kind of transport is this?"

Cocteau's eyes shot fire at Wilson. "It's captain to you. And what did you expect, a luxury liner?"

"What are *they* doing here?" Wilson gestured to the elderly passengers. "Half of them look like they'll drop once we hit the g-force."

"Oh my god," Cocteau hovered over him. "You want to get us kicked-off?" she hissed. "Who do you think pays for all this?"

Wilson looked at the man next to him, already sound asleep.

"Yes," Cocteau said. "Honorary members. You and I both know what that means. And SIC is going to utilize any transport that others are paying for. Part of my job is keeping this transport running, which means keeping the top dollar happy. And honestly, I don't think either of us is very good at that, so don't push it. Keep quiet and behave until we get to the moon orbiter. Am I clear?"

Cocteau did not break eye contact. It was evident that she was someone who was not afraid of confrontation, and Wilson did not want to push his luck. They had a long trip ahead and he wasn't in the mood for interactions with anyone, especially Cocteau.

"You are as glass," he said. "We have an understanding."

Cocteau stood straight. "Good."

She disappeared into the flight deck as the rest of the SIC crew finished strapping down their highest-paying customers.

"Alright everyone," Cocteau's voice sounded over the graveled intercom. "Let's make sure we're all strapped correctly. This transport's a rough ride till we reach our connection at the moon orbiter. Don't worry; those of you who are joining us for the final destination will enjoy a much smoother journey after the transfer. If you have not and are interested in upgrading your package to the 'Venus Viewing Experience', speak to one of the helpful SIC crew members. You'll know them by their gold insignias. Please take the time to listen to our safety instructions, and enjoy the SIC experience. Ah, yes, and I highly recommend any and all supplements offered to you today."

Wilson mentally prepared himself as multiple SIC employees dressed in white suits spread through the cabin, reviewing safety measures of the transport. He had been in enough simulators to know what happened next.

Two more crew members emerged, both women. A young women carried a silver platter of cerulean pills, the other a platter of water cups, enough for a sip or two. They began administering them to the passengers.

The young woman presented a pill to Wilson.

"Ah-ha, no thanks," Wilson said, raising his eyebrows. "I'd rather keep my mind intact."

"Um—" The young woman looked to the older one carrying the water. Her supervisor maybe? The supervisor nodded her head and Wilson was passed.

The pill—the new drug it was called—the new reality.

In a fast-paced world, anxiety ran high and morale ran low. And then came the pill, a savior to the fatherless and unaccountable. Slowing all body reactions and blocking neuropathways, complete relaxation came to those who desired it. But as with all miracle drugs, the pill was abused and lost its way among the needy and found its place among the wanting. And as time passed, it was rarely seen.

Then it became the solution. SIC, with their first transports, could only take passengers with optimum health through the atmosphere. Weakened immune systems and the promise of heart failure spelled out lawsuits from the most affluent patrons. Not profitable. To ensure their safety, SIC utilized the pill.

Many of the retirees' eyes dropped, drowsy from their dosage.

Wilson knew the thrill of the G-force would be too much for those compromised. Although his bias to the pill made him wary, he knew it preserved their lives.

All the SIC crew members disappeared.

"Doors sealing," a pleasant voice spoke through invisible speakers around them.

All the doors to the transport snapped shut. Electronic pulses sounded as Wilson heard the familiar pull of the doors sealing and the cabin pressurizing.

"T-minus nine minutes," Cocteau's voice said over the intercom. "Means we'll be on hold for about forty-five minutes folks."

She continued repeating information on the current weather forecast and other safety protocols.

T-minus didn't reflect real-time. They were checkpoints that had to be met before lift-off. Mission control could start and stop the clock for as long as they needed to complete the necessary steps in each checkpoint.

There was no reason for Cocteau to repeat all that information to them. After all, they were just the passengers, and most were asleep. Wilson knew though, that SIC required its people to give the full experience to their customers to avoid further litigation. Heaven forbid if all information was not relayed to them in their unconscious state.

"T-minus seven minutes and thirty seconds," Cocteau sounded again.

Had forty-five minutes passed already? At this checkpoint, there was no going back. Back in the early days of NASA, this was the point when the scaffolding path allowing people to board was retracted. Now, with transports parked neatly atop towering SIC hubs, it was only a formality. No going back once seven minutes and thirty seconds hit.

"T-minus five minutes."

The rumble of the transport's engines sounded. Pressure and blood rushed to Wilson's head. He looked across the line of unconscious passengers, to the round window across from him. The world outside turned as the transport tilted into take-off position.

"T-minus 2 minutes."

The checkpoints were coming quicker. His seat vibrated beneath him. Wilson felt cold.

"T-minus 31 seconds."

Outside the sun was bright. Its rays shined through the window, across his face. He squinted as it warmed his cheeks.

"T-minus 16 seconds," Cocteau sounded. "Water system activated."

They needed water to cool and protect the transport. Otherwise, the acoustical power behind the engines would shake it apart. Before Wilson left NASA, they had been working on alternative methods of protecting the shuttles. The project was quickly shut down when SIC formed a new plastic-metal alloy that absorbed sound efficiently, only requiring a third of the amount of water a shuttle did.

"T-minus 6 seconds," Cocteau's voice seemed an echo as Wilson gazed at the light of Earth's sun.

It was too quick.

"I'm not ready," Wilson said. "I'm not *ready*."

No one listened.

"T-minus 5-4-3-2-1," Cocteau's voice was fast and loud over all the noise. "Final engines running and rocket boosters ignited."

And the wind was knocked from Wilson.

Like a weight being pressed against his head, neck, and chest, the g-force of lift-off pinned him to his seat, securing him in place. His feet felt as though cement had dried them in place. He could no longer feel the strength of his safety straps.

It hurt to keep his head turned, looking out the window across the row of seats, but Wilson fought it. His neck would be unforgiving later, but he had to see. No artificial screens of a simulator could compare to his window. The sky was rushing away fast—faster— *faster!*

His neck gave out. His head was pinned back, the safety cushions of his seat protecting him from a concussion. Even though he couldn't turn his head, he strained his eyes to look.

From the corner of his eye, he could see the world changing. The sky no longer azure, but darkening and disappearing. The world—his world—he'd always known, was departing. He was leaving it behind.

A sudden fear entered Wilson's heart as the world outside turned to nothing. A fear that made him want to see his Earth one last time, and the apprehensive thought: *What if I don't?*

Chapter 3: Moon Orbiter

Sit tight folks," Cocteau's voice sounded throughout the transport. "We're through the atmosphere. We'll arrive at Moon Orbiter Armstrong by 2100 hours. Once we're in the safe zone, you can release your safety straps and float around."

There was nothing like Wilson was feeling. Water training only went so far to simulate weightlessness.

He put his hand over his head. The ends of his hair brushed against his palm, floating on end. He smiled.

He looked out the small window. No clouds, no atmosphere—no Earth.

"Stars," he gasped.

He'd never seen so many. They seemed endless, layer upon layer of pinpricks of lights, some swirling and clustered together, others scattered across the dark abyss; the eternal lights.

A lock of hair fanned in front of the window. An unconscious woman's head bobbed, her long, light hair coming loose and spreading, blocking his view of the outside.

Wilson became aware of everyone else in the cabin. Most were still fast asleep, but some were waking and drowsy. Even with the straps, everyone seemed to float. Arms flailed inches above armrests, hair stood on end, shoelaces and necklaces—even though they were warned to remove jewelry—hovered as though they were possessed.

A loose, gold watch wobbled on an unconscious man's arm near the front of the cabin. It made its way up his wrist, over his hand, slipping right from his fingers.

Wilson laughed. What a sight all this was. He reached down, grabbing the emergency release cord that would let his safety straps free.

The bald man next to him suddenly gained consciousness, his eyes blinking slowly as they awoke.

He glanced at Wilson pulling on on the release cord. "I don't think you're supposed to do that." He sounded lethargic. "They'll get mad."

Wilson smirked defiantly. "Let them."

Wilson's straps came loose and he unbuckled himself. He pushed up from his seat.

Wilson always had the impression that floating in space was like floating in water. He knew it wasn't, but whenever he imagined it, that was what he felt.

The sensation was nothing of the sort. In water, one can tread and move along by creating friction with arms and legs. There is no friction or force to push against in space, so he just floated. He twisted so he could reach the ceiling and gripped one of the grab rails. He pushed off again in the direction of the watch.

"What is he doing? You're not supposed to do that!" Murmurs flooded the cabin as people awoke from their artificial slumber.

Wilson continued forward, pulling himself along, letting the absence of gravity take over

"Almost," Wilson said, when he reached the front of the cabin. He held the grab rail with one hand and reached for the watch floating inches from his fingers.

"Getting a little ahead of yourself there," Cocteau appeared in the flight deck entrance, holding herself in place .

Wilson pushed forward and grabbed the watch. "Someone lost something."

The man who had lost the watch stirred. He looked down at his wrist and looked frantically around the cabin.

Cocteau dragged herself along the grab rail from the flight deck to Wilson. She reached her hand out.

"It's okay," Wilson let the watch float in his hand. "I got this."

Wilson pushed off the ceiling down to the man.

"I believe you lost this," Wilson held the floating watch with two fingers in front of the man.

"Oh yes," the man fumbled. "Thanks. I remembered to tie my glasses on, you'd think I'd remember to tighten this."

He took back the watch.

"Keep an eye on that," Wilson said. "Looks expensive. You wouldn't want SIC to repossess the gold for wiring repairs. They'd probably make you buy it back."

The watch-man looked confused.

Wilson kicked off the floor and floated back to Cocteau.

"You're a real smart-ass, you know?" Cocteau crossed her arms.

"What?" Wilson unclasped a pen from his pocket and dangled it in the air. "They do use gold wiring in these transports. Hey, if I break this open will the ink splatter, or bead? I know the answer, but do you?"

Cocteau snatched the pen. "No loose articles in passenger possession while we're in zero gravity."

"That was my best pen."

"Stop acting like a child," Cocteau shoved Wilson away. "Go back to your seat. No wandering while outside of the safe zone."

"You care about my safety?" Wilson jested. "Gee, thanks."

"No," Cocteau's face turned red. "I have this little light that flashes when an idiot pulls their emergency cord outside of the safe zone. And I can't concentrate with that damn light constantly flashing in my face."

"Okay, okay," Wilson said. "You don't have to get so mad."

"Oh, this isn't mad," Cocteau brushed floating hairs out of her face. "You'll know mad. Don't make me come out again."

She pushed off the grab rail and disappeared back into the flight deck.

Wilson floated back into his seat and hovered over the safety straps. He buckled and tightened his straps enough so that any signifiers to the flight deck would turn off and he could continue his escapades around the cabin.

The bald man watched him. "Are you sure you want to do that? She seemed pretty adamant."

"I know," Wilson said. "Believe me, all that stuff about the safety zone is a load of crap. We're fine, I promise you; I'm the one with a science degree. That military meathead's not going to care as long as the system doesn't know. You want me to let you loose? I can do the same thing to your seat so it won't signal them upfront."

The bald man laughed. "You know, you were kind of a jerk earlier—still are—but I think we're going to get along just fine from here on out."

*　*　*

The small light above each passenger turned green, signaling that they were in the safe zone.

They cruised steadily to the moon, although Wilson felt no difference between cruising speed and post-liftoff.

Most passengers were content to just stay where they were. Some of the more enthusiastic passengers took advantage of the situation and released themselves from their seats.

Wilson stuck to the center of the cabin, being able to look out all the windows from that point.

SIC attendants eventually emerged, pulling along the grab rails and doing an airless dance as they approached each passenger. "Enjoy your refreshment," the attendants said with dazzling smiles. Bags of beverages were strung along their arms, and they would tear them free whenever a customer requested one.

Wilson was wary of their smiles. Most of the time a smile was a mask of true intentions. He avoided asking for water until his sandpaper mouth could take it no longer.

"Um, excuse me," he called. Cool recycled air blew in his face, as he licked chapped lips.

An attendant approached. She wore a tight , ivory SIC uniform, pants replaced by short skirts.

What a stupid uniform for anti-gravity, Wilson thought, knowing very well what some of the more perverted passengers were thinking and watching as she floated by. *SIC thinks of everything, don't they?*

"Refreshment?" The attendant pulled a bag from her arm. It read eighty-six proof of something. A concoction that probably included scotch, gin, or whiskey, and a mystery ingredient of SICs own making.

"Just water, please."

"If you wish." She clipped the string holding a water bag and handed it to Wilson. She smiled. "Enjoy your refreshment."

"Um yeah, sure," Wilson said, now wishing he had taken the eighty-six proof as she floated away. He twisted and broke the cap. The nozzle was designed to not allow any liquid escape unless sucked out by the drinker.

"Hey, Mr. space archaeologist," Wilson's bald seat neighbor called from behind him. "Watch this."

The bald man sucked from whatever drink he had in his hand. He released a clear glob from his mouth.

An attendant suddenly backed right into the glob of liquid. It shattered into smaller beads, engulfing the attendant. She kicked off with her foot from a nearby armrest, throwing them dirty looks as she floated away.

"Finally," Wilson said, feeling relieved. "One of them broke character."

The attendant returned with a bag and tube that vacuumed the beads of liquid from the air, still giving the occasional *'you better not try that again'* stare.

The initial novelty of no gravity wore off soon and people strapped themselves back in their seats. Time stretched on, hours feeling longer and longer. Snores filled the cabin as they all napped.

All except Wilson. He just wanted to float above everything, lying back.

It's what you've always wanted, her distant voice echoed to him, the woman always on the back of his mind. *You should do this.*

No, his memory answered back. Not with such little time left for us. I want to spend it all with you. A husband should stay by his wife to the end.

You know they won't ask again, she echoed. *I'm only holding you back.*

You could never do that.

Wilson closed his eyes and he was suddenly back at NASA, fifteen years earlier. He was sitting in a colleague's office, Timothy Newton, a physicist and administrator for NASA.

"Marshall you know how it is," Timothy said. "With the government outsourcing to private companies, this may be the last time we send people up. *No,* it will be the last time."

"I know," Wilson sat at Timothy's desk, his head down and his fists pressed against his temples.

"Then why?" Timothy said.

Wilson lifted his head. "I just can't go."

Timothy shook his head, rubbing his fingers on his temples. "Marshall, I know you want this more than anything. We paid for your training and I put in the good word as you wanted. The board said yes. And now you're saying no? Do you have any idea how that makes me look?"

Wilson stood. "How *you* look?"

Timothy put his hands in his pockets. "Come on, I didn't mean it like that."

"Do you have any idea what I've been through the past year?"

"Marshall—"

"Just don't," Wilson stood and made for the door. He stopped. "If you think that going up to space, is what I want more than anything, then you don't know me at all."

"You can't go on being a space archeologist," Timothy said. "Everyone knows it's a joke. Can't make any promises, but if you reject this mission, the only way you can go up is with one of those trashy space corporations."

Wilson knew what he was saying. If he walked out with a no to this mission, then his position would swiftly become obsolete.

He gave his defiant smirk as he grabbed the door handle. "Wouldn't want to work for those assholes anyway."

Beep—beep—beep.

Wilson's eyes flew open to the present as a green lights flashed and an alarm sounded through the cabin.

"Alright, guys," Cocteau's voice came over the sound system. "That's the signal. We're preparing to port so you will need to stay seated and strapped for the remainder of the transfer."

Attendants helped a couple to their seats as Wilson pushed from the wall back to his.

"Here sir, let me help with that," an attendant reached for one of Wilson's straps.

"*No,*" Wilson said a little too harshly, his mind was still encompassed by the memories of Timothy's NASA office.

"Humph," the attendant moved along checking everyone else's seats.

"Almost there," his bald seat neighbor was excited. "Honorary SIC." He gave a friendly punch on Wilson's knee.

"Please don't do that," Wilson shifted his leg over.

"Oh, sorry, don't mind me," the man said. "I forget you've got boundaries."

"Yeah, boundaries," Wilson swallowed. "Good way to put it."

The room darkened, all power being sourced to docking. Red, blue, and green lights flashed at different intervals, signaling procedures.

Looking out, Wilson could see glimpses of the metal walls of the moon orbiter— a SIC space station for tourists. It was in orbit above a dark gray terrain, covered in patterns of craters. The moon's surface.

A sudden jolt and everything dropped. Lights came back on and Wilson felt his weight return, pushing him into his seat.

"Gravity reestablished," a pleasant voice echoed. "Please await further exit instructions."

"Ha," Wilson shook his head.

"What?" the bald man said.

"You can't re-establish gravity," Wilson said. "you can simulate gravity, but you cannot make it. This moon orbiter must have a gravity simulator, but it doesn't make real gravity. You just feel like there's gravity from the centrifugal force of the generator. The advanced simulators do help with muscle atrophy, but it doesn't stop it; just slows it so you can spend longer in space."

The man blinked. "I ain't understanding a single word you just said."

Wilson sighed. "It's just not real gravity."

The bald man laughed. "Hey, if it looks like a duck, good enough for me."

"Looks are deceiving," Wilson nestled into his seat.

They waited.

Attendants helped the aged from their seats, escorting them to an entrance now open to a containment center that sanitized them before entering the moon orbiter. Wilson was forced to keep sitting while the paying customers exited the transport first.

"Well, the moon is my final stop," the bald man said as an attendant helped him up. "Not much to see going further from here."

"Sorry to hear that," Wilson said, but also feeling relieved he no longer had obligation to anyone but his solitude.

The man eyed him. "No, you're not. And I don't suppose you're much for names; ain't going to do us much good anyway." He paused. "I hope you find what you're looking for."

The bald man was guided out of the transport.

Wilson unstrapped himself to find Cocteau standing, arms crossed, staring him down like a hungry dog.

"Do you need something?" Wilson said coolly.

"Just keep your mouth shut next time." She glared "Come on, we've got a lot of briefing to do before the Venus transfer tomorrow."

* * *

Wilson relaxed on a tightly strung hammock. The living quarters were lined with them, anti-gravity straps hanging from the edges for night cycles.

Fortunately, his hammock was nearest to the hexagonal window that filled part of the quarters. The grilles were thick as beams, holding each pane of aluminum silicate glass steadily. It was currently pointed at Earth. He knew it would only be for a few minutes, but still, he marveled at the white and blue marble below.

He was the only one in the quarters right now, and he liked it that way. Being alone meant he could think.

It also meant he didn't have to be close to anyone.

Like steam from a kettle, the sound of the room hatch depressurizing caught his attention.

"Hard to find solitude on a station, but it seems you did." Cocteau entered and closed the hatch behind her.

"You have a gift for me?" Wilson said, eyeing the thick manilla folder Cocteau carried under her arm. "Unless that's yours, but you don't seem the reading type."

Cocteau didn't change her expression as she threw the heavy file onto his lap. Wilson sat up, brushing his fingers across the confidential seal along the opening.

"Am I agreeing to anything if I open this file?"

"Not this time," Cocteau said. "You already did that on Earth."

Wilson broke the security seal, weighing how much work he had ahead of him. He pulled out a schematic of the geographic surface of Venus.

"There's a lot here," he said, flipping through other data sheets. "You couldn't have sent this digitally?"

"SIC expects the data memorized by the time we arrive at the final destination." Cocteau put a hand on her hip. "And hard copy means no hackers can get it. Scared yet?"

Wilson continued flipping through the data documents, including one that recorded an abnormally large radiation fluctuation from the Venusian surface. "I wouldn't be a space

archeologist if I feared the unknown. What exactly am I looking for Captain?"

"You're supposed to be the genius here," Cocteau said. "You tell me. It's not like they tell me much of anything."

"Hmm," Wilson scanned the charts. Most of them were average with random numbers going off every so often. "This is just some— interesting data."

"Interesting?" Cocteau snorted. "SIC doesn't send for people for just interesting. Study up on that while you can; we're going into a night cycle soon."

Wilson knew what that meant: artificial gravity off.

The night cycles on the moon orbiter did not match the night cycles of Earth, but that wasn't the point. It was about conserving energy. To keep the station running at optimum efficiency, it utilized solar energy from the sun. SIC created an artificial calendar, or as NASA joked, moon time to keep track when the station went on minimal power to conserve and recharge.

It needed approximately 6.89 hours to charge to run an eighteen hour day cycle. Meaning that a full cycle on the moon orbiter was twenty-four hours and fifty-three minutes. Earth's time is rounded up to twenty-four hours from its twenty-three hours and fifty-six minute rotation, making a full cycle on the moon orbiter approximately one hour longer than an Earth cycle. Those who worked on the moon orbiter gained an extra seven hours for every week they stayed on the station, but lost hours when they eventually returned to Earth for leave.

And it gave Wilson the worst space lag of a lifetime, the illusion of time. What awaited him at Venus station?

"Hopefully, I'll get through this," Wilson pulled out a photo of Venus. He felt both curious and worried about the disconnect in so much information. "There's a lot, even at a glance, that doesn't make sense."

"It will," Cocteau said. "More will be explained at the Venus station when you meet the other experts."

"You sound like you know a lot more than you're letting on."

"Believe it or not,"Cocteau crossed her arms, "I did go to school for planetary science,"

"What kind of degree?" Wilson raised an eyebrow. Did she hear what he said earlier on the transport about his science degree?

Cocteau's face went sour. "All you academics are the same. As long as you've got a paper that says Ph.D., it doesn't matter what anyone else knows."

She did hear.

"I didn't mean—"

"I know what you meant," Cocteau barked. "Military 'meathead' ordering you about, yeah I get it. Just read up genius and be ready for tomorrow. It's going to be a long ride and we've only got two tourists to keep us company on the trip. Which honestly, is not enough to keep you occupied and out of my hair."

Cocteau depressurized the hatch and marched out of the room.

"Can't say anything right can I?" Wilson said, sitting back with the folder.

He knew he blew it with her, assuming she was all brawn and no brain. Getting along with Cocteau was a lost cause. Maybe if he treated her differently, they would be doing better at this point.

"She's the one who really recruited me," he said to himself. He watched the slim view of Earth disappear. "In all honesty, I'm not exactly easy to get along with either."

Maybe they do have something in common.

He set the folder aside. The view of earth was gone and only darkness remained; the unforgiving abyss like a deep ocean, flecked with stars too distant to know his existence.

Don't let me be the end of your life, her distant voice echoed again, his late marital companion. He remembered her hair. . .

Her face. . .

Her voice. . .

You will see me again, Her final words to him. *When you least expect it.*

"If only I could see you," Wilson said, imagining himself at her side again. "But I know where you're buried, and I'm never going to see you again."

Chapter 4: The Artifact

The journey to Venus station wasn't as simple as the one to the moon orbiter.

It would be days before they reached Venus and this transport was built for it. More luxurious than the moon transfer, SIC gave everything to bidders who paid the highest for this venture. With its own gravity generator, passengers could wander as they pleased through hotel-like quarters.

'*Goddess of beauty, Earth's twin*' sparkled along the corridors. Images of Aphrodite painted in Italian renaissance style were plastered everywhere. She beckoned wooing mortals, drawing them to her golden planet.

Sleeping quarters were also themed thus, and it made Wilson sick. The goddess of love constantly baring down at him served only as a reminder of the thing he no longer had.

The pressure of the oncoming mission also loomed over him. He studied the confidential files from Cocteau and nothing made sense. He was left with only a promise that all would be explained once they arrived at the Venus station. He questioned if his own curiosity would be enough motivation to continue reading through the dull data.

He often peered out the observation deck to watch their approach to the yellow planet. Each day it grew bigger. Venus become more than just a dot of a star, but something sizable and tangible. When its size grew to titan quality their approach became evident, and docking day arrived.

"Oh I am just so excited, nervous too," an obese, female retiree said. She stood in front of Wilson as they waited in the sanitation chamber. Ultra violet lights dimmed on and off and strange odors sprayed around them. They were promised that whatever was sprayed was not harmful to them, but Wilson still held his breath.

The woman clutched her husband's shoulder as she looked behind at Wilson. "Be sure to stack my bags in the proper order will you?"

Wilson fumed. "Lady, I've told you time and again, I am not your bell boy."

"You do work for SIC don't you?" The woman lifted her nose.

"Yes, but—"

"Then do your job young man," she furrowed her brow.

"I'm flattered you think I'm young."

"You haven't done a single thing I've asked this entire trip," she scowled. "I have a good mind to report you." She tugged her husband's arm. "Harold, report him will you? We paid more than our fair share for this trip and our honorary membership, and I expect compensation for his, well, demeanor."

"You do that." Wilson smirked. He should've told her that he was employed by SIC for scientific research—not customer service—but he took a small delight in hearing her requests and promptly ignoring them.

"Uh," she pursed her lips.

Red and green lights flashed with an alarm. Suddenly, pressure sounded and the opening before them cleared.

"Oh, this is exciting!" the woman giggled. "I'm just so excited."

"How excited are you again?" Wilson asked sarcastically.

The woman turned and glared at Wilson just before a female SIC escort entered the opening. She wore a gold bodysuit, the SIC insignia outlined on her shoulders.

"Right this way Mr. and Mrs. Smithson," the escort said, gesturing to the couple.

"Enjoy your stay Mr. and Mrs. Billion Bucks," Wilson waved as they left. The couple did not look back at him.

"Ouch!" Wilson felt a thump on the back of his head.

"Do you know how much you cost SIC?" Cocteau stepped in front of him. "Not that I mind pulling at SICs pockets— they're deep enough—but we're here to do a job. Not mess with people."

"I get it," Wilson said.

"Sure you do," Cocteau barked. "That's why you keep heckling the patrons."

"Okay, okay," Wilson shook his head. "You don't have to be so hands on you know. Are you ever not angry?"

Cocteau said nothing as she turned.

"Follow me," she motioned for him to come. "And move fast, we're already running behind schedule."

Wilson took a breath as they stepped onto the station.

The Venus transport was luxurious in a classical way, but this station was more.

High ceilings, walls and floors shined with modern chrome. A colossal sculpture of the goddess of beauty breathing life into model planets floated above them. A sweet scent filled the atmosphere from an unknown source, and hidden vents blew comfortable temperate air. Wide windows surrounded them, showcasing the stormy yellow planet below.

Wilson stopped, reading the words etched into one of the showcase windows. *'Come children of love and life, bask in my beauty, pleasure, and passion.'*

"This way," Cocteau ordered ahead of him. "This place is for tourists. We've got better things to do."

They passed a service counter, and Wilson glanced at the retired couple being checked-in by their escort.

"See, I told you he wouldn't lift a finger," the woman pointed at Wilson as he passed them. "He doesn't even have our bags!"

"Over here." Cocteau stopped in front of a service door beyond the counter. She dialed into a touchpad.

"Retinal verification please," a pleasant voice sounded through the door.

Cocteau held her face still, staring at the door until a musical trill sounded.

"Thank you," the pleasant voice said. "Voice verification please."

"Captain Marie Cocteau," Cocteau said carefully. "And one guest."

"Thank you," pressure sounded and the door clicked. "Welcome back to Venus station Captain."

"Yeah yeah," Cocteau said, shoving the door open. "These SIC AI's. . . " Cocteau mumbled into a trail of profanities as they entered.

The employee corridors were just that—for employees. Unlike the tourist center the ceiling was low and the halls narrow, though they still retained the chrome color scheme. There were no windows except for small round ones every so often.

Cocteau walked too fast for Wilson to stop and look at the planet. He felt goosebumps emerge as the temperature dropped.

"Employee service corridors conserve energy," Cocteau explained as they walked. "Makes up for the cost of the showcase side of the station."

"It's a little cold don't you think?" Wilson shivered.

"Space is cold," Cocteau said. "Get used to it."

They turned a corner, stopping in front of a door that read *'Command Control'*. Cocteau held her hand on a fingerprint pad and the door gave a loud click as it unlocked.

They entered.

The view in the command room stopped Wilson in his tracks.

The entire wall in front of him was filled with the yellow planet, a long window peering to the world below. SIC operators in headsets and white uniforms bustled between computers and operation counters, not even taking notice of the extensive site before them.

"Ah, Captain, you're back."

Wilson so mesmerized by the planet didn't notice Cocteau standing to order as man in uniform approached them. He too wore the signature SIC white, but his uniform was decorated with gold pins, showing a rank Wilson was unfamiliar with. He adjusted a military style cap, although it had no markings of any military Wilson knew of.

"A pleasure sir," Cocteau said. "I'm here with Dr. Marshall Wilson, the space archeologist from NASA."

The man's smile was aged. He scanned Wilson with his pale eyes set beneath thick gray brows.

"Admiral Matthew Jones," he said offering his hand to Wilson.

"Dr. Wilson," Wilson said as they shook. "Though Captain Cocteau is mistaken; I haven't worked for NASA for years."

"That's good to know," Jones said, throwing a glance at Cocteau. "We've had enough government interference as is already."

"Um, Admiral?" Wilson said baffled. "May I ask Admiral of what?"

"Oh, my title can be confusing," Jones said. "I'm not a military admiral. SIC has their own program and rankings within that program for those that run space operations. Kind of like how police have their own rankings separate from the military. Or like those ancient White Star liners. See, I know a little history."

"I understand," Wilson said.

"Good," Jones smiled. "I'm sorry to cut this meeting short, but I have to greet our new guests now that they're settled. Can't keep the cash flow waiting."

Wilson couldn't tell if Jones was joking.

"Sir," Cocteau held up a hand. "Someone was supposed to escort Wilson to his living quarters."

"You know this station," Jones said. "Why not guide our newest employee to the lab? We are a little behind. I believe that is next on the agenda anyway. I'll meet you there when I'm finished with our guests. If you'll excuse me."

Jones left for the service corridor.

"Great, I've been degraded to your babysitter," Cocteau huffed. "Lab is right over here."

Wilson followed Cocteau through a side door.

The room they entered was an extension of the command room with the windowed wall hovering over the planet. The floors and walls were tiled white with bright fluorescents shining on cabinets and counters. A long table filled with rock samples stood in the center of the room.

A woman with thick braided curls and wearing a white lab coat stood over a microscope, taking no notice of them.

"Hem-hem," Cocteau coughed.

The woman looked up. "Captain, you're here." She spoke with a thick Haitian accent.

"Yeah, yeah," Cocteau said. "I've got your archeologist, Gomez. We're just waiting on the admiral. We can get the meeting started because apparently we're a 'little behind'."

"I see," the Haitian woman approached Wilson.

He held our his hand. "Dr. Marshall Wilson."

Her dark, steady eyes looked into his, unblinking yet friendly. "Dr. Arianna Gomez." She spoke precisely with every word as she shook his hand. "Geologist and planetary rock studies. It's good to finally meet you."

Wilson looked at Cocteau from the corner of his eye; she crossed her arms.

"Well, this is all very new to me," Wilson said. "I've never been in space before, Dr. Gomez."

"Please," she smiled a calm, sweet smile. "Are we not colleagues? Arianna."

"Marshall," Wilson said, reciprocating the gesture.

Cocteau made a sound that was between a growl and a gurgle.

"Um, problem?" Wilson asked.

"You brainiacs and first names," Cocteau. "Get over the formalities and get to the point. We're burning daylight and we've got a lot to cover. Right *Gomez?*"

Most people would've been offended by Cocteau's direct nature, but Gomez simply blinked and gestured for them to follow. "Of course, right this way."

She brought them to the lab table. Its surface glowed with white light, highlighting the varying rock samples. Petri dishes of dust surrounded a disc-like artifact as the centerpiece.

Cocteau leaned against the wall, looking disinterested.

"I've spent years studying the geologic structure of rocks on Earth, the moon, Mars, and now Venus," Gomez said, taking a lab coat from a nearby rack. She tossed it to Wilson. "Venus has definitely been the most fascinating to survey." She pulled on blue latex gloves and handed a pair to Wilson. "You'll be needing these."

As he pulled on his gloves, Gomez leaned over the table, taking samples. "I want you to look at these."

"I know a lot about rocks," Wilson said. "But I'm probably not as much of an expert as you."

"Just look," she said, placing two small rocks in his hands.

He twirled the rocks in his fingers. One was gray, cut to show a bubbled, silver interior. The other was black, porous, and covered in dust.

"I'm guessing these are from the surface," Wilson said.

"Yes and no," Gomez said. "The gray one there was found on Earth. Came over through a meteorite and has the same chemical composition as the black one, pulled from Venus's surface."

"You've been to the surface?" Wilson never heard of anyone going to the surface, or thought it possible. Not even those from NASA's failed Venusian cloud cities could weather the terrain.

Gomez held out her hand, and Wilson gave the samples back to her. "More things are possible with SIC than you can imagine Dr. Wilson. SIC has some very effective rovers and transports."

Gomez leaned over the table again, this time picking-up the disc-like artifact from the center. She handled it as if it were more fragile than glass.

She held it out to Wilson. "I want you to take a look at this."

He took it. It was a coin, no bigger than his palm. It had a good weight, being made from solid rock, mother-of-pearl in color and smooth. He looked closer as the light reflected off of it.

"What?" Wilson's eyes widened. "There's something here."

On either side, almost like a hologram, the mother-of-pearl colors reflected a figure of a humanoid, a wide open mouth, detailed eyes, and symbols carved all over the body.

"Interesting artifact." Wilson turned the coin over in his hands. "Nice color. The design, it looks almost Aztec, with some Egyptian qualities? No, not Egyptian—maybe?"

Wilson couldn't put his finger on it. It certainly wasn't Aztec, not with this material. But it didn't look like anything from the east. And he didn't recognize the symbols from anywhere.

"I'm sorry," Wilson gave a nervous laugh. "I've never seen anything like this. Where did you get it?"

It certainly couldn't be from the surface. Wilson thought of molten rock rivers on Venus's surface. He remembered old science projects where metal cans were crushed as easily as wet tissue under pressure, just like the rovers that eventually imploded on the surface. He suspected where she was going, but was it true?

"Think of rocks." Gomez raised an eyebrow. "Can you identify the material?"

"I'd say," Wilson still turning the artifact over in his hands, "it could be from the same meteorite as the other rock. Except this one has undergone extreme heat and pressure as it's clearly metamorphic. But the carvings; they don't even look like they're part of the rock."

Gomez glanced at the window, the swirling yellow planet reflecting in her eyes.

His heart raced. She really was suggesting it.

"No," Wilson paused. "No—no—no—no! Venus? But how?"

Gomez smiled. "Our very same question."

"And hopefully one you can answer." Admiral Jones was in the doorway. "We're all stumped."

Cocteau stood to attention. "Sir."

Admiral Jones entered, but he was not alone.

Following behind him was a small girl with dark hair. She could've been more than eight years old, though she wore her hair up like an adult. Unlike the rest of the SIC crew, she did not wear the white and gold uniform. Instead, she wore a plain black dress, the color of the great abyss. From her neck hung a long chain, decorated with a pendant that mimicked a star. The glow from the pendent was just enough that it was noticeable, but not overbearing. She was anything but unusual, seeming to blend inconspicuously behind the Admiral. Yet, she still drew the attention of Wilson.

She sat in a nearby chair, observing the room. No one else seemed to care that she was in there, or even acted aware of her presence.

"Tell us your analysis space archeologist," Jones said.

The girl turned her attention to Wilson, her face expressionless.

"If this was found on the surface," Wilson said, pretending he didn't see the girl's gaze, "I'd say, that someone planted it on the surface. A hoax. An expensive hoax, but all the same with the money people pay to come here they have more than enough to spare."

"What we thought too," Gomez said. "But no. No one has access to the surface except myself, the admiral, and our SIC engineers. All of whom underwent extensive investigation, and were deemed to have no way of sending this down to the surface."

"Or so we *think*," Jones said. "Gomez and I disagree. There's always the slightest possibility. But it's unlikely that someone could've put that down there,."

Wilson kept turning the artifact over. The symbols, they were some kind of written language, unknown to him and he assumed anyone on Earth.

"Then," he said, not believing the sound of his own voice, "that means that this was on the surface, and always has been."

"Also, yes and no," Gomez said, lifting the artifact from Wilson. She placed it back at the center of the table. "I suspect it's more than just a flashy coin."

"Six months ago our sensors picked up unusual radioactivity on the surface of the planet," Jones said walking over to the window, looking down at the planet starting to pass from view. "At the site of a land colony."

"Wait," Wilson shook his head. "SIC had a land colony? You must certainly mean an air colony?"

Years before Wilson's time, NASA pursued a project: the Venus Air and Cloud Colonization, or VACC. They were praised for the huge success of the colonies, providing the most hospitable environment beyond Earth. Humans didn't even need pressurized suits at that elevation; only a layer and air masks to protect them from the sulfuric gasses. That was until budget cuts, lawsuits, and SIC lobbyists bankrupted the program. NASA shut down VACC.

"Thought you read the confidential pack," Jones said, looking at Wilson unpleased.

"The land colony," Gomez continued in her calm demeanor, "was built on one of Venus's highest peaks. SIC artificially built upon that peak until it reached a safe height into Venus's atmosphere where humans could thrive. An artificial mountain you could say."

"What materials could SIC possibly use to create such a structure?" Wilson asked.

"Rocks mined from the planet surface," Cocteau said, speaking-up from her cold silence. "With the assistance of pressurized and hardened metals, and acrylics."

"SIC created an artificial polymer that can withstand extreme heat and pressure," Gomez added.

"And SIC did this without NASA's, or anyone's knowledge?" Wilson said critically. "How?"

"Does it really matter?" Cocteau rolled her eyes.

"Anyway," Jones sounded slightly frustrated. "It's normal to pick-up bursts of radiation and implosions from our surface rovers. But this was more than that. SIC engineers were running a beta land colony with no problems. Then, an implosion."

"An explosion?" Wilson asked curiously. "How?"

"An implosion smart ass," Cocteau said. "Do you know the difference?"

"Captain, please," Jones said.

"I know what an implosion is," Wilson said. "Matter collapsing instead of expanding."

"All traces of the land colony collapsed," Gomez joined Jones at the window, the yellow planet no longer in range of the window. "Right out of existence, fifty kilometers above the surface where there is Earth-like pressure. No trace of it, at all. The entire top of the damn mountain disappeared right out of existence. In its place we found the artifact, perfect as it is now, no damage to it whatsoever."

"Our sensors still cannot detect what happened," Jones said, "And radiation continues to flux. If we were, to say, get a closer look, maybe we could find more answers."

Wilson rubbed his head. "You mean if there were someone physically on what's left of your artificial mountain."

Gomez and Jones looked at one another.

"Exactly what we're thinking," Jones said.

"Wouldn't it be more practical to send an AI unit," Wilson said. "It could take just as good a survey as any human."

"About that," Jones scratched his head. "SIC shareholders are still wary of them, after the AI war and all. The UN has banned private corporations like us from so much of the tech, we can't operate one effectively at the scale we need to do an effective surface survey. And we all know a human can notice and deduce subtleties that an AI unit can only mimic."

"What about the pressure?" Wilson said. "And the heat?"

"Oh, they've found a way around that," Cocteau stepped forward. "SIC always finds a way. Nothing is impossible for them." She sounded scornful.

Jones glared at Cocteau. "That's enough." He looked back at Wilson. "Our engineers have designed gear that should protect you for the duration of your survey of the mountain. The gear will work temporarily against the heat, and has been designed to withstand the pressure, giving you a biosphere where you can survive. "

Wilson still wasn't convinced. "Temporarily?" He wasn't keen on the idea of going to one of the deadliest environments mankind has explored with temporary equipment. "What use am I? Like I said before, I know a lot about rocks, hell that's what I live for as an archeologist. But I'm not a geologist, and I'm not knowledgeable on those kinds of artificial materials. I can't do a thorough survey of the surface."

"That's why I'm going," Gomez said. "You and I together will be able to analyze and see different perspectives. And the mountain isn't just artificial materials; like the captain said, SIC used what was available which is Venus's natural materials. We will have plenty to analyze. And we'll have our Captain Cocteau leading."

"Yep," Cocteau said, completely unenthusiastic.

Wilson tried to wrap his head around it. "This really is the chance of a lifetime," he said, staring at the coin. Such a small thing. First space, now a chance to explore the surface of a planet. It was everything he hoped for, and it sounded too good to be true. It had to be.

"The artifact," Gomez's voice shook from excitement, "is the discovery of the century. A possible creation by intelligent life. Intelligent life not from Earth."

"We still don't know that," Jones said.

Gomez glared. "Maybe." She looked at Wilson. "The most curious thing, though, is the age of the artifact. Those rocks you looked at, they're fifty million years older than the artifact."

Wilson was intrigued. "How do you know?"

"We did a carbon dating of the natural rocks in the area surrounding the artifact," Gomez said. "They were all mined from the same area on Venus and all of them were fifty million years or older than that artifact."

"Would the implosion affect carbon dating?" Wilson asked.

"No," Gomez walked back to the table. "Maybe a space archeologist can find something we overlooked, and explain how this artifact came into being."

"Or prove once and for all, that there is no trace of native life on Venus, and never was," Jones said. "Don't forget that."

It was only a moment, but Wilson saw Gomez's eyes flash a fiery glance at Jones.

"My exact thoughts sir," a flawless oxford accent echoed in the room.

A man, tall and dark, wearing a SIC white business suit entered. A shining gold tie-tack with the SIC insignia stood out against his chest. He approached the admiral directly, shaking his hand firmly.

"Ahh, Bitiir, finally someone who's on the same page," Jones gave him a pat on the back.

"And the one hoping to keep this operation going," Bitiir said.

Cocteau gave a cough, one that sounded like she was going to vomit.

"Captain Cocteau, a pleasure as always." Bitiir spoke as though something distasteful was stuck in his mouth.

"Right back at ya'." Cocteau forced a smile.

"Dr. Gomez," Bitiir nodded and she gave a polite nod in return.

Jones gestured to Wilson. "May I introduce, Dr. Marshall—"

"Dr. Wilson, yes I am aware, and it is a pleasure." Bitiir approached Wilson way too aggressively. He immediately held out his hand and shook Wilson's hand too hard. "Oh, I have been looking forward to meeting you sir. Abdul Bitiir, I represent the Space Intelligence Corporation and head the finances and objectives of this operation."

"He means to say he's their lawyer," Cocteau rolled her eyes. "He wants to meet you to make sure you don't screw-up your job."

"Oh Cocteau, always so negative," Bitiir's laugh rang methodically. "I am here to support you and your endeavors."

"If that's what you call it," Cocteau said under her breath.

"Support?" Jones laughed. "He keeps this entire station going. He allocated the funds and organized everything for the survey. Without him, none of you would be here."

"Nevertheless," Bitiir continued. "I want to make this brief. We can speak more during dinner. Tonight, all of us?"

"As delightful as that sounds, I will be occupied this evening," Jones said. "But I encourage the four of you to get together often before the mission. There's still a lot of preparation, and you will need to figure your training schedules and assign responsibilities. Captain, you can head that, can't you?"

"Of course sir," Cocteau said. "Already on it."

"Good," Jones said. "I apologize, but I need to be going. Very busy to keep a station running. Thank you for your time. Captain Cocteau and Dr. Gomez can finish filling you in on anything else you need, Dr. Wilson."

"Thank you," Wilson said.

The admiral left, the small girl following behind them. She turned, winking at Wilson before disappearing through the doorway.

"Um, can someone explain the kid?" Wilson asked as soon as the admiral and girl were out of the room.

"Kid?" Gomez gave Wilson a confused look.

"I'd better be going as well," Bitiir said. "Don't forget, dinner tonight, all of us, mess hall, dinner hour."

"How can we possibly forget," Cocteau said sarcastically.

"Looking forward to it," Gomez said. "Thank you Bitiir."

"Yeah, thanks," Wilson said. "See you then."

Bitiir flashed them a wide grin before exiting.

"We will talk more about our survey tonight" Gomez said. "I'm sure you're anxious to get settled into your quarters. It's been a long journey."

"Oh, he sure is," Cocteau said, nudging Wilson and gesturing to the doorway. "Let's get going. After all, we have a lovely dinner to get ready for, with one of your soon-to-be-favorite individuals."

* * *

The mess hall wasn't anything spectacular.

After all the special treatment on the transports Wilson expected it to be as grand as everything SIC made. But the employee mess hall was anything but that. It was a simple cafeteria line-up. It was in one of the inner corridors of the station, so it didn't even have windows to view the planet. The food was basic; typical rations of preserved and prepackaged food. He knew SIC had a growing center on board, but given fresh food was difficult and expensive to grow, such things were reserved for tourists eating in the more scenic eatery.

Sitting here he felt like he was at the university again, eating whatever leftovers he was able to schmooze from the chefs that day.

He scooped a spoonful of reconstituted vanilla pudding.

"Starting with dessert I see," Gomez said, holding a tray and approaching Wilson's table. "Not the conventional choice, but I approve."

Wilson looked up. She was smiling pleasantly at him.

"Oh yes." He almost dripped the pudding from his mouth. He quickly wiped his mouth with a napkin. "Please, take a seat."

"Thank you." She sat right next to him. He scooted over an inch, and wanted to hit himself the moment he did so. He had expected her to sit across from him. He was not used to people sitting close to him, let alone eating with him.

Gomez did not seem to mind him as she started on her dinner.

"Ah, here comes our dear Captain and Bitiir," she said.

Cocteau and Bitiir set their trays across from them. They had the same preserved mush.

"You both arrived early," Bitiir said sitting. "Did you come together?"

"I don't see how any of that is your business," Gomez said stoically. "Not to mention an inappropriate question among colleagues."

Wilson felt his face turn hot.

"Enough of that you two," Cocteau sat. "We've got better things to discuss and little time to do so."

"It's great eating together," Bitiir said enthusiastically. "Promote teamwork, goodwill, and cooperation."

"We are eating together because it's efficient," Cocteau said. "None of this rhetorical bull-shit. This is a working dinner. We need to finalize our training schedule. The VR room is always packed with tourists and we need to make sure our time is a priority. I've sent you all a copy of our training schedule. I will just need a signature from each so I can submit it for approval."

Gomez pulled out a small tablet from her pocket. She clicked and swiped. She then pointed it at a clear spot on the table and an image of their schedule projected onto it.

"A lot of red tape just for training," Gomez said swiping through it "But I guess SIC has its reasons and it all works out."

"No it doesn't," Wilson shoved more pudding into his mouth.

"What?" Gomez looked surprised.

"It all doesn't work out," Wilson said. "Things don't just work out."

"Seems we have a realist on our team," Bitiir did a silent applaud. "Good work picking this one Cocteau, I approve. It's about time we had someone who was real around here."

"You know very well I didn't pick anyone for the team," Cocteau said. "If that were the case, none of you would be going."

"True," Bitiir said. "*If that were the case*, SIC would be sponsoring a team of military dogs to survey the planet with their guns. A lot of good that would do."

Cocteau slammed her fork down. "You got a problem?"

"With the military?"

"With me!" Cocteau's nose flared.

Wilson and Gomez scooted back.

Bitiir wiped his mouth calmly. "Given your violent nature," he said steadily, "and your history with knives, yes I do. I consider myself a pacifist by nature."

Cocteau stood, hovering over Bitiir. He didn't flinch as he folded his napkin neatly.

"I'll see you all early tomorrow," Cocteau grabbed her tray from the table and stalked off.

"Angry one she is," Bitiir said. "Didn't even finish her dinner."

"She is the mission lead," Gomez said. "You could show her a little more respect, even if you're just here to monitor and support."

"Respect?" Bitiir looked like he was about to laugh.

Gomez said nothing as she took a bite of her dinner.

"Well, we're all here for the same reason at least," Bitiir said. "To protect the interests of SIC and to keep operations, and our jobs, going."

"You're here," Gomez said. "Could you please excuse us Bitiir, I'd like a word with Dr. Wilson. Preparations for our survey and geologic studies for the surface. Nothing that would be of interest to you."

"As you wish," Bitiir gave a bow of the head. "I'll see you at the meeting tomorrow. Good night." He picked up his tray and walked away.

"Great dinner," Wilson said, scraping the last of his pudding. "And people say I'm an asshole."

"Don't say such things," Gomez said. "We do need to learn to work together, if only for a short time. We're all in this to make going down to the surface possible."

"Either way, we to work in training time for the survey equipment," Wilson wiped his mouth and leaned over to look at the projected schedule. "Between Cocteau's crazy training schedule and all the meetings, I can hardly see any time. When do you think it would work?"

"Before we get to that," Gomez sighed, avoiding eye contact with Wilson. "I wanted to talk to you."

"Yes?" Wilson set his napkin down.

Gomez looked around the room.

Wilson looked where she was looking, trying to figure out what she was searching for. It took him a moment to realize she was looking at everyone passing their table, all the ears that could hear them.

"I just want to say," she looked him in the eye, "be careful."

She swiped on her tablet again. "Anyway, training time for the survey? I can fit it in. Don't worry, you'll get the hang of it. I designed a lot of the equipment myself. Very user friendly."

"Yeah, sounds good," Wilson said, trying to brush off her warning and not sound too scared of what it meant to him.

Chapter 5: The Training Room

Wilson carried his virtual reality suit through the changing room.

Cocteau reserved the VR room for Venus surface training all week. Although they'd been training in labs and athletic rooms the past few days, the virtual experience was to give them their final run-through before the mission.

Although Wilson would meet with his landing team later for the training session, he wanted an early start as to not make a fool of himself. There was no telling Cocteau's reaction if he fumbled the entire time.

He stripped down to the bodysuit provided to him by SIC. One of the requirements on board was for everyone to wear the official eggshell white bodysuit. It made for quick changes in emergencies and separated them from civilian tourists.

Wilson pulled on the sleeves of the VR suit. VR suits were sleek, black, and covered in sensors. The helmet was light, with a clear face shield surrounding the entire front and peripheral. The only thing that resembled the equipment they'd be wearing on the surface were the arm pieces, an Electronic Companion attached to the left wrist: an EC.

"Don't worry," a voice echoed in the changing room. "It will look and feel just like your Venus surface suit in the VR room. SIC is good that way."

It was Bitiir. He too carried a VR suit, EC, and helmet.

"The VR room is reserved for training only," Wilson said, pulling on sensor boots. "We only have a few days before going down."

"I know," Bitiir said confidently. He opened a locker across from Wilson and started to change. "Which is why I need all the training I can get before then."

Wilson tucked his helmet under his arm. "*You're* going down to the surface? I was under the impression it was only Gomez, Cocteau, and me."

Bitiir seemed to brush-off the passive comment. "Obviously. Thought I made that evident by bringing us together for dinner last night. It's my job to protect the assets of SIC, so naturally, I would be going. You didn't think SIC would just send you down without representation?"

"Uh, Gomez?" Wilson stood up. "She works for SIC."

"Humph," Bitiir pulled his VR suit on. "Hardly. She's always cooped-up in that lab of hers."

"And Cocteau?"

Bitiir laughed.

Wilson didn't move. Why would he laugh like that?

Bitiir put his helmet on, his dark eyes reflecting off the face shield. "Oh, you're not joking, are you?" He latched his EC. "Cocteau, well now that one's a doozy," He dialed into the EC, the soft song of electric signals as his fingers moved across its two-inch screen. "She may be leading the mission, but the board would be insane to send that one down without a leash."

"Leash?"

The power-up trill sounded on Bitiir's suit. "Don't forget to sync your suit before going into the VR room."

Bitiir headed for the VR entrance.

Wilson threw on his helmet and locked it in place. He dialed into his EC, the screen glowing with options and preferences for the VR experience. The signature trill sounded and he entered the room.

The VR room was small, plain white ceiling, floor, and walls. The screen on his helmet glowed with augmented reality options against the plain white. Bitiir stood off to the side, waiting.

"Time and date," a pleasantly deep female voice echoed.

Wilson pressed the button on the right side of his helmet, simulating an intercom. "Current sol and time."

"Location?"

"Ishtar Terra," Wilson continued "Maxwell Montes Mountain Chain, Skadi Mons."

Bitiir looked impressed. "Getting to know your geography. Good."

As he spoke, the room became bright. Suddenly, they were floating over Venus. Both Wilson's and Bitiir's suits pixelated into the Venus surface suits around their bodies. The suits, a strange material that reflected like silver, moved like fabric, but could withstand the heat and pressure of Venus. The way Cocteau described it earlier that day was that it would harden when required, but keep its fabric-like quality in the high atmosphere where the pressure was less. Within the suit was an atmospheric system that activated as needed.

Even the oxygen tank was superior. Using secretive innovative methods, SIC created air tanks that condensed the oxygen without turning it into liquid. It was regulated by the suit to give just the right amount of oxygen to the user, allowing more time in hostile environments and eliminating the ever going fear of suffocation.

A cursor with the SIC insignia appeared over the planet, closing in on the upper hemisphere. It outlined the Istar Terra mountain range and glowed. They zoomed-in even further. The great mountain Skadi Mons glowed, growing larger and pulling them onto the surface.

Compression sounded in Wilsons helmet. Although he knew this was all simulated, SIC's VR simulator was unparalleled to anything he experienced. This was nothing like the VR theaters on Earth that frequently broke immersion; this was real.

The sky was orange with a glowing yellow undertone. Long shadows stretched from the unforgiving sun that peaked faintly behind layers of hazy cloud, as rigid rock structures grew from the surface, towering over them; monuments to the lifeless landscape. Volcanic fumes spewed somewhere in the distance and the air became hot.

Wilson moved his foot, kicking a smooth rock from his path. The VR suit triggered pressure exactly at the point of contact. The rock skipped away, stirring-up dust along its way.

"Wow," Wilson said, finally amazed at something SIC created.

"Fascinating, isn't it?" Bitiir walked ahead. "If I hadn't known better, I'd think this was all real. You feel the pressure change, don't you? Yes, they've even pressurized the cabin to truly simulate the surface. A typical summer day on our twin planet."

"I guess there's no better way to train for the surface," Wilson said, wandering around. "Given that it's the most dangerous environment humankind has ever explored."

"Oh this," Bitiir pointed around them, "this isn't for training."

Wilson turned. "Then why are we here?"

"Convenience," Bitiir said, stroking one of the rock structures. Something in his voice made Wilson uneasy, too calm for comfort. "And it's actually what I wanted to talk to you about."

A rush of anxiety gripped Wilson, a subconscious warning behind the faux pleasantries. Wilson pressed buttons to end the simulation.

"Lockdown override, level two access," Bitiir yelled.

Wilson continued to press his EC, but nothing responded.

"Seriously?" Wilson huffed. "What are you doing? Keeping me hostage?"

"I just want to talk," Bitiir approached with open arms.

"End simulation," Wilson yelled. "Uh, level three override."

Nothing happened.

"Won't work," Bitiir said. "It recognizes only my voice. Only I can end the simulation."

"So you are keeping me hostage!" Wilson turned to walk away, but there was nowhere to go. Just endless Venusian desert.

"Where are you going?" Bitiir laughed. "I know it's pretty deceiving, but we're still in the VR room. You haven't actually moved more than a foot from where you first started."

Wilson stopped. "I don't want to talk to someone who has to imprison me just to have a conversation."

"You're not imprisoned," Bitiir said. He sounded like he was trying to be charismatic, a sense of pristine within his oxford accent. "It's just secure. There's no chance of someone coming in to overhear our conversation. It just so happens that we can't leave either."

Wilson fumed, unconvinced of Bitiir's sincerity. "I'll rip-off the helmet," he said.

"Oh really?" Bitiir smiled. He punched into his EC. An abrupt change in pressure and Wilson felt a weight pushing from all sides and forcing him to his knees. His breathing became harsh and his ears plugged as the pressure in the cabin continued to increase. Bitiir was forced down too, but didn't seem to care.

"As you see, you still can't leave even if you take your helmet off," Bitiir smiled. "Might as well have a bit of scenery while we talk."

Wilson glowered at Bitiir's delight. Bitiir continued tapping his EC as the cabin pressure equalized.

Bitiir came to his feet and looked-up. "Time change: sunset."

The room darkened. The sky above changed. The orange and yellow sky that surrounded them disappeared. Shadows dispelled as the surface reflected the twilight blue of the setting white sun in the distance, fading into a sulfur yellow.

"Gives new meaning to a blue moon doesn't it?" Bitiir put his hands on his hips, a wide smile and teeth aglow as lights switched on within their helmets. "But there are no moons visible. Blue planet maybe? Has a nice ring to it, don't you think? I think Earth is referred to as the blue planet though."

Wilson scowled.

"Ah, don't be like that," Bitiir said. "These are the kind things we have to think about."

"It's ridiculous," Wilson said. "Say what you've got to say then let me out of here."

"Seems like Cocteau's rubbed off on you," Bitiir's manufactured hurt expression made Wilson feel sick. "Can't say I'm not disappointed."

"*Bitiir!*"

"Alright, I get the hint."

Was I dropping hints? Wilson thought, irritated.

"Like I said before, this room being used for training is pure convenience," Bitiir paced. "Same with the research labs, artifact transports, all of it serving the bigger picture."

"And what would that be?"

"This room was not created for training purposes," Bitiir said. "All this," he gestured to the denim colored sky, "is entertainment. To ensure profit."

"Profit?"

"What did you think SIC is?" Bitiir spoke as if Wilson were a child. "How do you think SIC can even afford all this? You saw firsthand who transported with you from Earth. As long as they keep flowing, then we get our profit to keep things running. You don't work for NASA anymore Marshall Wilson; we do things differently here."

"Clearly."

Bitiir stepped in front of Wilson. "You see, the international government has a nasty habit of wriggling their noses in things they don't understand. Like this station; looks good if we have some kind of research going for the 'betterment' of mankind, but really, results are shown in numbers. And those numbers come from coin, figuratively speaking.

"SIC has a number of honorary members and stockholders that have shown interest in the failed air colonies. What if that failure that could be reinvented somewhere else, like the surface? There's enough interest that these members already put money down on missions they hope to participate in one day using this planet."

Marshall didn't like where this was going. "Untrained retirees on the surface of Venus?"

"Not unescorted of course."

"Do you have any idea how dangerous it is to send down a young healthy, trained astronaut to the surface, let alone an oblivious tourist?"

"We have waivers, protections in place," Bitiir said.

"And they said Icarus flew too close to the sun."

"Imagine," Bitiir sounded like a used car salesman, "a life long dream of exploring other worlds, finally at your fingertips. Exotic lands beyond your wildest dreams worlds away. You of all people should understand that dream."

"The planet is dead," Wilson said. "There's nothing exotic about death. My only interest is scientific."

"You're missing the point!" Bitiir's face turned wild, wide eyes and a quivering mouth. He took a breath and composed himself. "Point is, there are those who have already invested in this venture, and there are those who are willing to invest more. Without this venture, this station is shutdown, gone. All that goodwill research and scientific betterment of mankind will end—even though I'm sure your science is more self-interest. The moon is no longer enough; people need more. And you are the key."

"Me?"

"Yes you," Bitiir said. "You see, that artifact Gomez picked-up on the surface has caused some, well, roadblocks in SICs current venture."

Wilson shook his head. "I see."

He knew better than anyone how international space law worked, especially as a space archeologist. Any evidence or hint that indigenous life once existed or does exist on a foreign world immediately becomes a protected zone; the planet becomes untouchable to development. And more importantly, secured against any private corporations like SIC.

"Now you understand," Bitiir's tone softened. "You cannot allow that artifact to shut down this operation. You're right, it's a dead planet, and it must stay that way. Progress for the sake of progress cannot be stopped."

"The artifact exists," Wilson said. "You cannot change that."

Bitiir pressed a bottom on his EC and Wilson felt the heat increasing around him.

Bitiir sighed. "I'm not the villain."

Fire.

Wilson was suddenly surrounded by a stream of glowing lava. He fell over, burning.

He hit the floor. The simulation ended.

Wilson blinked, flat on his back in the blank white room. Bitiir stood over him, offering a hand. Wilson rejected it, standing up and turning his back.

"Just remember who's in control," Bitiir said from behind, "and who you should be pleasing. I am protecting what I love and care about. That survey cannot show any evidence except that the artifact is a hoax. Remember who's in control."

Chapter 6: To the Infinite

Wilson couldn't sleep.

He was in bed, shirtless and waiting for sleep to come. It didn't.

All that goodwill research and scientific betterment of mankind will end, Bitiir's words repeated angrily in his mind. A knot formed in his stomach the more he thought about it, knowing that Bitiir was right.

Am I really the one to stop this? He thought about Venus station and what a miracle it was to exist, even after the air colonies failed. Was the artifact, which was more than likely a hoax, worth all this?

A flash of Bitiir's toothy grin. *Just remember who's in control.*

Beeping.

Wilson sat up, pulling a shirt on. Someone was ringing his quarters. He reached over and pressed the intercom button by the bed. "Come in."

He switched on the light just as the door slid open.

"Dr. Gomez?" Wilson tripped as he wrapped a blanket around himself.

"Please," Gomez stood in the doorway. She was still in her full day wear, but her hair was loose, curls spiraling in natural form around her head "Have I not already asked? To you I am Arianna. We are professionals, but we are also colleagues of SIC and will continue working closely together."

"Um, yes, sorry," Wilson said, slipping on socks. He let out a frustrated grunt when he realized it was upside down.

"It's okay," Gomez put up a hand for him to stop. "You don't need to do all that on my account. I'm sorry to wake you, and bother you in this late hour, but I must speak with you privately. The cafeteria the other day wasn't a good place to do that."

"Wasn't sleeping anyway," Wilson sat up straight on the end of the bed. "Honestly, you're the only person around here I like talking to."

Gomez smiled. "Thank you. May I?"

"Please," Wilson gestured for her to enter. She closed the door and stood across the room.

"You can sit," Wilson pat the end of the bed. "I don't bite."

"Alright." She came and sat down once again, like in the cafeteria, closer than Wilson intended. "I'm sorry, I just don't want to make you feel any more uncomfortable than you already are."

"You can say that again," Wilson huffed, pulling his blanket tightly around himself. "I'm starting to wonder if I should feel safe in my own bed with everything going on."

"I understand," Gomez said. "I apologize for any part I've played in that. We hardly know each other and I've already put much on your shoulders." She paused, looking down at her knees. "You know, since I was a little girl, I've always had a passion for rocks."

Wilson loosened the blanket around him. "Um, I'm glad? Sorry, why are you telling me this?"

She chuckled. "I said we hardly know each other. All we've ever spoken about is this job. Hard to work with someone if you don't build a relationship with them, even if it's a professional one. Sometimes someone has to take the first step, and I don't mind. Oh —I should correct. It's rocks *and* math I loved."

"Rocks and math" Wilson nodded. "Good thing you became a geologist."

"It is, isn't it," she beamed.

"Where did you grow up?"

"I was born in Haiti," she said. "But Florida's my home. I spent most of my life just outside Miami."

"Pretty close to a SIC hub," Wilson said. "Easy recruitment."

"Yes," she smiled, looking down at her folded fingers. "My family never had much. And you know, SIC gave me a way out. I know on the outside what SIC may look like. It's a company run by people, so it will never be perfect. But it also means it will never be wholly bad either."

"I guess." Wilson wasn't sure where she was going with this. He looked at her, her face in a calm concentration, as though remembering.

"Ah, look at me," she lifted her head. "How about you? Why space archeology? You don't meet many researchers in that field anymore."

Wilson sighed. "It was all the rage when I started studying archeology. You'll start calling me old man if you remember how long ago that was. But come to think of it, that's not why I got involved in the research."

"How then?" Gomez's eyes narrowed, a look of pure interest. Even if it was feigned, it drew Wilson in, and he wanted to tell more.

"It all started with my mother," he continued. "She was Creek you know, though I may not look it. I take more after my father. And that's about as much as I know. She never talked about her heritage. She was the kind of person more focused on the present. She distanced herself from her culture and pushed for me to do the same, to be more like my father's side."

"What?" Gomez's eyes widened, shocked. "Why would she do that?"

"Old fashioned thinking," Wilson shook his head. "She feared how I'd be treated. I tried to convince her differently but she insisted she knew better. After she died I tried to look into our family history, but no luck. Everyone just saw me as some guy pretending to be something he's not. So I figured if I couldn't connect with the culture, maybe I could with the history of it. And that's how it started. With an interest in one history, and then more."

Gomez blinked slowly. "I'm sorry. That's very sad."

He shook his head. "No, not sad. Unfortunate." He dropped his blanket to the floor. "Maybe if things were different, I'd know more. But then again, I wouldn't have gotten involved in archeology without it, let alone space archeology. One of those pick your poison situations. I'll never know for sure."

Gomez touched his elbow. "Thank you for telling me, that couldn't have been easy. But I do feel we know each other a bit better now."

They locked eyes.

"Well," Gomez dropped her gaze. "I understand that you couldn't make that situation right. But maybe there is one you could."

Wilson picked his blanket back up. "I figured this was more than a social call."

Gomez did that smile of hers again. "Listen, what I'm about to tell you, please keep it between us, from one scientist to another." Her smile faded. "I know how the other crew members feel about me, and I don't think they would approve of what I'm about to tell you."

"You mean SIC," Wilson said.

Gomez shook her head. "Be careful to not judge SIC too harshly. You *are here* because of them."

"Yes," Wilson said. "I've also been threatened with my life and reputation because of them."

"That's what I need to talk to you about," She grabbed Wilson's hand, staring him down with her deep, warm eyes.

"I know what they're pressuring you to do," she said slowly. "And I am asking you—no, I'm begging you—please don't do it. This artifact, the coin, is possibly the greatest scientific find in our human history. And I simply cannot let SIC take that away from mankind— away from me."

"And if I do, what will you do?" Wilson said. "Members of SIC are awfully good at threats. And now you know something about me."

Gomez gave a slight smile. "I'm not like other members of SIC. You too are a member of SIC and you're not like the rest of them. We are scientists, you and I. We understand our obligations. No matter what Bitiir has told you, please remember that."

Wilson pulled his hand away and crossed his arms. How did she know what Bitiir told him? Was she bluffing?

"And if I don't remember that?" he said. "I kind of like keeping my head intact, as well as my reputation."

"Then know this," Gomez continued, "that you will rob all of humanity of the greatest scientific achievement. I will feel sorry for you and all the regret you'll have to endure."

"Wow," Wilson laughed and shook his head. "That is quite the guilt trip. If you're serious Arianna, then you're probably the only truly good person on board this station."

Gomez's eyes seemed to twinkle, brighten. "Thank you Marshall, but I'm certainly not as selfless as you think."

"You don't need to worry about me," he said. "I'll remember what you've told me, and I will also remember that you are the first person since I've taken this job to treat me with some amount of dignity. I truly hope this all goes well for you Dr. Gomez."

Gomez stood. "Thank you." She patted him on the shoulder. "Good night Dr. Wilson."

He took a sigh of relief when she left. He threw himself back onto the bed.

I'm not supposed to think that way anymore, he told himself. That was why he called her Gomez in the end, a way to set a boundary, keep his distance.

What if I don't want to, he thought. As much as he preferred being alone, sometimes it was hard.

His room was still, silent. Only the hum of station itself was present.

Marshall, a whisper spoke to him.

He jumped.

This was no memory. It sounded clear, as though in his room.

"Who's there?"

Marshall. He heard it again. This time it sounded like her whispering, his dearly departed.

He stood. It was emanating from somewhere.

"Whoever's messing with me," he said aloud, this is cruel."

He looked around.`

Nothing.

He sat back on his bed. *I'm losing my mind.*

He grabbed a remote hanging on his wall and switched on a viewing screen that stretched across the wall before him. Every living quarter had one—made up for lack of windows for employees. And he was lucky enough to have a room to himself.

The viewing screen played feeds of Earth terrain, oceans, and of other planets. Supposedly it lifted the morale of those on extended missions. He pressed buttons and flipped through the live images until he reached one.

Venus.

The live feed of the planet looked too real to him. Could he really be floating above it, just as this screen showed? And would he really be visiting its surface in just a few days time?

Marshall. . .

He held his breath. This time it sounded like it came out of screen, from the planet.

He switched it off.

Someone's defiantly trying to intimidate me, he thought. *Probably one of Bitiir's tricks. There's no way that came from the planet. That's just laughable.*

But a thought on the back of his mind: *What if it did?*

* * *

A few days later. . .

The landing bay on Venus station was small compared to the rest of the station.

And the transport within the bay was too big.

SIC boasted that they created the most innovative travel through their space transports. From being mechanical wonders, to bringing comfort and efficiency, the transports were more sophisticated than any other transportation technology created by humankind.

From Wilson's experience, this was true. His experience traveling to the moon orbiter and Venus station were already beyond the technology he worked with at NASA.

He stood in full Venusian gear—with the exception of his helmet—in the landing bay. He and the rest of the landing team waited in the small space that was not taken up by the massive transport.

SIC employees buzzed from every direction. It was morning, according to Venus station time. Sparks flew, metal clanked against metal, steam rising from last minute touches to the hull of their oversized transport. Maintenance workers appearing in and out of nooks and crannies, preparing the pride and joy of SICs mechanical wonder: the Infinite. So named, for the infinite possibilities it possessed.

First of its kind, not only could the Infinite transfer people between the planet and station, it could travel within the atmosphere to multiple locations and landmarks. The true miracle was that it had no need to land on the surface to take them back to Venus station; it could launch to space from midair. A machine that could convert between space travel and worldly travel with ease. It was something Wilson only dreamed of in science fiction, and yet it existed.

"Get ready for the ride of your lives," Cocteau said tucking her helmet under her arm. "I've got a few things to prepare as the Infinite's just about ready. Make sure your EC's powered up and set to your personal settings."

She stepped away from them, taking a tablet from one of the SIC engineers and reading through it.

Wilson stood with Gomez and Bitiir, none of them speaking to one another. He fumbled with his EC, taking longer to input his personal settings rather than acknowledge them. He already had awkward encounters with both of them and preferred not to have another. They too, seemed to have the same idea.

"Alright, come on," Cocteau gestured for them to follow. "Time to load up."

There was a hatch along the side that created easy access into the cockpit of the Infinite. Within the cockpit were two rows of seats, two by two, cramped and surrounded by advanced dashboards.

Wilson only had a basic understanding of it from their recent training. The idea was for him to know enough to get them back to Venus station if something happened to Cocteau or Bitiir, the ones who actually had advanced training in the Infinite's functions. He doubted he if he actually could.

Wilson and Gomez took their places in the second row as Cocteau and Bitiir sat in the front with the main dashboard. A windshield spread across the front and roof of the cockpit, giving them a view of augmented operations and countdowns.

Wilson watched as Bitiir dialed into the dash in front of him. *All that goodwill research and scientific betterment of mankind will end. . .just remember who's in control.*

He looked at Gomez pulling her safety straps over her head, brushing a hair out of her face. *We are scientists, you and I; we understand our obligations. . . I simply cannot let SIC take that away from mankind—away from me. . .*

Something burned inside Wilson. Bitiir's and Gomez's words repeated incessantly in his mind, battling one another to occupy his thoughts.

"Wouldn't it make more sense to send a medic instead of a lawyer," Wilson said defiantly. "You know, if something happened to one of us down on the planet. Something *unfortunate.*"

"Oh, you know you would miss me down there," Bitiir said. "Plus we have two doctors aboard."

"Not medical," Wilson said under his breath.

"Knock it off you guys," Cocteau said, pressing a headset against her ear. "I am trying to listen to this channel and you are making it impossible with your passive aggressive shit."

Wilson scowled. "Is it really arguing if it's passive aggressive?"

Cocteau growled. "Don't be a smart ass."

Bitiir applauded. "Yes, Cocteau, you take charge now."

Cocteau looked at Bitiir and glared. "Don't be a kiss ass."

"You know, let's just not talk to one another unless it has to do with the mission," Gomez said. "I think that would be best."

"You always know best," Bitiir scoffed. "Don't you."

Wilson couldn't help but smile. "Dr. Gomez, you really are the only good person here."

"She's right," Cocteau barked. "*Shut-up!*"

"Captain Cocteau, do you read?" a voice came out of her headset.

"Yes," she said. "Sorry, please continue with the countdown."

Cocteau continued to press buttons as Wilson sat back, waiting for the final countdown to begin. He stared absentmindedly into his gloved hands.

He remembered holding *her* hand. A dearly beloved, parted from him.

It will be over soon, her voice echoed, the woman in a distant memory. Her laugh rang just as musically as it always did. *"Don't let me be the end of your life. . . You will see me again when you least expect it."*

"Final countdown about to initiate," Cocteau said.

An alarm sounded and Wilson glanced through the windshield. SIC engineers ran for the exit, clearing the landing bay.

"Brace yourself folks, it's going to be rough going down," Cocteau clicked on signals flashing across the glass. "Venus has a thick atmosphere."

"Platform is cleared, captain," said the voice in Cocteau's intercom.

"Helmets on," Cocteau ordered. She pulled off her headset and switched it for her helmet.

Wilson took the helmet from his lap and locked it in place over his head. Although the cockpit would've been enough to protect them, they wore helmets as a safety measure if something happened during the transfer.

"Landing bay cleared," said that same voice that had been in Cocteau's headset, but now sounded in their helmets. This would be how they would communicate for the rest of the mission. "Final countdown initiated."

"Gotcha," Wilson said, testing out his intercom. "Everyone got that?"

"We got you," Gomez responded.

"T-minus—" the final countdown began. The bay doors in front of the infinite slowly parted.

First, there was light.

Blinding sunlight filling the entire bay. Wilson squinted, hearing the signature trill of his EC charging, already soaking up whatever energy it could from the solar light. The bay doors finished opening, the entire sight filled with a vision of the swirling glow of the sulfur yellow planet.

Although Wilson knew it was his imagination, he could feel the heat of the fiery inferno emanating, pulling them in.

Then a whisper.

Marshall. . . you will see me again. . .

"What?" His heart skipped. It was the same whisper he heard from before, calling to him. He heard it clear as day, but not from intercom in his helmet. The whisper was everywhere, as though it were sent from the planet below.

Marshall. . .

"Did you hear that?" He surely couldn't be the only one to hear it.

"Hear what?" Gomez said.

"I hear a lot of things," Cocteau said. "And your voice shouldn't be one of them right now."

"Never mind," Wilson said, dismissing the whisper's existence. Stress. That's what it was. Stress from the mission. "It's nothing," he told his team and himself.

He'd been ruminating about *her* since that night he heard the whisper in his quarters. The closer he was to the planet, the more his late wife was on his mind. He avoided thinking her name, hoping it would stop the intrusive thoughts. It was getting harder to distract himself from her memory. Not that he ever tried to forget her, but distractions always made things easier.

Everything around them rumbled, the infinite vibrating. The sounds of the transport preparing to take-off overtook everything. Wilson could no longer hear the countdown.

"Ready to drop into hell?" Cocteau's laugh was drained out. Was she actually enjoying this?

Sudden pressure and Wilson felt like they were falling. They were no longer in the bay, but speeding forward, plunging into the great hostile before them. Wilson only saw space for a moment as his vision blacked out, the immense pressure increasing.

Darkness. Everything silenced as he felt a weight pull at his eyes, keeping them shut.

Wilson forced his eyes open. Red and yellow sparks drifted across the windshield, everything around them becoming a firestorm.

The force of gravity along with the Infinite's thrusters pulled the transport into the planet's atmosphere.

"*Heat shields holding!*" Wilson barely heard Cocteau yell. Everything was heating up and he heaved each breath. Perspiration stuck to his arms and face. He could no longer see out the windshield, the fiery atmospheric blaze devouring them.

"Slowing descent," Cocteau announced flicking up some switches. "Successful penetration of the planet's atmosphere."

They jolted forward and the blaze died.

Wilson panted, feeling like he just ran ten miles in a matter of minutes.

"We made it?" He looked around. The Infinite was gliding steadily through a thick, sickly yellow clouds—the Venus haze.

Guiding systems flashed on the glass in front of Cocteau.

"Looks like sleeping beauty decided to join us," Cocteau said. He could feel the smirk in her voice.

"Um yeah," Wilson was confused. "These new transports are really something else, getting here so fast."

"Fast is a relative term," Bitiir said. "If you remember from training, it takes a lot more than a few minutes to go from the station down to the planet.

"What are they talking about?" Wilson turned to Gomez.

"You—a—sort of passed-out for a bit," Gomez said uncomfortably. "Are you alright?"

"I'm fine," he huffed. Humiliation stung his chest. He felt like he blackout for only a moment, but it must've been for an hour or two. Back in the early days of space travel, shuttles would take twenty plus hours to go between an orbiting station and a planet below. SICs name went big when they announced their transports could do it within a couple hours.

"You more than passed-out," Cocteau didn't sound worried. "You were down for the count. Rough night, huh? Don't worry smart-ass, we'll be careful not to wake you next time."

"Ha-ha," Wilson said coldly.

He didn't want to admit it, but he wanted to impress them, prove that he was right for this mission. More than anything, he wanted to show-up Bitiir. He was getting used to Cocteau's taunting, but Bitiir's silent gloating made everything burn within him all the more.

They floated through the Venus haze, guiding systems flashing as Cocteau dialed into the dashboard every so often. Their surroundings were surreal, like they were floating through an unending cloud of jaundice fog.

Static sounded in their helmets.

"Venus command. . ." a garbled voice with more static.

"I knew this would happen," Cocteau said. She was using that voice where Wilson couldn't tell if she was sarcastic or serious. "They'll still be able to monitor and listen, but I don't think we'll be able to use two way communication. Great day for flying, isn't it?"

"Should we go back?" Gomez asked. She sounded disappointed at the idea.

"No need," Bitiir said. "We expected this to happen."

"Isn't that kind of dangerous?" Wilson asked.

"Who ever said this mission was safe?" Bitiir chuckled. "That's why we hired the best of the best. Orders are to keep going if this happened. It was unavoidable with the thick atmosphere and all. We'll be extra vigilant to check-in at rendezvous times."

A signal chirped on the dash.

"Destination approaching," the pleasant electronic SIC voice sounded around them.

"See, not all is lost," Bitiir said.

The Venus haze cleared just enough for Wilson to see.

Ahead of them, gleaming through the vaporous clouds were three massive disc-shaped silver solar balloons. So dauntingly big, they made the Infinite seem like a child's play toy.

More haze cleared and a floating city emerged beneath the balloons.

Wilson held his breath. He'd never seen anything of the like. The city hung steadily beneath the balloons, the shadow of buildings growing like industrial stalactites. The buildings were all interconnected by maintenance corridors, making the city a human formicarium.

NASA named the city Cerberus, guardian to the planet and the shining jewel of NASA's colonization successes. The three solar balloons that held the city afloat gave to its name all the more.

The VACC program created these air cities. Although abandoned, the cities still floated aimlessly in Venus airspace. Within them were research labs, living quarters, and all equipment and supplies that NASA couldn't afford to bring back after the project was defunded. Cerberus was one of two cities Wilson knew of; a ghost of a dream.

As they approached, the Infinite dropped in elevation and Wilson saw columns of scaffolding surround the city, shivering in the torrent of winds.

Sun rays peaked through the clouds, shining on various docking bays that held airships, no longer in use and unable to operate. They glittered with the same silver solar material as the balloons, back propellers eaten away from sulfuric gasses and lack of maintenance. Wilson wondered how NASA ever funded such a project. He mourned the airships, knowing they were all empty shells.

He glanced at Bitiir.

"Awe-inspiring, isn't it?" Bitiir said.

"Yeah," Wilson answered. He looked at the insignia on his suit, anger quickly replacing the empty mourning. A cold desire for retribution chilled the core of his chest.

"Of course, innovation would've never allowed it to last," Bitiir said. "The city was a good first step, but could never be the permanent solution. Too much maintenance and too expensive. *Just look!* The airships are already falling apart. There's no telling how everything else held up."

"We'll find out soon enough," Cocteau said, flicking switches. "Preparing to dock."

"The dock should hold," Gomez said. "It hasn't been that long since SIC checked. Should be safe enough."

"I hope so," Wilson said.

Cocteau steered them into an empty dock, one meant for an airship. The design of the Infinite made it slip easily onto the dock, better than a glove.

"Tapping into the city's docking systems," Cocteau announced. "Bitiir, I need you to start putting in the access codes."

"Got it," he said, typing into the touch screen on the dash. Augmented signals flashed across the cockpit window.

"Fingers crossed," Gomez said.

"Why?" Wilson leaned forward trying to see the access codes. He knew he didn't need to know them, but the feeling of knowing something SIC kept from him made him feel elated.

"SIC's been keeping an eye on the air cities," Gomez said carefully, "but their life support systems haven't been in use for quite some time. If we can't get the systems to power on, we won't be able to safely connect the transport to the city. We'll have to return to the station."

"Regardless, we're keeping our helmets on," Cocteau said, focusing on her task of hacking into the city's systems. "The life support will be enough for us to finish docking, but not to walk around like it's a holiday. We'll still need to flush the cockpit of the transport with clean oxygen before we return to Venus station."

They waited as Cocteau and Bitiir continued to type into the dashboard.

"How does he know how to hack into the city?" Wilson said. "Isn't that the job of a computer tech?"

"Because I'm privy to certain information that most aren't," Bitiir said, also focusing on his task. "Ah-ha!" he exclaimed and pressed a button. The dock began moving upward.

Wilson looked up and saw the shaft above slowly part.

"Really, what would you people do without me here?" Bitiir laughed.

"Oh I can think of a lot of things," Cocteau said.

For once, Wilson fully agreed with her.

"Don't be jealous," Bitiir said. "After all you're not the jealous type—not with your temper. That's more of Gomez's thing, isn't it?"

Gomez said nothing.

"You're one cocky son-of-a-bitch," Cocteau said. "Shut up before you piss-off everyone."

"Have it your way," Bitiir said. "I've put up with enough abuse. You'll all appreciate me eventually. Wilson's learned to."

Wilson held his breath, knowing that anything he said would only backfire at this point.

They continued to rise into the parted shaft above them. It seemed awkward, their transport going through an entrance made for giant airships. Cocteau kept reassuring them it was safe, at least as safe as SIC deemed.

White lights suddenly came on around them as they came through the opening. The shaft below closed.

"Air flush and cleanse in progress," the pleasant voice on the dashboard announced.

"Remember, doesn't matter what that thing says," Cocteau said unstrapping herself, "life support systems here are not stable. Keep your helmets on and let your suits do the job of filtering and cooling the air. Revert to your oxygen only in an emergency. Those air tanks are for the descent and for the surface. Once I open the hatch, until we can properly flush it, the air in the Infinite will be contaminated."

"I was only able to get us minimal emergency power for this section of the city," Bitiir added. "Just sufficient enough to keep us docked and to power essential functions at central command."

"Good," Cocteau said. "We're not staying long. Our next objective is to anchor the city's location through the command room. Then we'll take a maintenance shaft to begin our descent to the mountain. From there, Gomez and Wilson will take over for their survey. *Stick together*. No wandering."

Cocteau pressed the necessary codes and unlocked the escape hatch to the Infinite. With a twist and kick to the hatch, the cabin depressurized and opened. Cocteau jumped out first, followed by Bitiir, then Gomez. Wilson jumped out last, still feeling uneasy about his 'temporary' equipment from SIC.

Their feet echoed. Even though the bay lights were supposed to light their way, Wilson wished they were off. Seeing the sheer size of the docking bay, empty and lifeless, made it all too morose. As though they were walking through a graveyard with no gravestones.

"This way," Cocteau said, leading them through an opening. They entered a narrow, poorly lit corridor, the dim emergency lights seeming to fade as they continued.

Ahead was another dimly lit entrance.

"We'll cut through there," Cocteau pointed toward the end of the corridor, "the courtyard. Straight across it will be the command center. Remember, stay together. *No distractions, no detours*."

They approached the entrance and pushed the door open.

Vertigo took over as Wilson felt like they stepped out of the city and into the swirling atmosphere. They floated amid the thick clouds of Venus, yet did not fall.

But they weren't floating. They stood on a glass floor that overlooked the planet beneath. Wilson couldn't help but feel that they were walking among the clouds.

He only heard rumor of this place: The Grand Courtyard, capital of the cloud cities. Its beauty was different than anything aboard a SIC vessel. Everything was effortless; nothing extravagant, artificial, or elaborate. The beauty came from the planet itself, the simplicity of seeing it for what it was and not from the kind of accents SIC always put on everything.

In the center of the courtyard hung a ceiling fountain, carved into an abstract shape and looked like it once flowed gracefully to the floor beneath it. Now it was a husk, the years of no use showing. All around them the walls opened to different entryways, various parts of the city that were meant for high volume traffic. Wilson wondered which ones led to the libraries and research labs, untouched since the abandonment.

Their feet echoed through the wide courtyard. They passed the fountain.

Wilson stopped.

He stepped over the raised ledge that surrounded the floor beneath the ceiling fountain. All dried up, it was roughly thirty feet in diameter. He approached the center.

He reached above and touched the tip of the ceiling fountain, dangling delicately. Even through his glove, he could tell it was fragile, that unused years had taken a toll on its fortitude.

"You think SIC will allow it to flow again?" Wilson heard Gomez's voice through the intercom. She was standing across from him, on the other side of the fountain.

"Maybe, if they could get it to one of their planned surface colonies," Wilson said. "But then again, it was built for something, everything that SIC stands against. Why should they preserve anything like that?"

"Right you are Dr. Wilson," Bitiir's voice boomed over theirs. "SIC's already pulled the research they need and has superior plans beyond this dump. You'll see, and you'll be proud to know that you're a part of it."

"*I said no detours!*" Cocteau yelled. "Brainiacs, catch-up. Not supposed to leave anyone behind, but I will if you don't keep up. Last thing I want is for you two to get into something you're not supposed to and send the city crashing to the surface. *Come on!*"

They finished crossing the courtyard to an entrance larger than the others. Above it read 'Passage to Central Command'.

"We've wasted enough time sight-seeing," Cocteau said. "Up we go."

Through the entrance they climbed stairs, up to a locked metal door.

"Allow me," Bitiir said smoothly as he dialed into his EC. The door powered up and the sound of an electronic lock unhitched. He gently pushed against it and it swung open.

"What can I say?" Bitiir took a slight bow. "Have I proved my worth on this mission yet? Am I more than—what did you call me Cocteau? SIC's babysitter?"

"Yeah, yeah," Cocteau said taking the lead. Wilson knew it must've taken all she had not to shove Bitiir over as she walked past him.

They entered the control center. It was a small room, but laid-out as a living map of the city, packed full of panels to control every aspect of it.

"We're looking for maintenance," Cocteau said. "Maintenance has the access to anchor the city and to give power to the shafts we need."

"Here," Gomez said, pointing to a panel that hung off the wall. "This one looks to be it."

"Bitiir, do your thing," Cocteau said.

Bitiir approached, once again dialing into his EC.

"Won't let me without your command code," Bitiir said to Cocteau.

She dialed into her EC, and the maintenance panel came alive.

"Alright, let's anchor her," Cocteau said. "Bitiir, get on that. Gomez, help him. Wilson—*come here!*"

Wilson jumped. Had he done something wrong again? He felt rather useless at this point, not being as tech savvy as he always wanted to be. He observed at one of the layouts of the city, hoping to look too busy to face Cocteau.

"Wilson," Cocteau barked. "That was an order!"

Wilson tore his attention from the layout and approached Cocteau.

"You know, I'm not one of your military cronies," Wilson said. "You can't order me about like one of them."

"Cut the bullshit and give me your arm."

Wilson raised his right arm.

"Other arm, smartass." Cocteau sounded frustrated.

He raised his left arm. Cocteau grabbed it, pressing his EC against hers, dialing into it.

Bitiir looked over his shoulder at them. "Captain, what are you doing?"

Cocteau ignored him and continued to dial, Wilsons EC bringing up the syncing signal.

"Captain, I asked what you are doing? Bitiir stopped his work at the maintenance panel.

Gomez stepped aside. "Um, Captain, are you—"

"Shut-up," Cocteau said, focusing on her task. "I don't answer to any of you."

"You certainly do," Bitiir sounded offended. "Answer me—what are you doing?" He stepped toward her.

"Watch it Bitiir," Cocteau pointed at him. "Down here, I'm leading the mission, and what I do and say is law. Unless you really want to challenge me on that. Lawyer like you should know."

Bitiir stepped back.

Cocteau released Wilson's arm.

Wilson looked down at his EC. It didn't look any different.

"I'm not going to suddenly start breathing in sulfuric gas am I?" Wilson said.

"Not likely," Cocteau said. "But now, if something happens to me, your EC will automatically take command of the mission and of the emergency power of the city."

Bitiir's mouth dropped. "Are you kidding me?"

"I know I have one hell of a sense of humor," Cocteau smiled, "but I'm serious."

"He doesn't even know how to use that thing!" Bitiir yelled at them. "Even Gomez has more access codes that he does. He's only here for the survey, nothing more."

"Which is a lot more than what you're here for," Cocteau glared at Bitiir.

"This goes against protocol," Bitiir said. "I should have those commands."

"Liar," Cocteau said. "You know the protocol and that you very well cannot hold command codes, plus all the access codes. It's dangerous to put them all in one place. Gomez is already the backup for your access codes, so it only makes sense for Wilson to be the backup for my command codes."

"Why sync my EC now?" Wilson said. "Why didn't you establish this back on Venus station?"

"I had to finish downloading the commands for the city," Cocteau said. "And I couldn't do that until we were closer to central control. Bitiir and Gomez have the access codes, but none of it will work without the command codes. You're my backup if anything happens to me. Don't be a smartass about it."

"Um, thanks?" Wilson gulped. He had no idea that Cocteau held him in such high regard.

"No thanks," Cocteau said. "You were just the logical choice."

"Sorry to break up this lovely confrontation," Gomez said. "But the city is ready to anchor and the maintenance shafts are ready for us. We don't want the city to drift too far from our mountain."

"Good," Cocteau said. "Finish the mission. Let's go team."

Gomez followed Cocteau. Wilson went to follow, but Bitiir grabbed his shoulder.

Wilson looked at his face. With the intercom on, there wasn't much they could say without the others hearing, but Bitiir's expression was enough. *Just remember who's in control.*

Wilson shoved off Bitiir's arm. "Come on, we have a mission to finish."

Chapter 7: Doom

Earth's twin. That was nickname given to Venus, long before the age of space exploration.

Not just for its similar size, but as humankind evolved to understand creation, they began to understand the creations of both Earth and Venus. But even as twins are created in the same womb, they will still possess slight differences, even if only in personality.

The same was for Earth and Venus. Both were organized within the same creation cycle in the beginnings of the solar system. Formed from the same materials brought in from their mother Sun and father gravity.

In the end, they took different evolutionary paths just as human twins take different walks of life. Venus, being ever so slightly closer to the sun is naturally hotter and receives more solar radiation than that of the cooler Earth. A slower rotation allowed the heat from the sun to evaporate all the water on Venus, creating a greenhouse effect that trapped all the gasses from tectonic activity.

Overall, Earth's distance from the sun and fast rotation gave it all the advantages it needed to evolve enough to support and sustain life.

Such things were on Wilson's mind as he crouched in the dim, narrow maintenance passage. He was at least six inches too tall for the passage. His neck and shoulders ached as he helped Gomez pull a maintenance bin that barely cleared the ceiling; its wheels screeching and scraping against the dense metal floor.

Even slightly crouched, Bitiir walked nonchalantly in front of them. He followed close to Cocteau who held her EC arm in front of her, mapping and directing them. She led them through the myriad of confined passages, bringing them to the outgoing ones that connected to the city's scaffolding.

Cocteau flashed a light in Wilson's eyes. "We're here."

He heard a crack in his spine as he twisted to look ahead.

I'm going to feel that tomorrow, he thought.

The team stood in front of an enclosed threshold, a sealed doorway that stood as a barrier between them and the violent winds of upper Venus. In the center of it a small square window flickered dimly, swirling with the tumultuous weather that awaited them.

"Watch it," Cocteau said, pressing her EC. The maintenance passageway shook. Like chalk scratching iron, a wall lowered from the ceiling behind them, cutting them off from the city.

Cocteau pointed to the threshold ahead. "Once I open this," her eyes bore at them like high beams, "you're going to feel a lot of turbulence. Feel that sway? That's not from us walking down the passageway; *that's from outside*. Winds reach 250 kilometers up here. Gear up and remember your training."

Like mountaineers preparing for a steep climb, they took out an assortment of hooks and harnesses from the built-in packs of their suits, Using drill bits, Gomez secured the maintenance bin to the floor. She opened the wardrobe-like doors, presenting rolls of thick silver wire, SIC's finest descent cables. They each attached a cable to the harnesses along their backs, as well as additional wind gear from the chest.

Cocteau lifted her head. "Secured?"

"Secure," Bitiir and Gomez responded.

Wilson nodded his head.

"She needs verbal confirmation," Bitiir sneered ever so slightly that any unknowing listener wouldn't notice.

Wilson clenched his jaw, refusing to give Bitiir the satisfaction of his annoyance. "*Secure*," he said, enunciating each syllable.

"Brace yourselves," Cocteau said. She typed into her EC.

The sealed doorway parted.

A shockwave of wind abruptly knocked them back. Like a bomb bursting open, a thousand wistful wind voices howled, warning of the torrent before them.

"Remember your training!" Cocteau yelled above the wind howl. She stood, not even swaying at the sudden exposure. She stepped beyond the open threshold with ease.

How in God's name is she so strong? Wilson thought as another wave of wind pushed him back. He and others pushed through, their cables slowly unraveling from within the maintenance bin. The pressure of the wind like a constant, unwelcoming hand pushing them back.

Wilson felt the magnetic gripping of his boots take hold as his feet dragged along the metal surface beneath. He hauled himself onto the scaffolding platform outside

It was as though he entered the center of a tornado, the wind going in no one direction. Although the metal on the platform was treated with resins and stains to protect it from sulfuric rains, the platform was still worn, corners warped and eroding away. He looked up, the Venus haze dimming the view of the scaffolding layers above him.

"Venus, " Bitiir yelled over the windy tempest. "Truly the goddess of beauty."

Droplets pelted swiftly across the visors of helmets and the thin material of their suits, both completely unaffected by the rain's acidic nature.

"Doesn't seem much of a beauty to me," Wilson said looking over the side, down into more swirling haze and resisting the nauseating sensation brought on by vertigo. He couldn't see more than a few feet ahead. Only the gripping in his boots kept him from blowing off the edge. "Seems more like hell."

"Hell isn't hot," Gomez's voice was oddly calm over the intercom, as though there were no storm at all. "It's cold—empty."

"Will you guys quit the small talk," Cocteau yelled, signaling to them to come forward. "We need to prepare for the descent."

The descent.

That was the part that terrified Wilson.

In the abandoned air city they were safe; a minimum of fifty kilometers up from a surface hotter than the boiling point of lead. Although they were not dropping the full fifty kilometers to the true surface, the artificial surface on SIC's man-made mountain would still be dangerously hot and risk the dangers of high pressure.

SIC was willing to send living people down, but kept their precious Infinite up in the air city, safe from lasting harm. Their suits protected them from the sulfuric gasses and acidic air, but Wilson still doubted if the atmospheric adjustments would be enough once they reached their destination. Would this new acrylic compound in their suits really be enough to protect them during the survey?

"Anchored just in time," Cocteau said, displaying the readings on her EC. "The mountain is positioned perfectly. We'll be able to descend at an angle with the minimum amount of turbulence."

She seems confident enough, Wilson thought. Or she just doesn't care anymore.

Gomez dragged out a large silver spool that their cables ran through. It was no ordinary spool; it was completely enclosed, only allowing their cables through an opening at the bottom. It had buttons and dials to a computerized motor within it.

Wilson and Bitiir held it in place as she drilled it onto the edge of the platform.

Gomez finished with the last bit and stood. "This should ease our descent," she said and wiped her arm across her helmet as though she were wiping sweat from her forehead. "The software should detect errors and give us a more controlled fall."

"Alright, just as we practiced in the VR simulator," Cocteau said, tightening her gear and lining up along the edge. The others followed suit.

"Release your magnetic boot grips to jump the platform." She patted her harness. "Your cables are made with the same compound as our suits and should be able to withstand the heat as we near the mountain's surface. But don't get cocky. It's still going to get hot and we're going to be blown around.

"On my call, three, two—release!"

She jumped, falling into the mustard yellow mist and out of sight. Gomez and Bitiir followed.

Wilson hesitated.

"Wilson, descend!" Cocteau's voice yelled into the intercom.

He searched for his team through the Venus haze. He didn't move.

"Wilson, do your job!" Cocteau yelled again.

How could she tell? He held his breath.

And leapt.

It was the strangest sensation. Venus's gravity was similar to Earth's more than any planet in the known universe. But even with such similarities, Wilson could feel that his presence here was alien, that he did not belong in this world of sulfuric clouds. He should've been on Earth, and he reminded himself that he was the stranger here.

He was a fly trapped on sticky paper, the winds whipping him around, the planet trying to flick him away before he could land on her sacred land.

Muscle memory from descent training kicked-in: arms out and elbows at ninety degree angles. Feet flat, toes pointed, and thighs positioned higher than his pelvis.

He thanked every fiber in his body for his years at NASA, the athletic training for the space mission he never went on. It gave him the physical prowess to withstand this ordeal, even if he'd never be as strong as someone like Cocteau.

His wind gear activated, a fine feathery fabric fanning beneath his arms and legs creating wind resistance. The gear was supposed to steady the descent, enough to give back control of his body. But it felt useless against the power of Venus's breath.

Gravity kept him going down and the cables slowed him to a controlled fall, or else the winds would keep him spiraling in its torrent forever. Exhilaration filled Wilson as he felt the temperature and pressure of his suit change, fighting against the atmospheric changes. The uneasiness of the clouds made him doubt if there truly was a hard surface waiting for him beneath their wall of atmospheric gasses.

Miraculously the descent cables did not tangle with one another. Memory of a mention scratched at the back of his mind; a complex algorithm in their gear that kept that from happening. He didn't really care at this point, feeling on the edge of death as his suit strained to stay connected to his cable, his wind gear's constant clashing with the tempest.

"One kilometer," Cocteau's voice sounded.

Wilson's EC beeped, signaling a slow down to their drop. He felt increased pressure pull on his back as the cable stopped his descent. Although the advancements of the suits made the pressure change for them smooth, they still needed to give their bodies and suits time to equalize, or risk barotrauma—the bends from descending.

He floated in midair, a kite pulling against its strings.

"We'll be at the site of the land colony in no time," Cocteau said. "Just keep your wits about you. Don't get tired."

The pressure loosed, and the fall began again. Wilson tasted his own perspiration from his upper lip as they continued the same pattern, stopping every so often to adjust.

The Venus haze began to clear, and he could make-out the faint outlines of his team.

"Not much further," Cocteau announced after some time. "Clouds clearing and winds calming."

"Calming?" Wilson yelled. "Calming! *We're going to die!*"

"Get a grip," Bitiir said. "For upper Venus this is calm. It'd be worse without your wind gear!"

"Surface sighted," Gomez announced.

"Read you, Gomez," Cocteau responded.

Wilson reached a point where the haze thinned significantly. He could now see his team clearly. The wind around him slowed as he crossed an unmarked threshold in the air.

"Remember, since we're not on the true surface," Gomez's voice explained smoothly in the intercom, "there will still be winds pulling on us at the high elevation. Your suits should activate a surface gripping, like they did with the magnetic grips on the platform."

"H-how are you so composed?" Wilson asked, amazed at how unshaken she was by their descent. His muscles ached from holding the same position, and his voice shook from panting.

"Like Captain Cocteau said in training," she continued in her calm demeanor, "keep your wits about you. I completely trust SICs equipment for getting us to the surface. It works."

"Really?"

"She helped design it," Bitiir said. "You'll be safe enough. Though that makes me doubt if *I* should trust it."

Wilson, as shaken as he was, let out a small laugh.

"See, I can be funny," Bitiir said.

Their descent slowed as Wilson saw glimpses of volcanic rock. Before he knew it, his feet scuffled against the rough dark surface, his boot grips activating and steadying his balance.

The Venus haze was still around him, but thin enough that he could see beyond. Like the darkest cloudy day on Earth, sunlight glowed behind the layer of clouds above, lighting the mountain they stood upon.

He stepped to a nearby ledge.

And looked down.

The mountain was a black peak above a simmering world below. As updrafts pushed the Venus haze aside, he glimpsed the true surface below. Gasses rising, molten rivers cutting through black rock, and lightning striking in the distance, it was a nightmarish fantasy. Though void of life, the planet was far from lifeless.

The thundering of weather systems echoed, a booming voice bellowing from the winds above. Rain bled from cells in the distance, like upturned mushrooms disintegrating into the land. Winds gusted at him, telling him to step back, not to come too close, or be drawn in forever. Bursts of droplets spat onto him from the wind's voice and he heeded its warning, stepping away from the ledge.

Cocteau drilled an anchor into the hard ground. The team detached themselves from their harnesses. They hooked their cables to the anchor and tied additional wind gear to it. Although still attached to the air city above, the city's flight controls would keep it anchored in place as to not snap the cables.

"Your call, brainiacs," Cocteau sat next to the anchor. "This is where the land colony is supposed to be and where you found your little artifact, Gomez. Begin your survey when ready. Just keep in mind that there's a downpour approaching within the hour and I'd rather not experiment too much with the 'temporary' effectiveness of these suits. Melting is not preferable."

Step by step, Wilson and Gomez pulled surveying equipment from their packs. Small angular cubes that easily attached to their ECs. Insignificant to the untrained eye, but essential to the surveyor.

With the wave of a hand or the touch of a finger, the software contained within the cubes would activate and send electrical pulses through the surface; scan with invisible eyes any abnormalities along the terrain. Then download the readings directly to their ECs.

Wilson walked the perimeter of where the colony once was. Jagged and full of trenches, he recalled historical images of world wars; desolate lands once populated by cities, brought down to rubble as though they never existed. As much as he knew he was on Venus, he pictured himself on Earth, navigating these sites. How gruesome humans once were, that they could create regions that mimicked the hostile environment of Venus so perfectly. And now working for SIC he wondered, are they still?

He slipped up and down rocks, kicking up dirt and splattering it across his suit. Although void of water, the dirt had a stickiness to it that got everywhere and anywhere.

And the smell, although filtered by the suit, was overwhelming. Chemical stink as he called it, amplified by the unfamiliar stenches that surrounded him.

His EC beeped steadily, receiving readings; nothing out of the norm for the Venus surface. SIC used materials from the surface to create this level of the mountain and his surveying tools proved it. Nothing picked up on the artificial materials to create the former upper levels of the mountain. No readings or signs that there ever was a land colony. Not even the faintest hint or evidence of the biological life it took with it when it disappeared. It truly was gone out of existence.

Wilson crawled out of a trench, a set of feet blocking his view. He looked-up.

Bitiir stood over him, hands on hips. Through the darkened glass of his visor, his face lit up, twitching with his smile.

Remember who's in charge, his voice reverberated in Wilson's mind.

"Anything Dr. Wilson?" Bitiir asked.

"I'm getting nothing," Wilson said frustrated as he pulled himself out and onto his feet. "Even from a space archeologist's standpoint, I have nothing." He tried to brush Venus dust off him, but it stuck. He wiped his EC. "But the readings—"

"Readings?"

"Yes," Wilson said. "The readings do show that the materials here share properties to the artifact, and it's all natural. Nothing artificial."

"But couldn't it also share properties to materials on Earth, if we did a survey at right spot?" Bitiir said critically. "Couldn't it?"

Wilson hesitated.

"Dr?" Bitiir's smug dripped with gratification.

"Yes," Wilson gritted through his teeth.

"So it proves nothing," Bitiir said. "Dr. Gomez, you finding anything?"

Gomez appeared out of a nearby trench, panting heavily.

"Nothing," Gomez's voice lost some it's steady calm, her composure breaking. "I refuse to believe that there's nothing here. We did not spend all this time getting down here to find nothing."

"Believe what you will my dear," Bitiir sounded too gleeful. "But it seems that there is nothing of significance needing preserving, which leads us to conclude that the artifact is a hoax."

Wilson dug at the ground with his foot. "It was no hoax."

"Are you blind?" Bitiir gestured all around him. "There is nothing here, nothing! Dust, rock, sulfur, that's all we've ever found on Venus, and that's why the colonies failed."

"Then explain why an entire colony just disappeared," Gomez pointed up. "There's supposed to be a compound here and it's gone. Lives lost! Is SIC going to answer for those lives?"

"Are you sure it's really gone?" Bitiir said. "People go MIA in space missions all the time. You know storms and radiation can mess with—"

"We're in the right spot," Cocteau cut in, sounding more than a little offended, her feet heavy and stocky as she approached.

"Finished our little break, did we?" Bitiir said coolly to her. "I'm just saying—"

"You're just saying," Cocteau gave a sarcastic laugh. "You're always just saying. All those people are reported MIA? Give me a break! Did anyone even know they were down here? It's just like all the other bullshit that SIC has you say with their arm shoved up your ass."

"Really?" Bitiir gave a full laugh. "Aren't we one to talk. If anyone knows about being one of SIC's puppets—"

"You never know when to stop," Gomez spat. "Either of you! Think of the lives and careers your ruining—*my career*—"

"I'm the one saving your skins," Bitiir's voice enraged. "Do any of you think you'd be where you are without me? You have no idea how much I've done for *you*—"

They converged on one another, continuing to argue.

Wilson walked away, keeping his distance. Even if he still heard them in his intercom, he wanted no part of it.

He had enough of all this. The mission was a waste. Why was he even here? It was his dream to go into space, walk on other worlds. And now that he was on the surface of another world, it didn't feel like he was anymore. Being here, or being on Earth, it changed nothing. He was no better than Bitiir; just another one of SICs lackeys, here to do a data dump and save them from whatever lawsuits they dug themselves into.

And it made no difference. He would never find what he was truly looking for. Not here, not in space, or on his homeworld.

A vision flashed across his eyes: the smile of a woman, her lips slightly parted as he brushed her hair from her face. A whisper slipping from her mouth. *Marshall,* she called.

She was gone, and no matter how far he traveled or went, the emptiness of her would never cease, and would follow him to the end of time.

He looked to the west. The horizon was hazy over the mountain, continuing on into a vast uncertainty that was the desolate world he now walked upon.

And in that uncertainty he saw a wisp of smoke appear.

Smoke? Wilson squinted his eyes. That couldn't be right. Maybe a microburst of wind and dust, or volcanic gasses, but certainly not smoke.

Wilson looked down at his EC. Nothing came up for atmospheric disturbances. "Venus command," he pressed the emergency signal on the side of his helmet. "Are you reading anything?"

Only static. They were too deep below the atmosphere to reach anything in orbit.

"Um, guys?" Wilson tried to talk over the argument still continuing in his intercom. "Are you seeing this?"

"Not now, Wilson," Cocteau growled. "Bitiir, I've got a right mind—"

"Right mind for what?"

"Get a grip captain," Gomez actually sounded angry. "I've put my life's work into this planet—"

"Um, guys," Wilson looked to the horizon again to make sure he was seeing what he was. The smoke was gathering, massing into a wall, building. "You should really look at this."

"Not now Wilson," Cocteau sounded again.

Everyone continued arguing.

"Shut the hell up and look!" Wilson couldn't take his eyes off it.

"For crying out loud," Cocteau said. She looked west. *"What the hell is it?"*

All turned and looked. The smoke had become a massive wall getting bigger and denser. The sun reflected a lurid green in the smoke.

"That's not getting bigger," Wilson said. "It's getting closer."

"Back to the anchor," Gomez said. "Fast."

They all turned, running in the direction of the anchor.

"What is that thing?" Bitiir yelled.

"Don't know," Gomez panted. "But I've never seen anything like that before. That shouldn't be here—not at this elevation."

Wilson looked down at his EC. There were still no readings for the anomaly.

"Less talk, more run," Cocteau yelled.

Suddenly the ground vibrated, knocking them all over.

Earthquake? Wilson thought.

"Get-up," Cocteau yelled. "That thing is getting close and—"
Boom!

A sudden wave hit them and Cocteau's voice cut-out. The power-down signal went-off and cut-out the same time as Cocteau.

"No, no, no!" Wilson scrambled to his feet. His suit was getting hot and his air reserves suddenly kicked in. His checked his EC; it was off.

"Shit, shit, *shit!*" He knew this would happen. The main systems on his Venus suit failed, and he only had a few minutes before the reserve power would completely drain trying to run the entire suit; reserves were only enough to run parts of the suit, not in its entirety. He was going to be crushed by the heat and pressure.

"Gomez, Cocteau!" He panicked, looking to them. His team all the same look of panic on their faces, realizing the failure of their suits.

What hit them? It acted like an electromagnetic wave. If that was true, then their reserve air and power wouldn't have kicked in. It no longer mattered, because Wilson could hear his life support systems shutting down piece by piece, as the reserve power drained.

"What do we do?" he yelled, forgetting no one could hear him. Another system failed and the grips on his boot released. He now had to fight the winds with his own strength.

The cloud was almost upon them, traveling faster than the wind could carry.

"We need to run," Wilson tried to signal his team, but they all struggled from the lack of grip on their boots. They tried to run against wind and pressure that pushed them back, like a child trying to walk for the first time.

Suddenly they were engulfed.

Wilson could no longer see his team. He was on the ground, unable to stand as pressure pushed against him. Green smoke surrounded him.

"*No, no, no!*" Wilson coughed.

He watched in horror, unable to move as the smoke penetrated through his suit. He held his breath, but he had to breathe. He could feel tingling as the smoke came through his skin, burning through the nostrils of his nose, and seeping down his throat into his lungs.

And saw nothing as it overtook his eyes and burned away his sight, and bled into his mind.

END PART I

PART II: Inferos

Chapter 8: A Night in Hell

Marshall Wilson squeezed her hand. It felt real.

"It will be over soon," the voice of his dearly departed echoed in his mind.

"I know," he said aloud as though she were there. "I just didn't think it would be so soon."

He saw her grin; dry thin lips, once full before the sickness came.

She laughed. "Always break expectations, don't I?" Her laugh rang just as musically as it always did. *Don't let me be the end of your life. . . You will see me again when you least expect it.*

Then pain. In his chest, in his head, and through his spine. Wilson thought for a moment that he was back on Earth, sitting at his late wife's hospice bedside again, that she was truly there. It was like he had awoken from a dream, reliving every agonizing moment of her passing.

But that was just the emotional pain. There was also physical pain running through his body. His eyes were open, but darkness told him he was blind. The stillness was deafening, hearing nothing.

Where was he? He tried to remember.

I'm in my NASA lab.

No—I'm lecturing at the university.

No—I'm reading charts on the moon orbiter.

His mind wandered.

Wait—he transferred to the Venus station. Did he go down to the surface? Impossible, no one can survive the surface of Venus. But he had, and then—

Then came the ringing.

High pitched, stinging his ears. He could hear someone yelling, screaming. He tried to answer back, let whoever was screaming know they weren't alone, but the pain in his spine increased when he tried to speak, numbing his throat.

He tried to move, but his arms and legs were restrained. Was he standing? No, he was kneeling, wrists and ankles firmly in place on a ground he couldn't see.

He tried to move his head, but something around his neck held his head down.

"Gomez?" he gasped. "Bitiir? *Cocteau*—I'm here—*help me!*"

He kept trying to push his voice out, but his throat constrained.

Suddenly a glimpse of light.

It was still dark, but his vision was somewhat returning. He tried to look-up again, but whatever was restraining his neck pushed harder.

He saw the outline of his hands bound to the ground. He lifted his eyes slightly.

An outline stood before him. It was too blurry to see details, but there was something—someone—there.

He blinked, trying to focus his eyesight. He pushed his head against the restraint on his neck, but it wouldn't allow him to move any further. He could only move his eyes, hairs dropping in front of them, skewing his vision even more.

"Where am I?" he demanded. His voice was hoarse, like he swallowed gravel.

The outline shifted, taking a step closer. Legs? They had to be, but they didn't look right, even in the dark.

High pitched ringing started again as Wilson heard the screaming. Pain soaring up his back, through his limbs. Was he being tortured? He couldn't focus on anything but his agony and the the shrieking. As much as he tried, he was still unable to call out to the person screaming.

Then it all stopped.

"P-please," Wilson begged to the outline in front of him. "What's going on?"

The outline didn't move. Wilson strained his eyes further to make out what it was.

He froze.

He couldn't breathe as he stared at the legs before him.

Long, spindly, bent unnaturally like an upright canine. He could hear mechanical clicking as he became aware of the restraint on his neck. They were long fingers, cold, hard, like ice against rock. He could feel them tighten as he struggled. It was useless; the grip was stronger than anything he'd ever known.

Pain erupted up through his back again as the high pitched ringing made his ears feel on the verge of bleeding. His sight blacked-out as the screaming continued.

The visions started again: flashes of his late wife squeezing his hand, his career at NASA, Cocteau recruiting him, the moon orbiter, holding the artifact in his palm—

And the memory of Bitiir's snide expression as he mocked Wilson's suffering in the VR room. Taunting him with simulations of the scorching Venusian surface—the flaming molten surface and he was drowning in it!

Vermillion lava consumed Wilson, crushing his body from the pressure and gases. He felt himself dying. He wanted desperately to live, but death also meant relief; it meant seeing *her* again.

Abruptly the vision stopped.

His pain receded.

And the screaming ended.

The grip on Wilson's neck disappeared. He blinked and his eyesight returned.

The dreadful being was gone.

"W-water," he coughed.

With his neck free of the death grip, he looked around. He tried to stand, but his hands and feet were still restrained to the ground.

"H-hello?" he said, hoping against his intuition.

No one answered back.

"Who's there?" he asked. Please, he thought desperately, let the person screaming answer me.

He could make out walls, like those of a cave. Small, windowless and doorless.

And Wilson was the only one in there.

Chapter 9: Survive

Marie? Marie Cocteau! *You listen or so help me.*"

Captain Cocteau felt the slap across her face, just as firm and strong as the day it happened.

"God damn," she swore as the memory faded. Her father's hand felt real—*too real.*

Cocteau couldn't see anything, it was utterly dark. She was flat on her back, strapped down to something. A stone table?

She had no idea where she was or what was happening. Pain soared up her spine, but she did not scream. No matter where she was or what drugs were pumped into her, there was no way she was going to break, *not ever.* She felt memories of the past trying to break through, like an outside force was exerting itself into her head.

Really? Bitiir's laugh was as present as ever. *Aren't we one to talk. If anyone knows about being one of SIC's puppets, it's their dog. And you still need your bark collar.*

Recollections of her court martial, a curved knife between her knuckles, a pleasant face masking sinister intentions; all memory fragments trying to piece together.

She walled them off, like she'd done so many times before. People tried to break her and never succeeded. *Never.*

And was why she was here now.

None of it mattered. It never would because one word coursed through her; the very thing that created her, that made blood pump into her veins. One word that brought her further than any living thing possibly could.

Survive.

She had an obligation to survive, a responsibility to her team. Without her survival they were done for, she knew it. Deep in her bones she knew that everything depended on her.

"Keep trying bastard," Cocteau clenched her teeth, her skin crawled and boiled. Even though she couldn't see, she knew someone else was with her. A stranger probing her mind.

The pressure in her head forced the vexatious memories through. A long forgotten childhood she's chosen to forsake. Her father's disappointing gaze, school kids calling her freak, the humiliation of losing her first fight, the showers at base camp—

Knocked down by her father—knocked down by bullies—knocked down by rapists—

Survive.

She clenched her teeth so tight they felt as if they'd shatter. "You're gettin' nothing from me!"

Images of every time she punched back. She learned long ago that she could always punch back. *"You're gettin' nothing from me!"*

Her strength returned,

And she punched back just as she always did.

And broke free.

Whatever was holding her down, Cocteau ripped through it. She felt the surface crack beneath her and whatever link was connected to her brain was gone as memories dissipated.

She pushed off the table, landing on a warm, hard surface. Fully aware again, her eyesight returned.

Dim white lights strobed from an unknown source. A plangent sound echoed all around in rhythm to her heart. Was it an alarm?

She was free of her restraints and that wasn't good for whoever tied her down.

The light distortion made it impossible to see her surroundings in full. It all seemed like endless dark beyond the flashing light. Standing up, her body felt light only wearing her SIC bodysuit, all other gear gone.

The air all around burned her throat, drying it to the point she felt she could breathe fire. Just like the days she spent in deep desert missions. She was slick with sweat, her hair sticking to her scalp. Behind her, a clear table reflected off the strobing lights, broken with the shattered restraints that held her.

Then a high pitched ringing.

"Ahh!" Cocteau fell to her knees. She grabbed her ears as the ringing stung them, piercing like glass through flesh. From the corner of her eye, something reached for her.

Cocteau dodged, the sound of the ringing keeping her from standing straight. A dark limb brushed against her.

"No!" she ordered. The glimpse of a monstrous hand. Long fingers with too many joints spread in front of her face.

I've never been afraid, the memory of her youthful lie reverberated. *Never will be.*

And she was still afraid, like all those times before and buried so well. Everything felt like slow motion, though she knew only seconds passed.

Whatever was happening had nothing to do with SIC, and nothing to do with the military.

Only fools fear the unknown, she remembered Wilson saying back on the moon orbiter.

Cocteau held her breath. *I'm no coward.*

The monstrous hand reached for her again. She ducked away. More oversized limbs appeared, indescribable in the fast movements they made.

She positioned herself—hunched, holding her right fist in her left hand. She lunged forward, ramming her right side and stabbing her elbow in the direction of the dark limbs.

She hit something.

Not a wall, but a mass—the being, a creature to which the limbs belonged to. It was hard, like metal bones. She caught sight of a shining gold torso and a skeletal structure, her head only reaching what she assumed was a chest.

Still holding her fist, she shoved her elbow again into the creature.

It stumbled but didn't fall. Even with all her might, it still stood, head and face hidden in shadow, reaching spindly fingers at her.

But it did stumble, Cocteau thought, as she dodged again. *A weakness.*

She had to work fast, assuming this thing could predict as well as she could. She lunged forward again, but this time she aimed low.

She hit its lanky, misshapen legs.

It worked. The disorienting ring completely stopped and the creature hit the floor.

Something small and round flung into the air, hitting Cocteau in the head.

"What the—" Cocteau's chest froze as she realized what flew from the creature It was a coin, just like the artifact in Gomez's lab.

Her face angelically dancing at the forefront of Cocteau's mind. *It's more than just a coin,* she teased.

Gomez was always right.

Cocteau searched the warm, dark ground for the coin, hoping it could do something. It had to. She was out of options.

The creature stirred, its limbs scraping against the ground as it stood. Now she was out of time.

Her hands frantically searched the ground.

And just as her heart sank, she felt the coin under her wrist.

Cocteau grabbed it, holding it between her thumb and index finger, into the flashing light.

What felt like an infinite, wall-less room was no more. Out of the dark appeared a green light. She saw that she was in a wide, enclosed grotto with no apparent opening. The light emanated from a small holographic panel, like a translucent emerald floating on the other side along the wall.

Cocteau ran for it, the light from the panel growing brighter as the coin neared it.

She felt the creature approaching fast, it's unnerving wrath too similar to the paternal one she broke free from long ago.

She reached the panel.

She went to touch it, but her hand passed right through the holograph. As it did, the panel turned into a dial with distorted, unearthly symbols swirling around it. Nothing was readable.

She danced her fingers through all the symbols. They need to reveal something—*anything* useful. Desperation held her hostage.

Suddenly, another light.

The outline of a door in the form of fluorescent arch appeared on the wall beside the dial. The light spread, the door slid into its surroundings, creating an opening.

Survive.

She made a run for it, her foot brushing against the hard body of the creature just behind.

Survive.

She ran down a long, windowless corridor, unable to make out details except for the rock. Basalt? It was rough beneath her bare feet.

She kept her eyes ahead; looking back would only slow her down. Even curiosity of that creature was wasn't enough to make her look back.

She barely noticed bullets of light zipping past her as she ran evasively, keeping her head low. The creature couldn't be far behind, including any backup it gathered along the way.

I will survive this.

Chapter 10: Blinding Light

The restraints released from Marshall Wilson's wrists. Something pulled him to standing position.

His prison was still too dark to tell where he was. His hands were pulled behind his back, hot metal binding them together like handcuffs.

He felt another hot band wrap around his head, covering his eyes. He felt a rod stab the middle of his spine, pushing him forward.

Wilson halted.

"Where are you taking me," he demanded of his captors.

The sticky static of electricity cracked behind him. The rod stabbed him again, but this time a dry pain seared up it. It paralyzed him with pinprick sensations throughout his limbs.

The rod was removed and the sensation stopped.

He was pushed forward again.

He pushed back. "I'm not going till you tell me what's going on here. Is this some sick idea from SIC—"

He was stabbed again and pushed forward.

"Alright, alright," Wilson started forward. "I get the idea."

He could tell that there were others around him, even if he couldn't see. He heard their awkward joints bend with each movement, their feet dig into the rough, solid earth beneath them. Wilson's bare feet tugged and scraped tender flesh against the uneven and sharp surface, as though the ground had been crudely dug by a rusted shovel. He tripped a couple times, and his captors stabbed him merciless with electricity

Every so often he felt the cold grasp of long, hard fingers on him, handling him to move in different directions. He didn't realize it before, not till their icy fingers touched him, but he was hot. More than hot, he was burning. The trickling of sweat slipped down his limbs, making the walk all the more uncomfortable..

"SIC really has gone too far," Wilson said nervously. "I don't know who you think you are, but this is disgusting. All because I was doing my job. Is this Bitiir's idea of intimidation? He's got another thing coming setting this up—"

"Dr. Wilson?" Gomez's voice was right next to him.

"Gomez?" He was shoved, pushed to move faster. "Gomez!"

He knew he sounded hostile, but Gomez was one of them, one of SIC's people. He had trusted her. "Tell me what's going on. What's the big idea?"

"I-I," Gomez's meek voice shook to the left of him. "I don't know. I can't see. They put something over my eyes. T-they hurt me, Wilson, *hurt me!* I saw things."

"Sure," Wilson said unconvinced. "You saw things. Like me, drugged and tortured. And for what? Being honest? Doing my job?"

"*No,*" Gomez didn't sound like her usual calm self. "Please, t-trust me. I'm scared enough. This isn't SIC, I swear."

"Sure," Wilson stopped, holding his ground.

A sudden shriek. He heard crackling electricity and Gomez screamed. Was she being stabbed by electricity as well? He couldn't trust the act.

They moved forward in silence. Wilson was angry. He left everything he knew behind for this mission. The promise of a dream, the excitement of space exploration. And for what? He couldn't even see. He didn't even know if all this was real.

You've done it Marshall, he thought to himself. *You've got yourself into this one, and against your better judgment.*

They were pulled to a halt. Hands wrapped around Wilson's arm as he felt the binding around his head loosen. Light flooded and his eyes adjusted.

Wilson's heart stopped.

This was a nightmare, it had to be.

There was no other explanation for the beings that stood around them.

Their captors weren't of Earth.

They were in a poorly lit corridor, glowing a sickly yellow green. The walls and floor looked like they were carved right out of the rock of the Venus surface. And it was the garish corridor that reflected in their eyes.

It was the creatures' eyes that got Wilson first; large, deep, expressionless black holes of nothing. The eyes took up more than half the faceless head. Wilson looked into them, seeing his terror mirrored back at him. And the body stood larger than any human he'd ever known, towering over him and Gomez by at least two feet. The body of a mutilated exoskeleton, a shell of shining gold and copper bones hiding whatever dread was beneath. All atop long, gangly canine legs, just like the ones Wilson saw in his lonely prison.

All he could do was stare, motionless as one of creatures walked in front of them, holding up a coin like the one in the Venus station lab. A green holographic panel appeared on the wall. The creature's spider-leg fingers trilled a pattern into it.

Four more surrounded Wilson and Gomez, holding rods that crackled with blue static on the ends. Guards to keep them submissive.

"We're still on Venus," he whispered horrified.

Gomez gulped. "Yes," she whispered. "We are." Her hands were also bound behind her back. She was barefoot and only in the bodysuit that they wore under their Venusian gear. He realized that he, too, was still in his bodysuit.

"You think they'll let us talk?" Wilson mouthed.

"Doesn't look like they're stopping us," Gomez said, glancing at the creature dialing into the holograph. "I don't think they care."

Wilson shuttered. How powerful were these beings that they didn't care if their prisoners spoke with one another? Didn't care if their prisoners plotted against them, even before their very eyes? Didn't care enough that they allowed their prisoner's eyes to be uncovered and see their surroundings. Were they really in that much control that such things did not phase them?

"What are these things?" he asked, even though he knew Gomez didn't have the answers.

"I don't even know if this is real," she said. "They did something with my head and I don't even know if I'm alive."

Wilson sighed. "I don't either."

They locked eyes on one another, her dark, deep ones looking into his. The comfort of a mutual fear they both shared.

High pitched ringing broke their gaze as they grimaced at the sound. Wilson forced his eyes open against the sound, seeing the lead creature in front of them acknowledge the others. The ringing stopped.

That's it! Wilson thought. *Communicating! That's what they're doing.*

A white light illuminated an arch in the wall closest to them. Then it disappeared, leaving behind an opening. Inside was dark, impossible to see beyond it.

They were pushed into the opening.

"Gomez, I figured it out," Wilson said excited. He shook, elated at his discovery. "They're communicating. It's how they communicate!"

"The ringing?"

"That's why we heard it," Wilson said. "They're communicating at some kind of high frequency."

She nodded. "They—the Venusians."

Wilson and Gomez were forced forward and the opening shut with the wall reappearing behind them.

The ground beneath became smooth and the air turned cold. Wilson shivered, unable to adjust to the abrupt change. There was a dim, cool glow, reflecting polished volcanic glass floors and high cathedral walls. The air smelled dry, dead as though the cold would draw out their very souls. The obsidian walls and floor made Wilson felt like he was floating in the great abyss, his head reeling.

Then a whisper. . .

Marshall. . .

Wilson felt a pulsating sensation with the whisper, the sound of his name clearer than before. His eyes were drawn to the source of the call.

Far in the center of the room all was an orb, no bigger than a human fist. It sat perfectly upon a plain black pedestal. All the light in the room emanated from the orb, mimicking a dim star in the far reaches of the beyond.

Marshall. . .

He couldn't look away as it called his name. Neither Gomez or the Venusians gave any indication of hearing what he was. Could this be the thing he'd been hearing while at Venus station? The thing stealing the voice of his dead wife?

The Venusian's high pitched ringing started again, but instead of cringing, Wilson tried to listen. It pained him, but he had to try. What were they saying? What were they discussing? Gomez looked like she was going to be ill.

They were pushed toward the orb. As they neared, Wilson noticed a subtle pulse from the light, just as with the whisper, as though it were alive.

They were forced onto their knees on either side of the glowing orb, their hands chained to the ground behind them.

"What do you think?" Wilson said. "Do they worship it?"

"I don't think they worship anything," Gomez said staidly looking at the orb. "They have no masters."

One of the Venusian guards grabbed the back of Gomez's neck.

"*Hey.*" Wilson tried to stand, but his restraints held him in place.

The lead Venusian held out its coin, another pedestal rising from the floor beside them. Another green holographic panel appeared above it.

The orb grew brighter, spinning on its axis.

Wilson felt power surging from the orb, just as if he were standing too close to an electrical station. His and Gomez's hair stood on end as it spun faster, warped energy growing in diameter around it.

Suddenly, it became still, light pulsing in place, in rhythm of a relaxed heartbeat. A ghostly arm of light stretched from it, right into Gomez's face.

"No!" Wilson fought his restraints. "What are you doing?"

The Venusian behind Wilson pushed him down, shoving the side of his face onto the floor. It wrapped its bony fingers around his head, holding him down.

Gomez's eyes were transfixed on the light.

"Stop it," Wilson cried-out, trying shake out of the Venusian grip. Whatever the light was, it couldn't be good. "What are you doing? Look away Gomez, Look away!"

But she couldn't. By the lamented look in her eyes Wilson knew there was no way of pulling her gaze.

A twitch of a smile came from the corners of her mouth. Her eyes grew wider.

"Look away!" Wilson continued to yell.

But it was useless. He could see it in her. Gomez no longer heard him.

He knew she couldn't hear the sound of the stone pulsing. Or the complaints of Venusians as they shocked him with their poles, punishment for fighting against his jailers.

She heard no one because she was no longer there. Instead she was home—her real home—looking into her mother's face. . .

Chapter 11: What the Geologist Saw

'm sorry I failed you Ari. It is my fault. I want everything for you my love, so please let it go. . . let him go. . .

Those were among the last words Arianna Gracia heard her mother say before she died. Most people recognized her as Dr. Gomez, her chosen name. But titles made no difference to her or her mother. She knew who she was.

"Tell me about dad," little Ari begged. "Oh please tell me!"

Dr. Gomez could hear her childhood voice coming from her lips. It was no longer just a memory. She was a child again and everything unfolded as though she were living it for the first time. From the moment the orb's energy touched her she fell out of reality and no longer recognized the present.

Her memory was her new reality.

Ari and her mother were looking up at clouds, lying on a grassy hill, bright daylight blinding to those with uncareful eyes. It was a warm humid day. The breaking of Atlantic waves cracked in the distance, a constant reminder of the island they lived on.

"Ari," her mother Tamara sighed in that dismal voice.

"Please mom," Ari begged again. She sat up. Her eight-year-old mind could not wrap around the idea of why her mother never spoke of their father anymore. She remembered him, briefly, like a dream, and sometimes wondered if he was even real. She knew her mother loved him once, and that love still had to be there, enough to find him.

"Ari, I already told you," her mother adamant. "You don't have a father."

Ari grumbled. She hated what was happening. Her mother pretended like he never existed.

Back before Tamara stopped talking about him, she told Ari her Dad was the one who made it possible to attend Catholic school. He dropped her off her first day of primary school. That was the last time Ari saw her father.

Everyone at school knew that Ari was not a true Haitian. Although her mother was full blooded Haitian through and through, Ari wasn't. Tamara once hoped Ari's father could use his Mexican citizenship to take her away from island. After his disappearance that hope dissipated.

Until Tamara told Ari of a new idea.

"We're going to leave one day, I promise," Tamara said. "And we'll go to a place where you can be anything you want, where no one will care where you come from."

A place where you can be anything you want—her mother's promise was as bright as the light that now blinded Dr. Gomez's eyes. She tried to squint, bring her mind herself back to the present. But the power of the orb forced her deeper into her memories, her eyes transfixed on it.

"Look away Gomez, look away!" She heard Dr. Wilson's cries. They sounded far away and she couldn't see him. She tried to call back, tell him she was here; a kindred spirit and that she wanted desperately for him to trust her. He knew nothing of the broken heart she hid from her SIC colleagues. But his cries faded as another memory overcame her.

Ari and her mother left Haiti. In the dark of night, she said goodbye to her home, with only the stars as her companions as they traveled. They gained passageway to a new land where promises were made.

America.

They heard rumors about this nation. A land where even the most impoverished were rich, and where hopes and dreams came true. They chose to believe it.

"If anyone asks where you're from, you tell them you were born in Miami," Tamara told Ari as she tugged her hair with a smoothing brush, massaging oil and conditioner onto the strands.

Her mother wanted fresh braids in Ari's hair for school the next morning in Fort Lauderdale.

They sat on the crusty carpet in the middle of their apartment. They didn't have a couch yet, but her mother promised furniture as soon as more money came in. The smell of stale cigarettes was overwhelming when they first moved in, but Ari no longer noticed it.

"But mom, we're Haitian——"

"Shh," her mother shushed violently, yanking the brush from her hair. "Do you want to be taken from me? Remember the photos we saw in the landlord's office, on his TV? We are American now, and that is all people need to know. We don't have the money to do this the way they want, and never will. If people know where we're from, they will separate us and send us away to lord knows where. You know how hard it was to get here—*they don't.*"

Ari nodded, thinking of their journey; sleepless nights and evenings without dinner. Now they lived in an apartment, nicer than anything they had in Haiti, even if their neighbors always complained about it. Their home in Haiti had mud walls and floors, and a leaking roof made from scrap metal and palm leaves. Now she had a carpet, a tiled kitchen, and her own room.

"School can be fun here," Tamara continued, twisting and adding another elaborate braid to Ari's hair. "School will notice that you have an accent; they will question your language. You speak English now."

"But I don't know English."

"Remember the words I taught you," Tamara said. "It will be enough, and school will teach the rest."

"Yes mom."

"Look away!" Wilson's voice broke through the walls of the apartment, blinding light bleaching the memory from her mind. Gomez saw Wilson's outline through the light, drawing her back to the present.

"Gomez—Arianna! *Please*," Wilson's outline pleaded. "I don't understand, why won't you just look away!"

Then another presence. A voice without a voice, as though it came from the orb. No words were spoken, no sound to identify with. But there was an understanding, a question pressing against her mind.

How came you to Venus?

Through SIC, she answered, all inhibitions suppressed. She couldn't refuse even if she wanted to.

"Just stop looking," Wilson continued his plea. If only he knew the persuasive nature of the orb's power. She couldn't stop looking— she didn't want to.

What is your intent upon this world? Who is SIC and how came you to it? The voiceless understanding pressed against her, lulling her to dream of the past.

Her intent? What was easy. *To show them all,* her thoughts spoke to the understanding, *show everyone, that I am greatest at what I do, at what I am. As for SIC*—that one was more complicated. She didn't know how to answer.

The understanding pushed her mind and more visions of the past flashed across her mind.

"Où suis-je," Gomez said. "Où est-ce que je vais?" *Where am I, where do I go?*

"Gomez, *stop*—"

Wilson's outline faded and became someone familiar. A former principal. A strict elderly woman, but kind. She led little Ari through a sea of foreign words across the elementary school campus.

Ari exclusively spoke French when she was in Catholic primary school and Haitian creole at home. Now that she was in Florida, she was forced to change all that. Everyone spoke English and Spanish, two languages she knew nothing about. Even the small time she knew her father he hardly spoke his native Spanish with her. And the English words here sounded nothing like the few Tamara taught her.

American school was nothing like her old school. No one wore uniforms, kids were disorganized, and most didn't seem to care about why they were even in school in the first place. It was one big social party and that confused Ari.

The principal dropped her off in a classroom full of stuff. There was just so much stuff; toys, books, art, touch screens, and colors everywhere. Kids were frantically laughing and playing with electronic devices that showed them whatever they pleased. Catholic school was was quiet and no one spoke except the adults. She had only ever used old textbooks, paper, and pencils.

A tall, bony woman took Ari's hand and pulled her to the front of the room. Was this her teacher? The woman raised her hand and said something in English. The kids stopped and sat at round tables scattered nonsensically around the room. The bony teacher continued to talk in English so fast Ari couldn't catch any words. Everyone stared at her, a mixture of all kinds of people; some looked like her with their curls and braids, but none of them were Haitian.

The teacher stopped speaking and directed Ari to an empty seat. She placed a device with a wide screen in her hands and strange glasses on her face.

All the other kids put on their glasses and pulled-out screens and began working on lessons that made funny noises, making them laugh as they worked. Lights blinked in their glasses as they touched invisible buttons in the air around them. Did the glasses make them see things? Ari just stared at her screen.

Her spine crawled when she felt the presence of the bony teacher behind her. The teacher's hand reached over her shoulder and tapped the screen. Augmented reality came alive through the glasses as shapes and words spoke gibberish to her.

Ari still didn't get it.

Say something English, Ari thought. *Or they'll know.* "My name is Arianna, and I am from Miami."

It was the only English phrase she could remember. The bony teacher got that look in her eye; she knew.

The teacher headed to her desk and dialed into a phone.

Oh no, Ari thought. *They know.*

Should she run? Where would she go? Her mother wouldn't be home till late tonight. She was alone.

A stout woman came into the room a few minutes later. She spoke to the bony teacher, glancing at Ari every few seconds.

The stout woman approached Ari.

She smiled at her. "Est-ce que tu parles français?" *Do you speak French?*

It was French. What would happen if they knew?

Ari stayed mute for most of that year. While she was mute she could not stay in the big classroom; she was pulled, put into the small classroom with all the kids that spoke only Spanish. The lessons in that room were easy, especially the math ones. Even if she didn't understand what her new teacher said, she could still do them.

Then one day everything clicked.

Immersed in the language, English words did not seem to be spoken so fast. She could finally make-out the vocabulary with ease.

It's not so different from French, she thought. Not only could she understand English, she could also understand the Spanish that kids whispered to one another, hoping the teacher wouldn't translate what they were saying. She could.

Math also kept getting easier. So easy that she could finish in a matter of minutes what took other kids an entire lesson. She took tests in the small room at the front office. She could complete them all in English, French, and Spanish. Eventually, she was allowed to go back to the big classroom again, and she was often paired with students who struggled. She became the teacher where the teacher couldn't be.

Is this the SIC that brought you to our world? The voiceless understanding interrupted her thoughts.

No, she answered. *But they made SIC find me.*

The blinding light from the orb pushed Gomez further, to some years later. She was in junior high, the final year before high school.

"Metamorphism is the stage where rock undergoes a transformation," fourteen-year-old Ari announced to the audience in the school's auditorium. "Causation is immense heat and pressure that results in physical and chemical changes. "

Cheers and applause followed. It was announced she would attend the district academic-thon finals. Her teacher, a middle-aged man that specialized in sciences, placed a gold metal around her neck. He placed a silver one around Macie Williams, the runner-up.

Ari delighted at being first. Second to her was first loser.

A bell sounded from the intercom system. Students and parents alike dispersed from the auditorium.

Although Ari knew she wasn't there, she stayed on the stage and looked into the crowd of parents leaving. Tamara always worked. Strict schedules and a promise of keeping their legal status quiet kept Tamara from coming to any of Ari's school events.

Marcie was between her parents, both of them kissing and whispering congratulations to her at being second.

Ari's delight burned away, turning to envious fire as she stared at Macie's parents.

"Um, Ari, one moment please," her teacher called.

Ari jumped from the stage. "Yes?"

"Message from the front," her teacher read off a tablet. "You are to go directly to the counselor's office."

Ari put on her augmented glasses. It blinked red a notification to go immediately to counseling.

Probably another test, she thought, pulling them off. *There's always another test*. It was that time of year again when they flooded her with tests to see how smart she was. She didn't mind showing it off.

She headed to the front office, then through the narrow hall that ended in the counseling center.

She stopped dead in her tracks.

There was no counselor to test her. Instead, two people stood outside her counselor's office, in white uniforms and gold sunglasses.

Shit, they found me, she thought. Her mom warned her this day would come if she kept drawing attention to herself, but nothing ever happened. The elation of showing-up all the kids, especially the ones with the things she could never have, made her feel alive—validated. They could never have her brain, her smarts. And it was worth a risk she believed didn't exist.

How wrong she was. Ari's heart thumped fast as she thought of running to Tamara's work, warning her and leaving home forever. Starting over in a different school, different city, and different state. She turned to run.

"We're not from immigration," a voice echoed inside the office. "And we don't care about your status."

How did that voice know that was on her mind? And the accent was familiar. She paused.

"This conversation would be much easier if you would come in and take a seat."

Ari approached cautiously. She didn't want to leave Fort Lauderdale, not after all she accomplished, and she didn't want to go back to Haiti. The gold sunglasses of the brutes outside the door did not strike her as people from immigration. She decided to chance it.

She entered the office, the door closing behind her. Sitting at the desk where her counselor usually sat a large man—not overweight but thick in stature—with a shaved head and gray goatee. He wore a slick white suit, gold tie, and a gold pin of a comet on his collar.

"You're Haitian," Ari said sitting down. "I can hear it in your voice."

"Let's just say we have a lot in common, Ms. Gracia," the man said. His accent told her that he spoke Haitian Creole just like her. "I'm Emmanuel Stevenson. It's a pleasure."

He held out a thick hand to shake.

Ari hesitantly shook it. She shifted in her seat.

"I was born in Miami—"

"There's no need to lie to me," Mr. Stevenson said. "I'm not here to interrogate you."

"Why am I here?"

He studied her a moment. "I am from an organization, you may have heard of us. The Space Intelligence Corporation."

Ari did hear of them. They hung poster's promoting contests and programs all over the science wing of the school. She looked at his pin again and now recognized the insignia from the posters.

"Ah, you like it," he said. "We can get you one like it."

"You can?"

"Yes, *we* can," Mr. Stevenson said. "You see, we run the SIC Institute of science. A charter school, very prestigious, very expensive. Top students there earn full scholarships to university, as long as they major in a science degree. There's a program we run for students who, let's say, tend to be overlooked by their more affluent peers. Ari, we want you to join that program."

"How do you know if I'd be any good," Ari said suspiciously. "I never applied to your program."

"No need," he smiled. "We've seen your scores; we know you, Ari, and you would be perfect. This place has everything you've ever dreamed of in a school. You'll get a fancy uniform, and of course one of these pins. We have an astronomy center, the biggest telescope in the state, even better than the stuff at NASA, and all this for a student. You'll get to meet other students like you who are interested in math and science, and make friends who care about school as much as you do."

She did have trouble making friends here. No one cared about the things she liked, and they all despised her for no seemingly apparent reason. All the more she liked showing them up.

"Well, I have been liking science a lot this year," Ari said. "Especially rocks. Oh, and I've always wanted to see rocks from other places, like Mars or Venus. I really like Venus, but there's nothing there yet. "

"Maybe someday," he continued smiling pleasantly. "With someone like you on board, with your brain, that can become a reality. The school has field trips where you can dig, gather and study any kind of rock you like. Ari, we want to give this all to you. All you agree to is that by us providing your education, you come and work for us when all is said and done. Wouldn't being part of the SIC family be magnificent? Come to this school and you are guaranteed a future."

Future. That was a word that always lingered in the back of her mind. Even though everything came so easily to her, she always knew she would end up like her mother, working an under the table job, hiding her identity.

"I don't know," Ari said.

"You don't need to be afraid," Mr. Stevenson said. "SIC takes care of their own. Join the institute, and you and your mother will never have to worry about your status ever again."

It was too good to be true. No more looking over her shoulder, watching what she said. But Ari knew nothing came that easy, not without a price.

"I'm just not sure, sir," she said. "The school sounds fine and all, but what if I don't want to work for SIC when I graduate university? I just don't know."

"Ari, this opportunity is limited," he said leaning in close. "If you don't take it, your spot will be offered to someone else. Someone less talented, but won't hesitate to say yes."

The fire of jealousy flared in her. The thought of one of them, someone like second place Macie Williams taking her spot was unthinkable. Macie already had everything, why should someone like her get to attend the SIC school?

He placed a manilla folder on the table. "Ari, your father walked-out on your family when you were what? Three? Four?"

"He didn't walk-out," Ari crossed her arms defensively. "He went to take care of my grandmother in Mexico, to work and pay for me to go to school. And what does this have to do with your stupid school?"

Mr. Stevenson raised a disbelieving eyebrow.

"It's what my mother told me," Ari said confidently.

"Your mother still talks with him?"

"No," Ari huffed. "She stopped talking to him a long time ago."

"And when was that exactly?"

"A few years ago," Ari said, trying to be vague. What business was it of his to know about her family. She stood up to leave.

"You mean the year he stopped sending the money for Catholic school."

Ari stopped and looked at him.

Mr. Stevenson's expression no longer smiled and lost all persuasive kindness it held. His eyes bore into her as though to emphasize, *I already know.* "Ari, have you ever wondered what happened to your father?"

Ari squeezed her lips tight. She did want to know. She sat down.

"Ari, your father is not who you think he is," the SIC man opened the folder. "Do you know how he had the money for your Catholic school tuition? Because he was a substance trafficker. Ran all over the place. That was how he met your mother, to feed her addiction. And it was also the reason why he left."

Ari blinked. None of this was real, it was all a lie. "My father is not a trafficker, and my mother has no addictions."

"Really," Mr. Stevenson's lips curled. "Why couldn't your mother get you visas to live in the US? Why did you come the way you did? Why with all the hours she works, are you no better off than when you first arrived here? You know the answer Ari, and I think you've always known."

"No!" she yelled. All those days, her mother stayed hidden in her room, and would come out with sullen bloodshot eyes. The long hours she worked and Ari never saw a penny of it. She told herself it was stress, that Tamara was overtired and overworked. It was what she wanted to believe.

Mr. Stevenson opened the manilla folder.

Inside was a photo of her father surrounded by a family of loving faces, warm and welcoming. Something she never had.

"It's a lie," Ari she punched the table. She pushed the folder away.

"Ari," Mr. Stevenson chastised. "SIC doesn't lie."

"That's another family," Ari continued indignantly. "In that photo. My dad already has a family. He has me and my mom—*he has me.*"

Ari's lip quivered. She would not cry in front of this man that told her such awful lies about her parents.

She felt empty. She often daydreamed of her father, seeing him come through a door and how she would run to him with open arms, unable to contain how much she loved him.

And now it was easier to feel nothing.

She glanced at the family photo again. "Who are they?"

"That's a recent photo," Mr. Stevenson continued, "of his wife. And those are his kids. He's clean now, living in Texas and about as picture perfect as this photo."

"For them," Ari whispered to herself. He cleaned up for them— not me. I'm his mistake.

"Excuse me?"

"Is he good to them?" Ari asked a little too aggressively.

Mr. Stevenson looked at her steadily. "Very."

Covetous rage. Ari glared at the boy her father had his arm around. Was he the same age as her? Even though she wanted her father more than anything in the world, she hated him. She hated him for loving someone else, for not being hers.

Her insides turned into acid, eating away all her hopes.

"He never tried—" Ari tasted sick bile in her mouth. "—he never tried to find us. He forgot me."

"We can put you in contact—"

"No!" Ari yelled.

The room was quiet. She took the photo, branding the image into her memory.

Ari finally knew why she was hesitant in joining SIC. "He's not coming back. He's never going to help me, is he?

"Seems so," Mr. Stevenson said. "I am so sorry Ari. You deserved to know the truth. And you deserve better."

Ari sighed. She did deserve better.

"I want to be in your program," she said adamantly. "Give me the future my mother and father will never give me."

Mr. Stevenson cracked a small smile. "Ari, with SIC you will have your future and more, I promise you. You will have a family with us, with all the other members of SIC. Believe me, I know. I was in the program too. I'm like you."

"Like me."

"I know all this information is hard to digest," he continued. "How about we look at some paperwork."

"I want to start right away," Ari said . "Does your school have dorms?"

"Well yes—"

"Good," she said. "I want to stay in them. And another thing; I don't want to be Arianna Gracia when I go to your school. I want to be Arianna Gomez. You can make that happen, when you do my papers, right?"

"We can," the SIC man seemed surprised. "We certainly can for you Ms. Gomez."

"Thank you," Ari said. "Thank you so much."

Take that, Ari looked down at the boy in the photo. *I took his name, and I'm going to be better than you. Do what you want and be with him, but I have his name now. You'll see, I'll have everything you never had and will never get. I will be the best.*

The memory flickered out of view and pushed forward. What were these Venusian creatures that made her relive all the most painful moments of her life? Memories of her years at SIC started to appear before her—her expertise in geologic science, of planets, and of Venus. Everything she knew of Venus and the mysteries she uncovered at the Venus station flashed through her mind.

Including the face of a man she still loved.

"No," she said. "No more." She tried to wall off the memories but they were in too deep. They were taking everything she knew, ripping them away and tearing apart her soul.

And her mind slipped, lost in its lifelong sorrows.

Chapter 12: Truth and Key

Captain Marie Cocteau always lived her life for herself. She hated the name Marie and seldom told people about it. Cocteau also wasn't her favorite, but she tolerated it, more than she tolerated people for that part.

People never seemed to tolerate her. From an early age she remembered her frustration with the social norms of society, being assigned the things she should like and dislike.

Given her French Canadian background, she was a pale beauty that could've been the epitome of loveliness. But her bulky structure always overshadowed any femininity she had.

She took too much after her father; his face, his size and structure. Where her face should've been soft it was rigid and angular. Where her arms should've been dainty, they were thick and hard. Her height always towered over those around her.

Through grade school she wore dresses that itched down to the crinoline, shoes that pinched her toes, and tights that thinned her waist more than natural. None of it could hide who she really was—an oversized, masculine freak.

Despite hating everything that her sex was supposed to stand for, she was proud of her hair. Naturally dark and smooth like her Korean mother's, it was the one feminine thing she prided herself in. When she joined the military she refused to cut it, but instead kept it pulled back in a ponytail, out of the way and out of her life.

Your father will turn in his grave at the thought of what you've become, her mother's voice echoed day in and day out.

And so were the thoughts of Marie Cocteau as she hid. Of all the things that should've been on her mind, childhood pecked at it, like a scab that won't flake.

It wasn't easy, but she evaded *them,* the creatures that held her captive. She was sticky with sweat, back pressed against a shadow in the corner of one of the cavernous corridors. Her mouth was parched, and she could feel the fatigue and dizziness of dehydration setting in. She felt like she was in a volcano, the smell of eroded rock overpowering her senses.

What the hell are those things? She asked herself. *Not important. I need to find the others.*

She looked at the coin she clutched tightly in her hand.

Know your enemy, she told herself, squeezing the stolen coin in her palm. *The monstrous being used this to control things around them, make images appear from nowhere.* She used it, even by mistake, to free herself from her prison.

These coins aren't coins, she thought. *They're a key.* She thought of SIC and the access codes, key cards, the voice and retinal recognition systems they used. This coin was all that and those creatures would be sore for missing it.

She held the coin up, just like she did before.

Nothing.

"Ugh, god damn!" How did it work? She flipped it around to see the holographic designs. No one noticed on Venus station, but she had taken a closer look at the one in Gomez's lab. She was good at visual memorization, she had to be; she didn't become a captain without the ability to quickly scan an area and remember it.

The coin was much the same as the one in the lab, but reflected slightly different images. The humanoid in the center had a different face (if you could call it a face) and the writing had a different arrangement of symbols.

Distinct identification, she thought. *So they do see individuality, like us. Which means they have rank and hierarchy.*

There was a noise around the corner.

Can't stay in one place, have to keep moving. She gulped against her dry throat. *They probably know where I am. Can't be too many, or they would've caught me by now.*

She normally counted her enemies, but she couldn't tell them apart. Were they one? Two? Five? It was impossible to tell.

She was on the move again, silent steps. Her bare feet were beaten and scratched from the dark, rough, floor beneath. She was swift, staying ahead of the dangers that pursued her. She held out the coin, pressing it against the wall of the endless maze of sweltering corridors, hoping it would activate an escape.

She felt like she was going in circles, reaching no place, constantly fighting to stay ahead. She couldn't slack, couldn't rest even a moment, for she knew a moment of human weakness would be fatal. They would find her and she would not escape them again. Just as she was getting to know them, they also knew her. She panicked in her desperation for survival, and thus showed her cards too early, let them see her abilities too soon.

She panted, her head spinning. There had to be a way. She could not spend an eternity running from her enemy. This was hell, torture. She didn't run from anything. She was Captain Cocteau, the lone wolf who faced everything head on. Her insides twisted, hurt from the thought that she, Captain Cocteau, was running away again.

But she didn't know her enemy enough to face them right now. It was more important to survive than give into pride, as much as she hated it.

Chapter 13: Seen and Unseen

"Stop it!" Wilson yelled with the last of his voice at the Venusians. "Can't you see what it's doing to her! Stop— *please stop!*"

Gomez was gone, her gaze lost in whatever the orb was doing to her. It stole her eyes, life draining from her, almost gone. All that Gomez was deteriorated before Wilson. Her eyes glazed over, her face stiffened, her body going stiff. The arm of light around her released and she fell sideways.

"No!" Wilson cried, tears welling in his eyes. "How could you? She was perfect! How could you take her! How—"

Wilson was cut short as the light from the orb turned on him. The Venusian behind him held his head up, forcing him to look at it.

He tried to pull away, but he saw a flash, a flicker. *Her* golden hair, swaying in the wind on that beach long ago.

Marshall, she spoke to him.

"Justine?"

There she was, the woman of his memories beckoning him with her gaze. But her gaze changed; just as Gomez's face had stiffened, so did hers as she lay in the hospice bed. And everything that she was, was gone.

All the pain, the loss, the grief flooded into Wilson, a tsunami of emotion pounding against him, hitting him repeatedly like the violent waves of the shoreline. She was gone forever and there was no bringing her back; there was no hearing her words, no touching her soft face, holding her hand when it mattered. He was being ripped from the inside out, becoming too much, so much so that he couldn't contain his grief any longer.

"No!" Wilson screamed. Like a sharp knife from his chest he released his pain. Her image disappeared and the light probing Wilson shot from him, hitting all the Venusians in the room. He could hear their screeches, the confused ringing as they were hit with the light extending from him.

A sensation overcame him, like a feather brushing against his heart and mind. A thought, a conscious. Foreign as the feather of thought was, he felt at one with it. Then he felt multiple feathers, each extending into his own consciousness.

The Venusians. He could see what they saw, feel what they felt as they watched the power of the orb in terror. Not an orb, a celestial stone. Powerful and all encompassing. They also felt what he felt, reliving Wilson's most painful moments right along with him. Their individual minds were one with his, and each mind blacked out as it became overwhelmed.

The last of the confused ringing, the last mind still attached to his, fighting to stay alive.

Suddenly, the ringing stopped.

"You will die Earthchild, body and mind!" The last mind fell away.

Wilson was released.

His face was against the cold, smooth floor. When did he fall? So tuned to the Venusians minds he was unaware of what happened to his body. He felt drops warm blood spilling from his ears. His hands were still bound, but he was able to sit up. The stone only gave a faint, blue light now, just enough to see the Venusians around the room, on the floor and unconscious.

Are they dead? Wilson thought. The way their minds left him he could only assume. Or did he imagine the entire ordeal? He was too dumbfounded to understand.

Then he looked across from him. Gomez was lying on the floor, stiff and unresponsive.

"Dr. Gomez?" Wilson's voice shook. "A-Arianna?"

She didn't respond.

"Arianna?" It couldn't be—*she couldn't be*—

"Justine," he whispered. It was the first time he had the courage to speak her name in years. He squeezed his eyes shut trying to awake from the nightmare of his life.

"What the hell happened here?"

Wilson's eyes flew open from the familiar bark of a voice.

"Cocteau!" Wilson rejoiced. He was never so relieved to see someone he disliked in his entire life. "Captain! Is it you? Are you real?

Cocteau hovered over one of the Venusians. "Of course I'm real smart ass," she gave Wilson her usual glare. She was barefoot and in her bodysuit like him and Gomez, though more ragged. "You didn't think those bastards could keep me locked up?" She kicked the Venusian she hovered over. "What did you do to them?"

Wilson shook his head. He didn't know how to answer.

Cocteau approached him, staring at Gomez.

"Arianna i-is," he couldn't bring himself to say it. "She's—"

"Shush," Cocteau ordered. She walked over and kneeled over Gomez.

Wilson clenched his jaw. "Did you just shush me?"

Cocteau put up a finger for him to wait, her other hand pressed against Gomez's neck, taking a pulse.

"She's not dead," Cocteau stood.

"What?" Wilson held his breath. "Thank god."

Cocteau crossed her arms. "But of course a smart ass like you would think she is. I don't know if those *things* are dead or just knocked out. Either way, let's take these binds off and get out of here before we find out."

Wilson felt a sudden pressure in his head, a distant memory brushing against his mind.

"You need one of their recognitions," he said mechanically.

Cocteau gave him a look. "Recognitions?"

"The coin thing,' Wilson said, the pressure in his head increasing as foreign memories pushed their way through, making his jaw still and his eyes water. "Hover it there, next to the pedestal and the holopanel will appear."

"Holopanel? How do you know this?" Cocteau stared at him like she was watching a kitten being tortured. "My god Wilson, are you okay?"

"Just do it!" he snapped, feeling his entire body go rigid. The pressure in his head was increasing the more he thought about it, and he shook.

Cocteau followed his directions and the holographic panel appeared in front of her, glowing green outlines and orange controls with symbols.

"I don't know what any of this means," she said. "Wilson, you're not okay, let me—"

"Just get me out of these binds!" he yelled. "And don't call me smart ass again!"

"Fine," Cocteau said cooly. "Looks like I'll be pressing buttons and hope I don't kill you by accident."

"Wait—"The pressure in his head pounded, steady in beat with what he now knew to be a celestial stone. All that happened replayed in his mind. He saw the bright flashes of the stone probing him again and watched Venusians hit the ground around him, their thoughts filling him as he felt the echoes of the consciousnesses that touched him. But he wasn't Wilson anymore as a memory came forward. Out of body and towering over Gomez and himself, he looked into the holopanel controlling the stone, the interface for its power. His hand, a Venusian hand, dialed into it.

"The symbol in the upper right corner," he said to Cocteau, "press that one."

Cocteau pressed it and the cuffs holding him and Gomez came apart.

The pounding in Wilson's head faded as he brought his hands forward, rubbing his sore wrists. He was himself again, in his own body and mind.

Cocteau stared at Wilson, eyes wide and mouth open.

"Keep your face like that and you'll start to look like one of them," Wilson said, trying to stand. Cocteau came and helped him to his feet.

"How did you know that would work?" she said cautiously.

"Let's get Arianna," Wilson said, avoiding her question.

"How did you know, *space archeologist?*" Cocteau barked. "Answer me!"

"Because it said release," Wilson said apprehensively. "That symbol means release. I can read that entire panel."

"And?" Cocteau looked suspicious. "How long have you been able to do that?"

"I don't know," Wilson said, glancing at the unconscious Venusian behind the holopanal. *I saw through its eyes,* he thought. *Its memory became mine.* "It's like I always could. But no—it's only since I —" he nodded to the Venusian, "—did that to them."

Wilson started to shake. Cocteau let go and took a defensive stance, putting herself between him and passed-out Gomez. "Wilson, what's going on?"

"They were in my mind," he panted. Why did he feel so strange? His heart pounded as the flashes of the foreign consciousnesses went through his mind again, melding with thoughts of her, of his Justine. Grief, pain, and now anger. An anger that gave him a false sense of strength, but also the kind of anger used to shield fear. "They took part of me with that stone. I don't know, I don't fully feel like me; I feel like one of them."

Cocteau looked ready to pounce on him.

"Listen," Wilson said. "I can't exactly explain what they did to us, and I know what you're thinking. I am not compromised."

"That's for me to decide," she said eyeing him.

"I'm not going to hurt anyone," Wilson said. "If anything, I can help, we have an advantage."

"You feel like one of *them*?" Cocteau said unconvinced. "Seriously Wilson, what I am supposed to think."

"I can get us out of here."

Cocteau's mouth was stiff and unmoving.

"I can get us out of here," Wilson repeated desperately.

Cocteau signed. "Fine, but your weird little mind meld thing better not compromise our survival. You forget who you are and start acting like one of them, I *will* take you out."

"Alright by me," Wilson said. "Just one thing: don't let me forget myself."

Cocteau cracked a smile. "I'll do my best smart ass." Her smile faded. "Do you know what happened to Bitiir?"

Bitiir, Wilson thought. *Where is he? Why isn't he a part of this?*

Just remember who's in control, Bitiir's words repeated in his head.

Here Wilson was, in the most impossible, life-threatening situation and he felt his loathing against Bitiir stronger than ever. Bitiir made him feel weak, insignificant and humiliated. He'd blackmailed him, forced him into submitting into the wishes of SIC. And now was Wilson's chance to ensure Bitiir could never harm him or anyone again. His chance to keep him away from Gomez.

"Dead," Wilson said. "It's only me and Arianna."

Cocteau shook her head. "Damn it! How?"

"I couldn't say," Wilson said, rubbing his head.

They both glanced at Gomez on the floor.

"We'd better help her," Cocteau said.

They each took a side of Gomez, pulling her upright.

She stirred.

"I said I loved you," Gomez's voice was wispy, her eyes boring into Wilsons. "I said I loved you. She had to know who you really were."

"Um," Wilson stiffened nervously. "You never loved me."

"She's hallucinating," Cocteau said. "Come on Gomez, I need you to walk."

"People can be in different places at different times, you know," Gomez smiled. "You don't have to say it back."

"Hold her a minute," Wilson said, shifting Gomez's weight onto Cocteau. He bent over, took a recognition coin off one of the Venusians and pulled the holopanel back up.

"What are you doing?" Cocteau said. "These things could wake at any moment!"

"We do need to escape," Wilson said. "But we need to know where to escape to." He scanned the panel, his head feeling the pressure again. "Tell me, where do you think we are?" He already knew the answer, but he had to hear it aloud to believe it. And Cocteau's commanding voice would make it believable.

"Still on goddamn Venus somehow," Cocteau said irritated. "It's not like we were magically transported back to Earth! What are you doing?"

"Proving your theory."

Everything finally made sense to him. He didn't know everything the Venusians knew at once; he had to recall it, probe their memories for specific information. And there was a price to pay each time he looked, he could feel it. A physical price, as though his mind would overload from too much information at any one time. Something inside him would physically burst and kill him if he pushed too hard. He could read the panel just as easily as he could in English, but as he read, he felt the pressure increasing in his head again, his body shaking from exertion.

Wilson navigated through the symbols and found what he was looking for. He tapped it and a three dimensional, cone-shaped augmented map appeared, hovering over the holopanel. It glowed with green outlines and orange symbols of directional points spinning around it.

"Look at the holomap," he said. "This place is an underground compound, probably inside the original part of the mountain we were on."

He maneuvered the map with his hands, twisting through the various levels and determining their current position. "Wow, it's ingenious, the way it's designed. It's made of a series of levels that descend and surround one another, like a cone, all surrounding this —a celestial stone, the heart of the compound. I don't know what the stone is yet, but each level reinforces the previous one—"

"Stop admiring and cut to the chase."

"Alright, we're on the bottom, the detention level," Wilson pointed to the bottom of the map and used his fingers to enlarge it. "We are in the center, in the main interrogation chamber. We need to make our way to operations, the final level," he traced his fingers to the top. "Hmm, funny."

"What's funny?" Cocteau said, trying to hold Gomez up. Gomez looked around the room, her face clearly lost in some kind of wonderment.

"There are no barracks," Wilson said surprised. "A compound with no barracks or quarters for the inhabitants? Don't you find that strange?"

Cocteau blinked. "We're trapped in a cave with monster aliens and you find that strange?"

"Well, technically, we're the aliens as this is not our world—"

"How about our gear?" Cocteau narrowed her gaze at the holomap. "We aren't getting far without it."

"There's so many places it could be, I can't narrow it down," Wilson said, scrolling through more chambers and levels. "It would take hours, unless. . ."

A whisper of a voice that only his mind could hear. He closed his eyes. Like a feather tapping water, tendrils of memory touched him. He reached out to them, and the closer he got the more vibrant they became. He could feel the pressure in his head warning him he was too close. But he had to know and his enemies' memories became clearer. It was hard to make-out details, so he kept reaching further. . .*further.* . .

"Wilson!"

He opened his eyes. He was on the floor. *Don't tell me I blacked-out again.* He sat up.

"Seriously?" Cocteau snarled. "Don't do that again. You looked like you were having a seizure."

"Our gear is in operations," Wilson stood up feeling dizzy. "They wanted to keep our gear as far from our reach as possible so they put it in the level furthest from detentions."

Cocteau glared.

"I'll be fine," he said.

"Fine," she said resentfully. "How do we get to operations? I don't know if you noticed, but we're kind of trapped in a labyrinth of caves with invisible doors. Believe me, I ran around them enough to know. I found you by accident. Not to mention who knows how long we've gone without food or water. We're not going to last much longer without water in this heat."

"There's a system of lifts," Wilson said pointing to another area on the holomap "We can find them using the recognition coins. But they're guarded, not to mention the detention level is more so than others."

"We can't fight through without weapons," Cocteau said. "Find another way."

Wilson clicked through the screen. He paused. "Cocteau, did you notice we're breathing air?"

"Are you getting weird on me again Wilson?"

"No, but didn't you notice? It's clear that we never left Venus and yet we're breathing air without our suits on. Albeit, hot air, but livable and breathable."

Cocteau's face dawned. "There's a maintenance system."

"And maybe a maintenance system big enough for us to navigate through." Wilson found the symbol for life support and pressed it. "We can!"

A new holomap, this time showing a system of glowing red veins throughout the compound appeared. It simulated movement—airflow from a main source in the operations level. A direct path to follow. "There's a main shaft that goes between levels in the compound to control temperature and air quality for the rest of the system. It's small, too small for one of those *things* to fit through, but we might be able to squeeze through to move to the other levels and get our gear. There's an opening close to here, and we can get to it without being seen if we're quick."

"Let's do it," Cocteau said. "I don't want to be here when these things wake up."

"Don't worry, they won't." Wilson looked down at the Venusian closest to him, the one that had been operating the panel and the stone, knowing its fate.

You will die Earth child, body and mind, the voice from the Venusian repeated in his mind. With how exotic and alien looking these creatures were, he didn't expect the voices that spoke to him to sound so familiar. Had Gomez heard the same voices in her mind? Was that the reason she was in the state she was in now? What did she see that made her body and mind deteriorate right before them?

The Venusian memories crept into the chasm of his conscious. Unexpectedly, their voices did not sound as odd and sinister as they looked; they were ordinary—*too ordinary*. It was extraordinary how average the voices that spoke to him were. And it was the thought of how ordinary the voices were that worried him. And more importantly, made him feel guilt for their accidental deaths by his hand.

"Wilson?" Cocteau said. "Don't you be getting like Gomez. I can't have you both like this, especially since you can read Venusian or whatever it is."

"Right," Wilson brushed off the thought. "I'm ready, let's go."

Chapter 14: Lost

diots, Cocteau thought. *Smart idiots, but idiots all the same. And one of them has turned bonkers, and the other is well on his way to crazy town.*

You brought this on yourself, the past voice of Cocteau's mother Lucinda echoed.

"You will thank me," Gomez said wistfully below everyone. "Believe me, you'll be dodging a bullet."

They were in the dark, narrow maintenance airshaft. It slanted upwards toward the other levels, spreading the hot, breathable air. It was steep, but not so much so that it made climbing impossible; just extremely difficult.

There was no relief from the heat, even within the windy tunnel. It was carved out of rock like the rest of the underground compound, and emanated the planet's warmth. The only light they had were from the crudely cut openings, just big enough for them to climb into, but too small for a Venusian.

Feet pushed their backs against the hot, jagged walls to keep from sliding down.

Cocteau led the way in case they met trouble. As her heels dug down, she felt grateful for her rough calloused feet. She could only imagine how the brainiacs were doing with their delicate limbs. She heard their hard panting of dry air, chapped lips smacking incessantly.

Gomez hummed an unidentifiable song.

"Keep her quiet!" Cocteau whispered aggressively.

"I'm trying!" Wilson said in his voice just above a whisper. "She's about as reasonable as a two-year-old right now."

Gomez continued to hum, her insane songs echoing up to Cocteau.

This would be so much easier if we left her, Cocteau thought.

Being military blood and soul, and more so a captain, she wasn't supposed to think that way. But thinking and doing were two different things. She could think as much as she wanted, and as long as she never acted on these innermost wishes her conscience stayed clear.

"How much more," Wilson asked, his voice sounding more like a broken exhaust pipe than human.

Cocteau looked up.

She squinted at the slivers of yellowish green light that emanated from the airshaft entrances. They had passed at least two openings on their climb. "We're only a third of the way, I'm guessing."

It'd been strange following Wilson to the airshaft. He had led them down the dark cavernous corridors as if he knew the place by heart, and avoiding detection. He would stop them, holding a hand up to signal 'wait,' closing his eyes as if he were listening. Cocteau heard nothing. His body would turn rigid, then the fit would pass and he'd signal them to move on.

Cocteau felt unnerved by his sudden sixth sense. But he was their only chance of survival. Death was on the threshold, if not by the hand of the Venusians then by dehydration and lack of resources. Still, she trusted Wilson more than the others; he was truly a NASA man and not one of SICs lackeys.

"C-can't," Wilson from gasped below. "No water, no sleep, pain —I can't go on."

"Can't," Gomez repeated breathlessly.

Great, last thing we need right now, Cocteau thought. "Listen to me—you're alive. You're both soldiers now, which means you have a duty. You have a responsibility to stay alive and I have a responsibility to keep you alive. Do not give up and fail the objective."

"Which is what?" Wilson said snidely.

"You have a duty to get out of here and report back to your families, friends, and SIC."

No one moved.

Cocteau looked down and gave them the look. It was the same look she'd give her soldiers whenever they talked of giving up or were overall negative on the outlook of an objective. She knew Wilson and Gomez probably couldn't see her face, but she had to believe there was still power in the expression. If not for them, then for herself.

Suddenly she heard shifting, backs and limbs scraping against rock as Wilson and Gomez continued to climb.

Good, Cocteau thought as she continued her ascent.

The speech and look never failed. All she had to do was mention duty to family. People always got emotional about family in the oddest way. It never made sense. Even the most cowardliness of her recruits would run into the line of fire if it was in the name of family. Cocteau just accepted it'd just be another thing she'd never understand.

"You need your family," Gomez's crazed whisper rippled up to her. "You need your father. Believe me, I know."

"Shut her up!" Cocteau said. "Or we're all dead." *Especially about things she doesn't understand,* she thought. Cocteau felt a throb on her left cheek.

Got to have one to get it, she remembered an old friend say to her once about family, the name long forgotten.

Whatever, I don't get it, and I don't plan on having one, Cocteau told the nameless friend. *I worked too hard to get out of family; don't need another telling me who I can and can't be.*

"Stop!" Wilson's whisper echoed up.

Cocteau froze where she was. One of the airshaft openings was in arm's length.

The light from it disappeared.

Someone blocked that light.

Dammit, Cocteau thought. As long as they were quiet they could avoid detection and wait it out.

All was silent.

"Yes, but I didn't mean cut-out your family," Gomez cried out. "You need your family—*you need your father!*"

The opening filled with monstrous screeches, Venusian arms reaching out. Cocteau dodged a long finger.

"Drop!" she yelled, not even taking a chance to see the creature that peered down at them. She launched herself, sliding along the edge of the shaft, razor rocks tearing the back of her bodysuit.

A blast sounded and pieces of rock dropped down on her face. They were being shot at.

"Oomph," she slammed into Gomez. They stopped.

"Are you crazy?" Cocteau ducked as something else shot at them, shards of rock bursting over her head. "Keep going!"

"Jump in here," Wilson's voice tunneled up to them.

Cocteau looked over Gomez and saw one of the openings they passed earlier. Wilson's head peering out of it.

"Slide down," he said reaching his arms out. "I'll pull you in."

Another shot and more rock rained on them.

Cocteau kicked Gomez, shoving her forward. Like a nightmare slide, Gomez slid down. Wilson caught and pulled her through the opening.

"Come on," Wilson beckoned.

Cocteau ducked her head as more blasts sounded. What were they shooting at her with? It didn't sound pleasant whatever it was.

She could make it, slide right on down and slip through the entrance.

"Agh!" she yelled, one of the blasts coming close to her. It burned the right side of her shoulder. No bullets? It was like she was hit with pure heat and energy, scorching her suit and skin.

She launched herself forward.

"Do not touch me!" she shouted as she dropped.

And completely missed the opening.

The airshaft was too steep and she was moving too fast.

Wilson couldn't grab her.

"*Shit,*" she swore as she fell alone in the dark.

Chapter 15: Alone

N o!" Wilson shouted as Cocteau fell.

Gomez grabbed the back of his collar and shoved him against the wall.

"Arianna?" Wilson couldn't believe what she was doing. Calm, reasonable Gomez never lashed out at anyone. But her wide crazed eyes told him she was far from her reasonable self.

"She can't make it alone." Gomez released Wilson, then dove through the airshaft opening.

"Don't leave me," he gasped, reaching for her, but she was already gone.

He was alone.

Don't leave me, a past memory crept to the surface. *I don't want to do this alone.*

"I don't want to do this alone," he said aloud, leaning against the wall and sliding to the ground.

But he was alone.

Cocteau had fallen, Gomez left him, and he had no idea where Bitiir was. He paid no mind to the dim corridor he was in, so enthralled in the loneliness that encompassed his very being. He cared not if he was heard or if he was found. Nothing that happened to him could be worse than this emptiness. The emptiness filled him so that his body hurt, physically making every breath a chore, the pain balling in his chest unable to find a point of relief.

Don't let me be the end of your life, her voice said to him. He refused to think of *her* name. He didn't want to anymore, not when he was so alone.

"Stop it!" he said.

You'll see me once again. . .

"I won't see you again," he shouted to nothing. "You left. You left me—*you're dead.*"

Tears stung Wilson's eyes. The truth cut sharper than any Earthly weapon. Why did he come here? What did he expect to find on Venus? Certainly not this. Venusians were coming for him and he didn't care anymore. He had been looking for her—his wife—and she was long gone. Why was he looking for her? He knew he wouldn't find her on Venus, yet hadn't felt this close since her death. What was making him feel this way?

The image of the stone orb glowed in his mind, hearing her voice come from it, seeing her face starting to form from its light.

He heard high pitched ringing.

They were coming.

He stood, hyperventilating.

Maybe if he could see the stone, just one more time, get one last glimpse of her face that he craved—

—*No.* What was he thinking? Surely if he went back down to the detention level he lessened his chances of survival.

But the stone was there. *She* was there, waiting for him, just like she promised him on her deathbed. She promised him that he'd see her again. Could this not be it? He chose to believe it, even if it made no sense whatsoever.

She's not actually there, he told himself. It was wishful thinking, and unless he wanted to end up like Gomez, he knew he had to stay away from the stone. He hoped he had the strength to stay away.

He pulled out the Venusian recognition he'd stolen.

Marshall. . . the whisper of a voice echoed up to him from the shaft.

He ignored it. He waved the recognition, summoning a holopanel in front of him. He scrolled through symbols and pulled up the three dimensional map of the compound.

Whispers in his mind grew louder as he pressed the memories to interpret the map of him. They were discussing plans, ways to neutralize their prisoners, to contain them till they were no longer useful.

One is still contained; it must be moved for further extraction for its life is draining quicker than the others. It has information like the female did. One is still missing, and two are on the detention level; they will be dealt with soon enough. Find them, or your fate will be the same as theirs. Awake your comrades, for their usefulness is apparent in detaining these invaders who would claim our birthright.

He saw flashes of the Venusians he knocked away with the stone's light. They truly were dead. Their fellow compatriots inspected the dead bodies, anger seizing inside them.

Do not underestimate them again. The whispers were infuriated, they wanted blood for blood. *They want to escape, they want their tools; let us be smart and they will come to us.*

Rows upon rows of them.

He saw them all, Venusians, hooked up to machines pumping steam and liquids into their bodies. Some of them limbless as others used exotic mechanics to reattach parts to their bodies.

We are awakening. . .

We are coming. . .

Wilson opened his eyes. He was no longer looking at the map. He was on the ground, trembling, sweating.

That voice. Why did he know it? He shouldn't know it, but he did. It was a commanding voice, one that wielded true power, and he felt the impulse to obey it just as all Venusians do.

Marshall. . .

He heard the echo again and he sat up.

He crept to the edge of the shaft, looking down into its depths, its immovable darkness.

Marshall. . .

It was using *her* voice again, calling him to return and look for her.

"I'll find you," he said. *"I'll find you."*

Chapter 16: What the Captain Saw

I'm leaving," young Marie Cocteau announced.

Alexandre Cocteau laughed. "Is that so?" He didn't even look up from his handheld device. He was reading something, probably to do with stocks or money again. She didn't understand and did not plan on trying to.

She wondered how long it would take him to look up. "You keep forcing me to do stupid shit, then yeah, I'll leave," Marie said defiantly. She was twelve and dressed in her school uniform, skirt and all.

"Young ladies don't say *shit*, Marie," Alexandre puffed a cigar. He tapped his foot in time to popular music playing on his device, devoid of Marie's presence in his study. Framed photos of famous Canadian sports teams hung on the walls. A bay window that let in too much light surrounded him and his desk, turning his features into a dark silhouette.

Lucinda Cocteau entered the study. A petite and elegant Korean woman, she also carried an air of sophistication and old money. "Honey, here's your coffee and—my god!

She dropped the coffee mug, splattering its contents across the floor like a smashed egg. "Marie! What did you do!"

Alexandre finally looked up and his jaw dropped.

Marie Cocteau stood, arms crossed in front of her parents, with a black left eye.

Finally noticed, didn't they, Marie thought as she smirked inwardly. She knew what outward smirks resulted in.

"Were you—were you—" her mother started.

"Je suis sûr qu'elle ne se battait pas," her father fumed. *I'm sure she wasn't fighting.* He always spoke Canadian French at the height of his anger. "She must've taken a fall because she knows that a young lady shouldn't be fighting, *ever.*"

"Oh no, I was fighting," Marie Cocteau said, pleased that she managed to get him to yell in his previous language. "And for good reason. If those lousy turds think they can bully their way around, then they have another thing comin—"

Marie Cocteau couldn't finish as Alexandre suddenly had her by the ear. He hurled himself over so quickly she couldn't dodge him. She pulled from him, hitting his arms to let go.

"Cussing and now fighting," he snarled, batting her arms away.

"Alex, be careful," Lucinda looked like she was about to cry.

"I know what I'm doing!" he yelled. "You want her to keep acting like this? Like a boy? We already have a hard enough time making her look like a young lady, the least she can do is act like one. Next thing we know she'll start kissing girls and become one of those damn lesbians. Do you want that Lucinda? Do you really want no grandchildren?"

Lucinda backed away into the corner, sobbing. "No, no, just be careful, Alex—"

"Shut up," he said. "If you were doing your job as a mother Marie wouldn't be acting like this and I would still have my son."

Lucinda turned her face away, covering her mouth with her hand.

"And now for you," he said to the struggling Marie. "Marie, my little darling Marie. You've been grating my last nerve lately. When will you learn to start acting like a young lady?"

"I don't want to be a young lady!" Marie growled. "I hate it!"

He slapped her across the mouth. "Get used to it, you need help. You need me."

"I don't need anybody, least of all you!"

Captain Cocteau felt that pain across her mouth as she blinked her eyes open. Her father's voice still echoed in her ears. Everything was dark and her head pounded.

A patch of skin on her right shoulder stung where she was shot from the Venusian weapon; she felt it blister. The charred small of her the singed clothing still hung around it. *Second degree burn,* she thought. *Could've been worse if from a more direct shot.*

Someone shook her.

Cocteau jumped up, ready to kill whatever touched her.

"It's me, just me," Gomez cried. "Shh-shh, they're coming. They've been swarming out there."

"Gomez, what the hell?" Cocteau realized they were at the bottom of the maintenance shaft. She must've slid all the way down and hit her head along the way. It was too dark to see clearly, but she could tell that Gomez was right beside her.

"Go," Gomez tugged her shoulder. "We need to go."

"I get it," Cocteau said shaking her arm off. "Watch it, it's burnt there. When did you get so touchy?"

Cocteau's eyes finished adjusting as she felt around for the small opening of the shaft. She found it, the entrance so dim it blended into the wall.

She peeked her head out. Her chest sank. "Dammit!" They were on the detention level, back right where they started.

No Venusians were in sight.

"All clear," she whispered.

They crept out of the shaft into the dark glow of the cavernous corridors. Gomez followed, seemingly more aware and not acting as lucid as she had been. The faraway look in her eye was gone, as if the fall down the shaft had knocked sense back into her.

A scuffle and the sound of scratching footsteps.

Cocteau flung herself and Gomez against the wall.

She brushed her hand down the leg of her bodysuit and found the indentation of where she had hidden the Venusian recognition. She pulled it out.

Oh please let there be an empty room! She held it out as they slid along the wall.

The footsteps grew louder and quicker.

She desperately waved the recognition, just like she had done when she found Wilson and Gomez.

Gomez grabbed her arm, shaking her head. "It's not working."

Cocteau shoved her away. "It will—it has to."

She continued frantically, hearing the footsteps come. Louder and louder, moving ever closer to them.

She was confident to fight one of those Venusian things, but she doubted she could handle more, especially while taking care of Gomez.

"Stop!" Gomez grabbed Cocteau's arm again.

Cocteau tried to shove Gomez's grip, but was surprised at her strength. "You're going to get us kill—"

Suddenly, the familiar green holopanel appeared in front of them. She tapped the symbols that seemed to work to open doors . The glowing arch of an opening appeared behind them. As it slid open, Cocteau jumped in, dragging Gomez in with her. She pulled up another holopanel inside, and pressed the same symbol again. The the entrance suddenly closed, sealing them in.

It was dark, only the glow of the holopanel lighting their faces. They sat, catching their breath.

"Looks like we're in one of those holding cells again," Cocteau whispered. "Lucky this one's empty."

"Lucky?" Gomez said irate. "And how do you know what the cells look like? We were blindfolded."

Cocteau smiled.

"Of course," Gomez shook her head.

"What do you mean 'of course'?" Cocteau felt a flux of fury in her chest.

"You just have a way of doing certain things," Gomez said coolly. "Differently than I would've."

"Differently than you would've?" Cocteau shook, her face somehow getting hotter than it already was. Did Gomez really just judge her, after all she did to free them? "Oh, because you had things under such control before I saved your sorry ass."

Gomez's eyes changed; not in color or in size, but in maturity. As though she aged a decade or more in that split second. "You could've let Wilson help you, back in the airshaft."

Cocteau clenched her jaw. What right did Gomez have to say anything after what she pulled in the shaft? It was her demented ravings that ruined any element of stealth they had. They were here because of her, weren't they? This was Gomez's fault. "What's wrong with you?"

Cocteau didn't need to ask. Gomez's brain was fried, that's what was wrong with her. Nevertheless, she wished Gomez didn't act like an all-knowing dick about it.

"You know what," Cocteau stood, "I don't have time for this. I'm going to look for the lift Wilson talked about. And you can go off on your own or stay here. I don't care. Just don't get in my way." She fumbled through the holopanel, looking for the same map Wilson used.

Gomez stood over the panel, the glow under her face defining the fine lines around her eyes. "You know what your problem is?"

"Sure, why not," Cocteau threw her arms up. "I have nothing better to do than listen to the rants of a nut job."

"That's it," Gomez pointed. "You keep saying 'I'. You always try to do things on your own and never need anyone else's help, and you don't care who you hurt in the process."

"That's because I don't need anyone," Cocteau avoided Gomez's gaze, staying focused on her task. "I've always done well enough alone. I don't need anybody, least of all you."

Gomez was still, staring at Cocteau. "You're a lone wolf, Captain." She shook her head. "We need people, we all do."

"Whatever," Cocteau said. "I don't even know why I'm arguing with you. Arg!" She punched through the holopanel. "Where is that goddamn map!"

Gomez's lips tightened. "You're just going to leave me?"

You're just going to leave, really? Her father's voice erupted in her head.

"I *know* what I'm doing," Cocteau answered.

"I'm sorry Captain, but you don't," Gomez said. "None of us do. And if you would just listen to me I'll tell you where that lift is."

Cocteau stopped, frustration ripping through her like a rock through wet tissue. "You know where the lift is?"

Gomez nodded, a grin stretching across her face, a signal that her mania was returning.

"Oh my god," Cocteau closed her eyes and rubbed her forehead. She opened her eyes, giving Gomez the glare she often gave those she despised. "Like, do you really know where it is or is this the other weird Gomez talking?"

"I know," Gomez's lashes twinkled in the holopanel light. "If you weren't pulling me around out there I could've pointed it out to you." She spoke fast, all her words falling together. "And those weren't Venusians out there—it was Dr. Wilson getting off the lift—and because the way sound travels, the echoes made it sound like multiple footsteps were coming at us. I assume they designed the walls that way to scare potential escapees, like us. Ingenious—"

"Stop," Cocteau held up a hand and took a breath. "What do you mean it was Dr. Wilson? He's down here? *What the hell is he thinking!*"

"Some things needed to be said," Gomez's eyes glossed over, her mania fully returned. Her mind was lost again. "Some things needed to be said, you had to know, she had to know."

"God, I never thought I'd miss Wilson" Cocteau shook her head. "Come on."

Cocteau opened the door and they crept out into the corridor.

"Show me where you saw Wilson," she whispered.

"*Dr. Wilson,*" Gomez hissed.

"Fine, doctor whatever, where did you see him?"

Gomez giggled. "I didn't see him," her eyes grew wide and she tapped the side of her head. "I saw him."

"Where?" Cocteau grumbled, her fingernails digging so hard into her palms that they broke skin. She knew she had to keep her patience from this point on; it was no use reasoning or arguing with Gomez in this state of mind. They already wasted enough time with her being unreceptive to Cocteau's unfiltered nature. She had to be calm and direct, and maybe they would get somewhere. "I'm sorry, I mean where should I look for him? Please tell me or take me there."

Gomez guided her down another passage, around a turn to the next corridor. Sure enough, there was an opening in the wall, dimly lit with a platform within.

"How did you see this?" Cocteau asked. There was no way from their position that Gomez would've known the lift was here.

"I already told you," she said pointing to her head again. "I didn't see it—I saw it."

Cocteau kept a straight face. And for once, instead of the flurry of anger she often felt when frustrated, she felt something else. What if she had been the one with her head fried and Gomez caring for her? Patience never came easily, but for people like Gomez it was second nature. And the first time in her life, Cocteau felt something for Gomez she only ever felt for herself. A sudden moment of empathy stretched forth, a pity for one who was hurt beyond control or repair.

She heard the familiar scuffling of footsteps and instinctively crouched low.

"Dr. Wilson?" Gomez's eyes almost seemed to glow, her voice ethereal as though not her own. "Marshall Wilson?"

"Stay here," Cocteau whispered, ignoring Gomez's eerie voice, though her spine still prickled at the oddity. "And stay quiet." Gomez's unpredictability could put them in more danger. She needed to handle Wilson on her own.

She crept past the lift and looked down the next corridor. Halfway down, lit by the walls yellow-green glow, a dark silhouette moved smoothly, as though it was floating. The outline matched Wilson.

It is Wilson! Cocteau thought. *What the hell is he doing down here? He should've run!*

She crept down the corridor, Gomez now completely out of her line of vision. *Oh god, please stay put*, she thought knowing that it was a vain wish. But she couldn't lose Wilson—he was their chance out of this place with his new extraordinary sense.

Something didn't seem right about Wilson. The way he walked down the corridor as though an unearthly ghost possessed his body. She carefully walked toward the outline of Wilson.

"Wilson," she whispered to an almost full voice.

He took no notice of her, continuing on his path with slow steps.

"Wilson," she said carefully, trying to get his attention without causing a scene. "Hey, brainiac—smart-ass—"

Nothing worked.

"Come on, I can't lose you too," Cocteau said desperately.

Wilson stopped moving. He turned around, his darkened features gaunt, his eyes still.

"You cannot leave me alone," Cocteau said. "I thought I could do this on my own, but I can't, and I hate that I can't. But we have to survive."

Wilson blinked, an expression of normalcy returning.

"Cocteau?" he said. "Captain?"

"Yes, it's me."

"Where are we?"

"We're on Venus," she said. "Remember? In a compound. We're all back on the detention level; the maintenance shaft plan didn't work."

Wilson bit his lip. "No, it didn't."

"What are you doing here?" Cocteau said, trying not to sound as infuriated as she really was at him coming back down. "You should've continued with the objective. Gotten out and sent for help to save us."

Wilson looked away with a far eyed look. "The stone." He started walking.

"Stop." Cocteau grabbed his arm.

"I need to see her," he said pulling away from Cocteau. "She's there."

She wanted to slap Wilson, get him back to reality, but stopped. Gomez's words lingered.

You have a certain way of doing things. . . you could've let Wilson help you.

She should've let him help. She always barreled into situations, head strong and aggressively. None of that worked, and slapping Wilson back to reality would not work now.

Cocteau stepped in front of him. He tried to push forward, but she blockaded him either way he stepped.

Wilson's face was different. His eyes were bright, and he had a small smile. He never smiled unless it was at another's expense, to feed his ego that he hid well from others. The depressed, emotional sap he truly was, was no longer there. Here was a man who looked forward.

He still wasn't listening. He continued forward, pushing past her.

There was only one reason Wilson looked this way. The only reason anyone she ever knew looked this way. It was always because of the one thing she swore to never have and abandoned.

"She's not there," Cocteau said. "The person you love isn't there."

That stopped him. The look on his face melted away with her words, hopelessness taking over. Here was the Wilson she knew.

He fell against the wall. "It's hot," he said.

"Excuse me?"

"The wall, it's hot, it should burn," Wilson's voice shook. "But everything else hurts so much I can't feel it. Tell me, was this what it was like for you on deployments?"

"In some ways," she didn't like to talk about the things she saw in her deployments. "In other ways it was worse."

"Worse," Wilson laughed. "How can it be worse than this? These things, what they've done to us, our minds, only monsters can be that cruel."

"Monsters?" Cocteau was frank. "Dr. Wilson, it's clear that you've never fought a war—you don't know." She offered a hand. "I won't be leaving you alone again, soldier. Let's get out of this mess, together?"

Wilson looked at her. She half hoped he would have that hopeful expression again, or at least part of it. Whoever he was thinking about that entranced him to come back here wasn't on his mind anymore.

He clenched his jaw. He reached out and grabbed her hand. "Together."

She helped him to his feet.

"I'm sorry," he said. "You must blame me for putting us back where we started. I couldn't control Gomez like I said I would, the maintenance shaft was my idea, and that celestial stone did something with my head. I keep seeing their memories, and I no longer feel like me—"

"Damn the stone," Cocteau didn't want to hear any more of his sentiments. "Maybe it's time for us to stop blaming one another, including ourselves."

Wilson smiled. "That sounds good to me."

Chapter 17: Found

Gomez was nowhere to be found.

"Damn, I told her to stay put!" Cocteau kicked the wall next to the lift.

"You left her alone?" Wilson brushed his wet, sweat ridden hair from his forehead. "Of course she wandered off!"

Already worried enough about Gomez, there was no telling what she was capable of alone. He imagined a series of dangers that awaited her, defenseless without her full mind intact and without guidance.

"It's not like I could take her to get you," Cocteau said.

"Why not?" Wilson couldn't believe this was happening. "If you just—ahh!"

As if out of nowhere, Gomez fell against him, panting.

A wave of relief washed over him. "Thank god."

"I told you to stay put," Cocteau chastised. "Where did you go?"

"I-I," Gomez hummed nonsensically.

Wilson knew there was no point in lecturing Gomez. Reasoning while in her mania bore little result.

"It's okay," Wilson said, helping her steady herself. As much as he hated being startled, it meant that she was safe, that she was alive. "We're here now, you're okay."

Gomez stopped humming. She looked-up, doe-eyed. "Oh, I found you Dr. Wilson."

"You sure did," Cocteau said sardonically.

"We can't do this without him, you know" Gomez said dreamily, stroking Wilson's arm. "Or without me."

Or we could, Cocteau mouthed silently to Wilson.

"That's enough," Wilson said gently, pulling her hands off.

Cocteau paced in front of the lift. "Do you think it's safe to use this thing?"

"I think so," Wilson said twirling his recognition coin in his fingers.

"Think so?" Cocteau put a hand on her hip. "You were just on it."

"I know, it's just—" he trailed off, thinking about the commanding voice he heard, and the visions of mangled Venusians being reassembled.

"What's wrong with it?"

"Not with the lift," Wilson said. "It's with the Venusians. None of them are down here."

"Are you sure?" Cocteau said. "Because they were eager to snuff us earlier."

"They withdrew," Wilson said, his vision at the forefront of his mind. "When you and Gomez left, something happened. I heard one of them speaking. Not a memory, but a voice that was present. They've withdrawn from the lower levels. Their current numbers are not what we think; very few are awake."

"Awake?" Cocteau put her hands on her hips, "I know it's supposed to be good news, but you look like our death warrant's already signed."

"There are more," Wilson shook his head. "Oh so much more, and they're awakening them. Reinforcements, more than we can imagine. They saw what I did to the others with the stone, so they retreated to regroups. They're going to retaliate."

"Shit," Cocteau punched the wall. "How do we get this lift thing working? The longer we wait, the harder it's going to get."

"I'm not sure," he said. "I wasn't myself till you snapped me out of it, and I don't recall any Venusian guarding or using the lift. I think they're too distracted awakening the others. I put a dent in their numbers when I—um well—killed them."

Cocteau squinted at Wilson. "Killed? When did you kill one of those things?"

"When you found us," Wilson said. "Those Venusians weren't just knocked-out. They were—"

He breathed. He didn't like saying it. He wasn't one for killing anything. He even felt uncomfortable killing a fly. And knowing he caused the death of multiple, intelligent living beings, he felt like an imposter in his own body. "Somehow, with the stone, I more than their memories. I gained a part of them. I can hear them. I think they plan to cut us off, but they need to awaken their reinforcements. If we leave now, we have a chance before there are too many to overwhelm us. "

Cocteau looked worried. "It's not perfect, but this lift is our only way out. We can't do that shaft again, and there is nothing else. We will brace ourselves for whatever meets us at the top."

They stepped into the lift, but Gomez didn't move.

"Um, Gomez?" Cocteau said. "You need to come with us."

"You're a liar Dr. Wilson," Gomez's voice shook.

"What?" Wilson froze, her words an electric shock.

"Still alive," she said, firm this time. "And you won't say it, will you?"

"What?" Cocteau looked confused.

"Bitiir's alive," Gomez sliced each word through her teeth. "I saw him, Dr. Wilson. *I saw him.* They took him, up the lift. *They took him!* That's why I ran when the Captain told me to stay; that's why I ran."

Cocteau looked at Wilson. "Is this true?"

"I told you—"

"No excuses," Cocteau said. "Is Bitiir still alive?"

Wilson backed away from them.

"That's a yes," Cocteau said, disgusted. "What else do you know?"

Wilson parched mouth coated in sour sweet saliva. "He's alive, but I don't know where."

Cocteau closed her eyes. "Damn it Wilson, why are you doing this to me?"

"I'm trying to protect us," he said smugly. "You know how he is —"

"Shut-up," Cocteau ordered. "I'm trying to think."

"We need to find him," Gomez said. "Or I'm not going."

"Why do you care all of a sudden?" Wilson felt that burn inside him again.

Gomez starred Wilson down.

"New plan," Cocteau rubbed her face. "Wilson, use your recognition coin thing and pull up a map of the place."

Wilson waved his recognition and the holopanal's interface appeared waist high in front of him.

"Find Bitiir."

"Captain, really, I don't think—"

"That's an order!" Cocteau barked.

Wilson tapped and it split into multiple screens showing the compound levels. A red dot blinked at the top corner of one. He pressed it.

"Found him," he said cautiously. "He was here, but there's an order to relocate him four levels up from detentions. He's there now. Why move him?"

"Probably to prevent us from doing exactly this," Cocteau wiped a hair from her face. "As much as I hate the bastard, we need to get him."

Just remember who's in control, Bitiir's words seeped into Wilson's mind.

"I don't know if we can," Wilson said.

"Don't know if *we* can?" Cocteau chided, "or if *you* can?"

"He wouldn't do the same for us," Wilson tried to sound indifferent, but his voice quivered slightly. "There is no way we can save him without risking our own escape. Venusian numbers are growing as we speak. Who knows if we'll have access to lift again. Going for our gear and leaving is our best chance."

The pressure in his head increased. He waved his recognition again and the holopanal disappeared. *I have to be careful.* He rolled his shoulders, forcing the pressure to pass.

He offered a hand to Gomez. "Come on, we're going."

"No, you come on!" She snarled and slapped his hand away. "We leave no one behind! Isn't that right captain?" she mockingly saluted Cocteau.

Cocteau clenched her jaw. "She's right. We have an obligation."

"To what?" Wilson felt the stab of rejection. "To him? We go for him, we risk having all of us stuck in this hell hole forever!"

"Then risk it," Gomez said. "Or I am not setting foot out of here. Is it worth your soul Wilson? Is it worth his? Theirs? Going is the only way to make things right, to save us all."

"We're not saving him", Wilson said. "We're killing ourselves."

Gomez's eyes were in that far-off expression. She came close enough to touch Wilson, but kept her feet planted outside the lift. She pointed at his head. "Don't let them take you," Her voice was whispy. She slowly drew a line from his head, down to his chest. "The key is in there. They've seen it, I can tell; they fear it. Don't let them take you."

She looked into his eyes; he couldn't avoid them. They froze, piercing him like a needle to skin. Looking into them he felt like a scolded child. The Arianna Gomez he knew was still in there and what did she think of him now? He shuddered at the thought. This wasn't mindless Gomez asking them to go for Bitiir, but his Gomez, the one who welcomed him and trusted him before anyone else.

Could he really disappoint her?

Marshall, he heard the calling again. Was it real, or was it his imagination? Or did Gomez just say it? He couldn't tell and it didn't matter.

"I will find you," he said.

Gomez took Wilson's hand. "We will find him together. Then we'll be free."

He squeezed her hand. It felt nice to have someone hold it again. He held it, just the same as the last time he held Justine's hand. He knew it shouldn't, but it felt like hers and he would do anything to feel her touch again.

"Ugh," Cocteau rolled her eyes. "Gomez, just get your ass on board and we'll go get him."

Gomez dropped Wilson's hand and broke her gaze. It felt like a rip from his chest.

She stepped onto the lift.

"Are you ready, Dr. Wilson?" Gomez asked in her careful tone, a sign that her mania episode was fading, at least temporarily. Her eyes returned to their typical direct look, to being in the moment.

He shifted uneasily. He feared looking into her eyes again. "I am."

He waved his recognition and the lift opening shut.

Chapter 18: Through the Glass Door

He watched her.

Gomez stood, erect and strong. The lift moved at great speed, and yet she needed no support. Even with her mind slipping in and out, she seemed more in control than either Wilson or Cocteau.

Cocteau refused to look at him. He knew she was mad; they both were.

"We're going to stop soon," Wilson said, the pressure of movement lessening as the lift slowed. The hum around them turned deep, the rhythm in conjunction to the speed. "Brace yourself."

The lift was faster than any elevator he knew on Earth. How deep were they into the Venusian mountain? He was wary looking holomap when not necessary, afraid of losing his mind like Gomez.

"Are we stopping?" Cocteau said, still not looking at him. "I don't know, you're the only one that can read that Venusian stuff, and who's to say what you read and what you say are the same thing."

Wilson glared. "I get it, but I actually do want to save our lives. And anyways," he nodded at Gomez, "I'm doing this for her. She's the only good person involved in all this SIC stuff and look what's happened. If this were my way, we'd be heading straight up and out to safety."

"Don't be such a hero," Cocteau said. "I don't give a rat's ass why you do what you do, but you try lying to me again, you'll be the one left behind. The Dr. Wilson I know isn't a liar; he's too naive for that. I'm supposed to keep you in check and not let you forget yourself, remember?" She sighed. "Fine job I've done at that."

The hum of the lift filled their ears, exemplifying the disdainful silence of his colleagues.

"Why do I feel like I'm leaning back," Cocteau grumbled to herself as she pulled herself steady.

"Because we're not just going up," Wilson said. He knew she wasn't looking for an answer, but he had to say something, find a way to earn their trust back. "Remember what I said before? This compound is shaped like a cone, which means we are going up and in. The detention level is deepest, so it doesn't need as much to surround and protect it. The operations level is most vulnerable at the top, and has the most reinforcement from the other levels around it. Not to mention if you remember in the air shaft, there's a lot of space between each level—too much space," he held up his recognition. "I can show you."

"I get it," Cocteau tightened her upper lip.

Gomez continued in her way as though neither of them were there.

He looked at her. Her eyes were gone again, to the far away gaze, another mania episode preparing to set in. What was she thinking about? Why did her mind keep leaving for it? And what kept drawing her back to reality between episodes?

The lift came to a sudden stop. Cocteau and Wilson lost their footing, while Gomez stayed perfectly balanced.

"We need to find water," Wilson rebalanced himself, then sat against the wall. "I feel like I can barely stand, and it's not just the lift."

"You'll adapt," Cocteau said, completely unsympathetic. "Believe me, the human body can withstand a lot more than most realize. We can go two, maybe three days without water if necessary. Honestly, I don't think we've been trapped here that long. Few hours at most."

"You feel how hot it is?" Wilson huffed. "I can see steam coming off my skin."

Cocteau smiled. "There are other means of getting fluids if you didn't relieve it all already."

Wilson scowled. "You're disgusting."

"I'm a survivor," Cocteau said. "Wish you'd act like one."

"I'm the one worried about water."

"Did I say I wasn't?" Cocteau also sat against the wall. "Before we go anywhere, we need a plan."

Wilson blinked slowly. "Um, I thought this was the plan?"

Cocteau did her smile, the one that made him feel like he was nothing more than an ignorant pest. "Yes, but getting Bitiir is only half the plan. If he's locked in a room how do we get him out? If he is guarded how do we get past them? If he's violent, what do we do with him? What if he's dead, do we take the body? How do we make it back to lift? What if the lift is no longer an option?"

"If, if, if," Gomez said, joining them in the sitting circle. Her voice was unsteady, signaling that her current episode was set in place. "So uncertain of everything."

"Are you able to see where those things are on that map?" Cocteau pointed at Wilson.

"I can only see orders, I cannot tell who the individuals are." He used his recognition coin to conjure up the holomap between them.

This time it glowed red and gold, showing a three dimensional diagram of the entire compound. Orange blobs moved nonsensically through the levels. "These are heat signatures pulling power from the central power source, but they could be anything. There are a set of orders posted to pull everyone, with the exception of two, to the upper levels. The two exceptions are ordered to stay on this level and keep the prisoner contained." He tapped on their level, a section of map showing a circular maze of passages and doors. He traced his finger, mapping out a route for them to follow. "I assume Bitiir is here," he stopped his finger on a room full of multiple heat signatures and clear on the other side of the level, "where they're ordered to stay."

"If we follow that path we find Bitiir, but also those two Venusians," Cocteau traced her finger then stopped. "But there's that other path. It also looks like it could lead us back to the lift."

"It does." Wilson said.

"What if," she pointed to Bitiir's location, "we take that route to Bitiir—ah, but we have to do something about those Venusians. We have to make them think we are heading one way, but take the other. I am the fastest; I can approach while you two are still hidden, and bait them to chase me, making way for you two to free Bitiir."

"What if only one goes after you," Wilson said. "There's still another one to deal with."

"Two against one," Cocteau stood. "I can handle one for you, but I can't handle two. You and Gomez will need to get Bitiir and take it down. Its body is too hard to pierce, but their legs are weak and struggle to stand back up. If you can ground it, you can buy yourself time."

Wilson gulped. He and Gomez were physically fit enough to make it this far, but it didn't mean that he knew how to fight, or had it in him to do so. And did Gomez have it in her? Or would she succumb to her episodes?

"No," Gomez stood. Her face was hard, focused. "Captain, we are not as strong as you and will not be able to take down a Venusian like you can. I will follow in a second wave and distract the second Venusian while Dr. Wilson frees our Bitiir."

Cocteau snorted. "Umm—"

"Are you—" Wilson wasn't sure how to ask. It was sudden, Gomez speaking coherently. He knew little of mental illness, and the little he did know did not help him with this. "—all right?

"I am well aware of my state of mind," Gomez said. "Of the episodes I keep having. But it must be done, it must be this way." She paused. "And it has to be Dr. Wilson who frees Bitiir."

Wilson shook his head. "Arianna, you don't have to."

"Please," Gomez put up a hand. "However my state of mind is at that time, I will follow through; no matter what I am saying or acting at the time, I am still here and I know my mission. I may not be able to communicate as I wish when I am in an episode, but my mind is still my own. Do not forget that." She sighed. "I know it's hard, but you both need to trust me. Trust that I'm still me, that I will do what's right."

Wilson didn't like it. How long could Gomez hold-out before her episodes were too much? And when it came down to it, could he really free Bitiir? A burning sensation filled his chest cavity.

"Dr. Wilson," Gomez knelt on her knee and put a hand on his shoulder. "You must be the one to free him. I cannot, I do not know how to use the recognition coin as you do. Only you can free him. Do this, if not for him, then for yourself."

She stood and turned to the door, waiting for them.

"It's a plan," Cocteau said. "Is there anything else in that map we need to know?"

"There are some rooms scattered throughout this level," Wilson zoomed out so that the others could see, "I don't know what's in them, but we can hide if we absolutely have to"

He paused. A pulsating light drew his attention. "It's weird, everything relies on this central power source. The way it fluctuates in this diagram is nothing like I've ever seen." He opened a new section to the map, the bottom center. Light pulsed from that section, spreading up and to all other parts of the compound. Was that where the celestial stone was? Could it be the heart of the compound? He zoomed-in closer, strings of energy like neural tendrils zipping around. "It's so. . ." His words trailed-off as he saw the energy flow through the holomap, powering it just like the rest of the compound. He rubbed at the pressure in his head.

"Stop that," Cocteau slapped the recognition from Wilson's hand and the map disappeared.

"Really?" He picked it up. "You had to do that?"

"Yes," Cocteau said. "You see Gomez there, not even fazed by anything? The more you look at that shit the more you start acting like her. You should only be using that thing when we need it. *Stop frying your brain.*"

She was right. Reading their words, seeing their science, and thinking about the stone, he felt more drawn to everything each time he used his recognition. But he also felt more distant from himself.

His connection with Gomez drew him back right before they entered the lift, and was the only thing keeping him grounded now.

* * *

The corridor they entered wasn't like the lower levels.

Where the walls on the lower levels were poorly chiseled volcanic rock, these were polished, like black water smoothed over tarmac. Shadows of their reflections bounced off the low, rounded ceiling curved artistically to go seamlessly into flat walls. Their mirrored faces stretched into distorted and surreal shapes as they looked into etched images of strange humanoids, oversized with elongated limbs. The etchings continued in patterns along the walls, floor, and ceiling, the same story circling; repeating indefinitely.

Wilson touched the wall; it was warm.

"It's like glass," Gomez said gently stroking the it, tracing an etching with her fingertips. "It's warm, not hot like before."

"It's a lot like that room with the stone," Wilson said uneasy. *Too much like that room.* He nudged her move along.

"Metamorphic," Cocteau said, walking ahead of them.

"What?" Wilson said.

"Right Dr. Gomez?" Cocteau said pointed around them. "Metamorphic, volcanic glass. Probably obsidian. Though it shouldn't be here; you need crystallization to form this rock, even if it's a small amount. Venus doesn't have the oxygen to do that. I imagine that's what you would be telling us right now if you could."

Gomez paid her no mind as she continued stroking the wall as she walked.

"Loves rocks that one," Cocteau said. "Don't you worry Wilson, she'll come to. That's her pattern; she comes and goes. She'll be fine."

Wilson helped guide Gomez forward, but couldn't keep her hands from the walls. "Captain, you seem to know a lot about rock formations," he said. "Do they interest you?"

"Why ask now?" Cocteau didn't sound interested in making conversation.

"Why not?" He said. "We may never make it out of here. Sometimes it's nice just to say things aloud to someone, no matter who it is."

Cocteau sighed. "For some, silence is golden."

She continued to walk ahead of them.

"You told me once that you went to school for planetary science," Wilson said. "You would've studied the phases of rocks early on."

"I did."

"What made you want to study planetary science?"

Cocteau stopped. "I know what you're fishing for," She turned her head over her shoulder. "I'm not stupid. You're not going to earn my trust back that easily by feigning interest in my unfinished degree."

Wilson avoided eye contact. She was right.

They continued walking.

"Why did you quit your degree captain?" Gomez asked softly, still gliding her hand across the wall. "Why join the military?

Cocteau took a sharp breath. "If you must know," she put her hand on her hip, "I didn't just quit. I escaped. And joining the marines guaranteed American citizenship if I finished boot camp and served long enough."

Wilson was taken back. "Wait—you're not an American citizen?"

"Am now," she said. "Wasn't then. Why does it matter?"

"But you act and look so—"

"Looks are deceiving," she said. "I went to the University of Toronto egghead, not another planet." She paused a moment, chuckling. "Ha, another planet."

"My sense of humor is a little numb, so forgive me for not laughing," Wilson said, giving Gomez another nudge to keep her moving.

Cocteau raised her dark brows. "When is it not numb?"

"Obsidian!" Gomez exclaimed. "Dr. Wilson, its volcanic glass, made from the planet."

"Now she's caught up," Cocteau said. "Hope she starts registering soon, for your sake. You know, I did my desert training in the southwest, in New Mexico and Arizona."

"Um, okay?" Wilson was confused. Why was she telling him this? She made it clear that she was giving him the cold-shoulder.

"Yep," Cocteau said. "Met some kids messing around at the training site; almost got themselves killed till I intervened. A sorry lot they were. Should've called the MP, but didn't. Wilson, if you could've seen them. Just looking, I knew their lives. I didn't ask why they were there. They were the kind that had nowhere else to go. They'd risk their lives rather than go home. Well, a girl, maybe thirteen, was from one of the local reservations. Seemed more grateful than the others that I saved their lives. She gave me a piece of obsidian. Dark and smooth just like these walls. She called it an apache tear. Said it had a story behind it and to look it up."

"Did you?" Wilson said.

"No," Cocteau said.

"Why?"

"Didn't need to," Cocteau said. "Her being there told me enough." Cocteau was quiet. "I hope those kids found something better than I did at their age."

What was with Cocteau? Was she being affected by the celestial stone's power too? She only saw it briefly when she came for to rescue them, not at its full power like they did. Was just seeing it enough to affect someone's mind? Wilson broke out in goosebumps just thinking about it.

Cocteau jumped back, pushing Wilson and Gomez flat against the wall.

"Hey—"

She did a 'silence' motion with her hand, her eyes wide.

The awkward clanking and clicking of Venusian footsteps fast approached.

Wilson mouthed 'this way.' He pointed to a small alcove ten feet ahead in the opposite wall. On light feet and blistered toes, they dashed to it.

He used his recognition coin, scanning it in front of the wall to open the door that should've been there. Nothing happened

"Wilson?" Cocteau whispered.

"There's a room here," Wilson said in a hushed voice. "There is supposed to be a room here!"

The holopanel finally appeared, though smaller with more symbols.

Wilson punched the wall. "Dang it!"

"Dang it?" Cocteau rolled her eyes.

Gomez tapped Cocteau's shoulder. "I think he means damn it."

"It requires a security code," Wilson said.

The footsteps grew louder.

"I thought you said this level was empty except around Bitiir's holding," Cocteau hissed.

"They're living beings," Wilson typed random symbols. "They're not going to stay put."

He kept typing random combinations. It was no use. Looking at all the characters, there was no way he'd figure it out.

"Wilson—" Cocteau shook his shoulder.

"I know," he gasped. "I'm trying."

Venusian shadows stretched across the wall.

"Wilson!"

He closed his eyes. *I have to know it,* he thought. He knew Cocteau didn't want him to access Venusian memories anymore, but their lives were at stake. He searched, tried to feel for them, but nothing came up.

"Come on," he cringed as the pressure in his head started as it always did.

A memory came into view.

His heart thumped in time to footsteps. Not Venusian footsteps, but his own. Out of body, he observed himself from earlier, a male Earth child blindfolded with the metal band that the Venusian guardian fitted on him. A blindfolded Gomez was thrown next him. But this wasn't his memory. Wilson was no longer Wilson; he was the warden, the Venusian in charge of detentions.

He was observing the transfer of prisoners to extraction. This male and female Earth child are knowledgable. Extraction will make them give what they fight to protect. He ordered the lesser guardians to remove the blinders from the prisoners; there was need to hide their vision anymore. Their fear would make extraction all the more equitable with the celestial stone.

He took delight in seeing the Earth children's faces sink at the sight of him. If only they knew. They reached the entrance of extraction, and he waved his recognition. The panel appeared and it prompted him for his overlord pass sequence—a sequence only for the higher ranked.

"Wilson," Cocteau pulled on Wilson. "Wilson get up!"

Wilson was on the ground holding his head. Why did he always end up on the ground? Cocteau and Gomez pulled him to his feet.

"I know the code!" Wilson waved the recognition again and started dialing into the panel. "The pass sequence!"

"Come on—come on—*come on,*" he shook anxiously.

The panel disappeared as soon as he finished dialing.

The door was still shut.

"Run," Cocteau ordered.

Just as they turned, cracks in the wall glowed a brilliant yellow-gold, revealing the arched outline of a door.

It slid open.

Cocteau pushed them in.

Wilson dialed again and it closed behind them.

It was pitch black, the air so thick that every breath labored.

He felt Gomez's touch as she pulled his arm close to her. He could still hear the steps of the approaching Venusian. Its steps scurried close, like an insect scratching against fabric.

The dim glow from the outer corridor lit the obsidian door just enough to be translucent. He could see the obscure silhouette of a Venusian on the other side. Scratching and scraping footsteps came closer as the silhouette grew more defined against the door.

Wilson felt Gomez's breath; calm and steady. Her chest pressed against his arm, and the rhythm of her heart stayed steady. Cocteau held her breath.

Thump.

Thump-thump.

Wilson's ears filled with the sound of his heart beating faster with each movement of the Venusian. He watched its silhouette raise its arms, long spindly fingers fanning-out, like a spider stretching to its prey.

He gulped, pulling Gomez closer to him. His heart felt like it was being ripped apart. The Venusian fingers dragged lightly against the door, their slight tapping making the thumping in Wilson's ears move faster. So fast his heart was no longer in rhythm; just one sound, pushing against his ears and chest.

The Venusian's arms swiftly waved the outline of a recognition coin and fingers fluttered in a frenzy.

The pass sequence, Wilson thought. *He's pulling it up to come in!*

Wilson's knees buckled; his legs numb as anxiety surged throughout his body. He could taste it in his mouth.

Gomez's hand gripped his, her firm touch electrical, surging energy into him once more.

No, he thought. *I won't fall to the ground again. I will stand.*

Then time stopped.

In the split moment the Venusian dialed its pass sequence they waited; waited for their discovery, for their unavoidable recapture by its hand.

And nothing happened.

Whatever pass sequence it dialed didn't work.

He doesn't have the right pass sequence, Wilson felt a wave of relief. *He cannot enter.*

Then the high-pitched ringing.

"No sign of the Earth children," a muffled unearthly voice emanated from the Venusian, a voice that Wilson knew only he could hear through the ringing. It's silhouette dissipated, backing away from the door.

All became clear and the thumping in Wilson's ears alleviated.

"Do you think it's gone?" Gomez whispered.

"We're in the clear," Wilson breathed. "It's gone.

"How do you know?"

"I just do."

Gomez released her grip on Wilson.

Wilson conjured up the holopanel for the room.

He paused.

Trickling.

Something dripped near them.

"What is it?" Gomez asked.

"Water!" Wilson felt the word dry up in his mouth as soon as he said it. "It's water, my god it's water!"

He found the screen that controlled the lighting in the room and he punched through it.

The lights came on, bright and golden, radiating out of the walls from an unseen source. Wilson squinted and eyes darted immediately toward the source of the trickling.

Sure enough, as through it were part of the obsidian wall, a basin filled with clear liquid that drizzled as a steady stream above it.

He ran to it, filling his nose with the sweet smell. Who knew that water could have a scent? He felt the coolness it emitted, and he dunked his face in, not caring if it truly was water or not. He just knew that the cold felt good against his hot skin, and was the first relief since coming here.

He lifted his head out, splashing water down his back.

"Ha-ha guys, we have water," he said proudly. "Probably shouldn't have stuck my head in it until I was sure it was water, but it is. Come on over."

Wilson expected them to run for water as he did, but was not met with the same satisfaction. He turned, his team frozen in place, wide-eyed.

"Um, guys—"

He too froze.

And realized why a pass sequence was required to enter.

Before them was a long hall lined with Venusians.

Chapter 19: Service and Sacrifice

Marshall Wilson never considered death. Like anyone else he knew of death, but he did not register its existence or realize its inevitability.

That is, until that fateful day when death reflected in the eyes of his beloved. Death became real. No longer was it something he watched in movies, read about in books, or listened to in spiritual orations, but a physical reality of what is to come.

And he thought he was about to die in the instant he saw the long hall lined with Venusians.

I'm not ready. He was startled by the thought. *Oh god, I'm not ready.*

Hundreds of Venusians stood at attention, perfectly still.

Wait—Wilson took a step forward. None of the Venusians moved.

"Hey!" he yelled at them.

"What the hell are you doing?" Cocteau's face was murderously angry.

Gomez squinted her eyes curiously.

"Look," Wilson pointed, walking up to one of the Venusians. He grabbed its arm and shook it. An empty husk.

"What's wrong with it?" Gomez approached.

"I don't know," Wilson said. "But I don't think it's alive. I don't think any of them are alive."

Gomez stroked the abdomen. "Lifeless machine."

"Ick, what the hell is wrong with these things?" Cocteau said studying one of them, a disgusted expression on her face. "They've hung their dead with all the innards spilling out behind it."

Wilson poked his head around a Venusian. Sure enough, scores of blue and red veins coated in a clear gelatin spilled out the back all the way down the spine. It hung in a tangled heap and attached to the back of the wall, holding the lifeless Venusian in place.

"Is this what they do with their carcasses when they die?" Wilson asked no one, thinking out loud.

"What if it's not dead?" Gomez said, stroking the exoskeleton again. "What if it could never die?"

"Gomez, stop touching it like that," Cocteau said, her face flushed. "Alive or dead we don't know why they put them all in here. Just get a drink of water will you."

"It's like a mausoleum," Wilson said walking down the hall.

Memories of a dark day crept to his mind. A day when it was easier to feel nothing than to feel something. Rows of tombstones and a religious man reciting comforting words to an assembly of relatives. Freshly dug Earth stung him, trying to make him feel anything. He stared at the casket, highly polished mahogany—he spared no expense. How was he going to live without *her*? This was an unknown he'd never faced. Uncertainty was his only promise, and it clenched him like a rock in his abdomen. He saw no future; his mind blocked any premise of it like a thick fog and all became meaningless. As the casket lowered into the ground he chose to think of it as empty. It was easier that way. *She* couldn't spend forever there, deep in the underworld of earth and soil. She loved the sun too much. *She* couldn't be in there, *she* just couldn't be—

"Mausoleum?" Cocteau said brusquely, bring him back to the present. She just finished splashing her face with water. "Is that what those Venusian memories are telling you? Because this is more like a b-grade horror morgue."

Wilson glared. "No, it's my own assumption. They're intelligent —they feel—they have to do something with their dead. Tell me, do you have no reverence for anything?"

Cocteau shrugged her shoulders.

"Whatever," Wilson turned back and continued down the hall.

"Where are you going?" Cocteau called.

"We found water didn't we?" Wilson said, waving to follow. "Let's find something to take it with us."

Cocteau raised an eyebrow. "Finally, thinking like a survivor."

Wilson didn't need her validation. He used to seek the validation of others, but after everything at NASA, he stopped searching for it. He didn't want it. Even though he didn't want or need Cocteau's, it felt good. Was it because he actively sought her trust? He impressed her. And in the short time he knew Cocteau, impressing her, even in the smallest way, was hard earned.

"Water break's over," Cocteau said to Gomez as she splashed a handful of water into her face. "Finish up. We'll be back."

Wilson walked in the lead as they continued down the line of lifeless Venusians. Their motionless eyes seemingly to follow whichever way they went.

"How can they do that?" Cocteau asked.

"Watching," Gomez said. "It's always watching us."

"It? Us?" Cocteau's face scanned the line of eyes warily. "I don't like the sound of that."

"We'll be fine," Wilson said. "Just keep walking."

Wilson knew what 'it' was. The power surged through every part of this place, its pulsating presence becoming more evident the longer he spent in the compound: the celestial stone.

He felt it, its life giving energy flowing through the floors, walls, and ceiling. It was the stones's light that illuminated from the walls, the unseen force lighting their path. The power of the celestial stone penetrated everything and every level in this compound. Wilson wondered if it held the answers to what they sought. Why couldn't anyone find them? How could something like this stay hidden from NASA and SIC, and what did Venus have to do with any of it?

And more importantly, why was he here? What was he looking for? He had the inkling that the celestial stone not only held the answers, but probably was the answer.

Further on, the line of carcasses ended and were replaced by copper and gold devices, hanging from floor to ceiling and twisted in sharp gruesome shapes to almost no purpose. Wilson hunched his shoulders as the devices barred down at them. Their acute edges gave a warning: this is no place for you—*beware*, we are not your ally.

He stopped.

"Alright there Dr. Wilson?" Cocteau asked.

Gomez came and stood beside him.

"These tools," Wilson gulped, "don't some of them look familiar?"

Cocteau approached the wall to the left of them. "They don't look like anything I've seen."

"That one there, " Wilson pointed, "looks like a scalpel, if you look at it the right way, don't you think? And that one there, a lancet?"

Cocteau and Gomez looked to where Wilson pointed.

"I guess?" Cocteau said. "I don't know a lot about surgical tools; I only know what I've seen on the field, but these look more, I don't know, complex?"

"Death will walk," Gomez said morbidly, eyeing some copper straps dangling.

Wilson's eyes passed a giant screw and what he suspected were oversized surgical saws. "What in god's name are they doing down here?"

"I don't know," Cocteau reached up and pulled off one of the surgical saws. She made a stabbing motion with it. "But they look pretty useful to me, don't you think?"

"Yeah sure," Wilson said uneasy.

Cocteau grabbed a small curved blade with rings that fit between her fingers. "Now I like this one. Reminds me of one I used to have back in the day."

Wilson wasn't paying much attention to Cocteau. His attention was caught by a device on the opposite wall.

It was a small. A rectangular pack with loops and a gold cord extending from it. The cord attached to a copper ring the size of a small melon.

A number of them hung in neat rows. He took one carefully into his hands.

"What'd you find there?" Cocteau came up and took one. "Think it can hold water?"

"This," Wilson turned it meticulously, looking at the outward simplicity, different from all the other tools surrounding them, "this device is more than what it seems." He closed his eyes. Maybe if he tried hard enough he'd see just enough memory fragments without hurting himself, and piece together what it was.

"Stop that," Cocteau said. "I thought I ordered you to stop frying your brain."

"Shush!" Wilson two fingers to his lip, eyes still closed.

"Don't shush—"

"Shush!"

Gomez poked over Cocteau's shoulder. "I think we better do what he says."

Cocteau turned tight-lipped as glared at Gomez.

Unintelligible voices, whispers from foreign memories echoed around Wilson as his identity wandered. He could feel himself draining, trying to interpret the exotic memories of the beings that left part of themselves in him. The power of the celestial stone pulsed through the memories, images becoming clearer. The pressure he always felt lessened, and their thoughts came easier.

Then it dawned on him.

"It's a weapon," he said, opening his eyes. "The best I can describe is that it's a gun of some sort, but more than that. It amplifies, emits energy. It's an energy emitter."

"Good," Cocteau said. "Looks like our escape just got a lot easier."

"Really? I've never shot a gun in my life," Wilson said apathetically, holding the energy emitter away from him. "And I'm not about to start, especially not one made by them."

"Get off your high horse," Cocteau said, shoving the strange weapon back at him. "It's you or them, and for some strange perverse reason, I prefer you. Show us what to do."

Wilson clenched his jaw in distaste and turned the emitter over.

"You or them," Cocteau said again.

"Fine." He used the loops to attach the device his wrist, and ran the cord up his arm, connecting the metal band around his head. It fit perfectly right around his forehead. He felt a slight humming as the band on his head began to vibrate. Suddenly, he felt a drain in energy and he buckled to the floor.

"Whoa!" Cocteau reached to rip the band off of Wilson.

"It's okay," Wilson took a deep breath and stood. "It's just powering on. I can feel it; it's using my own body energy to work. It's amazing really, I can feel it drawing from me even now." He held up his arm and aiming his fist and energy emitter at an empty space on the wall. He took a deep breath and the humming on the ring-spun, increasing. Suddenly a piece of the wall blasted away, knocking a dozen tools to the ground.

The blast even caught Gomez's attention. She and Cocteau stared at Wilson.

"Give me one of those sons-of-bitches," Cocteau said, putting on the device just as Wilson did. She pointed at the same spot, mimicking Wilson in every way. Nothing happened.

"What?" Cocteau shook the pack on her wrist.

"Here, let me try," Gomez said, reaching for Cocteau.

"Uh, I think not," Cocteau said. "You shouldn't be handling a gun right now, not with your episodes." She turned to Wilson. "How did you get it to work?"

"I don't know," Wilson said. "It just did."

"Oh god, please don't tell me we're leaving our safety and defense in your hands."

"You have to concentrate," Wilson said. "It's a mind thing. You have to let it take your energy, like you're surrendering to it."

"I have never surrendered," Cocteau glowered.

"Yeah, well I've never shot a gun," Wilson said. "Today's a day for firsts. Try it my way, you'll see."

"Fine," Cocteau breathed, closing her eyes. "I'm surrendering. I'm surrendering to the power of the Venusian weapon."

"It doesn't work if you mock it," Wilson said

"Well, I'm not the kind of person that surrenders," Cocteau said frustratedly. "I've never won a fight with that kind of thinking. What kind of soldiers are these things that they have to surrender to win a fight."

Wilson shook his head. "A very dangerous kind: the kind that has nothing to lose." He looked down at the pack on his wrist. It didn't draw upon the celestial stone for energy like everything else in this place; whoever designed it purposely made it draw from its host, like a parasite controlling its prey. A bit of freedom lost in every shot taken. "The way this gun works ensures it."

*   *   *

They reentered the corridor they previously escaped, this time in their makeshift gear. Before leaving, they found small sacks attached to drill devices, and ripped them off to hold water. Though Wilson suspected that their original intent was to hold something much more sinister.

They crept along the walls, intent not to draw attention again. Both Wilson and Cocteau wore energy emitters and strapped whatever useful blades to themselves using gold and copper cords they scavenged. Even though the cords and straps were metal, they were flexible like fabric, making Wilson question what elements could make something so flexible, yet strong.

Cocteau only allowed Gomez a couple small blades, just enough to defend herself if needed. Gomez made no protest.

"Not much further," Wilson whispered. He was in the lead again, bringing them to the room he suspected Bitiir was in.

"Remember the new plan," Cocteau said. "And don't flake on me."

Wilson grumbled. "I know, I get it." Being the only one able to handle the energy emitter, the new plan was for him to shoot and kill the Venusians guarding Bitiir.

The corridor curved at a sharp angle, and they could no longer see far ahead of them.

"The room Bitiir's in should be right over—"

A blast hit the wall next to Wilson, shards breaking and raining upon them.

Cocteau grabbed his sleeve and pulled him into an alcove for cover.

All three were hunched together. Wilson peered around the alcove.

Down the corridor just before the bend, a Venusian, tall and barely clearing the ceiling, held its arm out, the box of an energy emitter on its wrist, humming with power.

Gomez screamed. "Marshall!"

Wilson ducked his head into the alcove just in time. An energy blast burst flew right where his head was.

Cocteau held Gomez back, her eyes hard. "Well?"

"Well what?" Wilson snapped. "My head almost blew off!"

Cocteau gestured with her head. "Shoot it."

Another energy blast hit the edge of the alcove, more obsidian shards scattering about them.

"I can't just—"

"Yes you can," Cocteau growled. "Aim your arm and shoot it."

"But it will—"

More shards darted at them as another blast hit the same spot.

"God damn it Wilson!" Cocteau shoved him over and aimed her arm around the alcove, trying for the Venusian.

Nothing happened.

"Arg!" Cocteau pulled her arm back before another blast shot at them. "Wilson, do it."

"I'll get—"

"Then don't give it the chance," Cocteau's brows curved in rage. "Shoot it, or I will kill you myself!"

"What if—"

"Shoot it!"

Wilson took a deep breath. *Here goes nothing.*

The mere split seconds it took for him to move, another blast shot at them and he ducked low. He aimed, the hum of his emitter drawing from him as he surrendered to its power.

He shot.

And missed.

It hit the wall next to the Venusian and did nothing. Not even a mark against the smooth surface.

The section it hit suddenly glowed with an arched doorway. It slid open and another Venusian appeared within it.

"That's it!" Wilson said. "Bitiir's in there."

"Shit," Cocteau said as she poked her head around and pulled it back.

"Execute them all," a raspy ethereal voice emanated from the Venusian in the doorway. "We have what we need. I shall dispose of this one."

Wilson knew Cocteau only heard ringing as the pressure in his head translated their words to him.

I shall dispose of this one. Wilsons chest tightened. *He means Bitiir!"*

A gaunt horror filled Gomez's face, as the Venusian turned to disappear into the doorway. If it closed, there was no way they'd make it in time before the deed was complete.

I knew this was a mistake! Wilson's thoughts ran at a top speed. *He was going to die anyway, and we risked everything to—*

He glanced at Gomez. Her expression sank and the tightness in his chest dissipated.

His mind went blank as his arm aimed. He wasn't thinking when he did it; he just did. He never believed in relying on instinct. Logic and reason were key in survival. But instinct took over as he surrendered to it, taking the place of all his logic and reasoning. The energy emitter pulled power from his body, fatigue making him lightheaded as it left him and hit the Venusian in the doorway.

It was enough. The strength from the blast hit it in the neck, snapping the head sideways and fell instantaneously.

Wilson's exhaustion made his knees give away as he slid against the wall of the alcove.

A screech from the remaining Venusian. It's screeching turned to enraged words in Wilson's mind: *Murderers!*

He knew what to do next. Wilson conjured up a holopanel, hoping the proximity was close enough to control the door.

And it was.

He dialed in his stolen pass sequence and the door slammed shut behind the remaining Venusian, locking it in place.

The Venusian scrambled, conjuring up its own holopanel, dialing and unable to open the doorway without the pass sequence.

"Nice!" Cocteau smiled. Her smile quickly turned to a grimace when she looked down at Wilson. "What are you doing? Kill the other one!"

"I can't," Wilson panted.

"What do you mean you can't!" Cocteau was frantic. "Now's our chance! Kill it!"

"I can't do it anymore," Wilson yelled. "I don't have the energy. It's taken too much."

The awkward clanking of Venusian steps advanced.

An energy blast flew past them.

Cocteau's face was hard. "Alright, back to plan A. I'll distract it and—*Gomez, what the hell are you doing?*"

In the commotion no one noticed Gomez slip away. She stood in the center of the corridor, stepping lightly out of the way of another energy blast.

"Tell them," she said, her eyes glistening, the corners of her mouth quivered. "Tell them, for once I wasn't selfish."

She darted forward.

Another blast and the smell of scorched hair filled their nostrils. It barely missed Gomez as singed hair gripped her scalp.

Blades flung in the air as she threw them at the Venusian.

"Here!" she yelled, her face frenzied, but her eyes focused. "Here! You've taken everything else from me! Take more!"

"Ari, no!" Wilson bit his cheek, the salty taste of blood plastering his tongue.

Another screech from the Venusian as it turned to her, away from the doorway. *Murderer.*

"Now," Cocteau ordered. "She's given you an open, go now!"

Holding back tears and regaining strength in his legs, Wilson pulled himself up.

"I'll take care of her," Cocteau locked eyes with Wilson. "Trust me. Now go! Rendezvous at the lift."

His knees ached as he darted forward.

Gomez's distraction gave him the time he needed. The Venusian didn't notice as he ran behind it within inches and conjured the holopanel and unlocked the door. The glowing outline appeared and it slid open.

He dove in.

He tripped over the dead Venusian and fell.

The Venusian fighting Gomez noticed and arms reached for him.

The side of Cocteau's body appeared just next to the opening.

"The lift!" she yelled.

And the door shut.

She closed it, Wilson thought. He quickly pulled up another holopanel and locked it with his pass sequence.

And now I'm alone.

He stood.

Faint light emanated from holographic screens projected against the dark surface of the walls. Lines and other readings quivered on them, fluctuating. Symbols blinked and Wilson read them: L i f e support readings.

Bitiir's life readings, he thought.

A small, rounded opening glowed with white light from another room.

Wilson walked over to it, his eyes adjusting as he stepped through.

He entered a room that glowed much like the one with the Venusian corpses, though this one significantly smaller and bare. All except for one thing.

A black, obsidian table stood in the center of the room. All manner of straps and wires attached to the one thing upon it.

Bitiir.

Chapter 20: A Life for a Soul

Wilson stood over Bitiir. He was helpless, weak, and at the full mercy of the Venusians.

And at the mercy of Wilson.

Bitiir's head moved, his neck thick with veins popping out from the stress of the restraints. His eyes wide, seeing only what was in his mind and not Wilson standing over him. His breathing was shallow, struggling and gasping for even the smallest breaths.

Remember who's in control, Bitiir's strong voice echoed in Wilson's mind. How could something so weak and pathetic have been strong enough to intimidate him?

"I know who's in control," Wilson's voice did not seem his own as it rasped, grating against his vocal cords.

He backed away. Bitiir was dying, there was no doubt about it. His parched lips told Wilson he was dehydrated, taking its toll. If Wilson waited long enough, the deed would be done and it would be the hand of the Venusian to blame, not his. All he had to do was wait.

You must be the one to free him, Gomez's voice said in his mind. *If not for him, then for yourself.*

"No," he said, the continued taste of blood in his mouth from where he bit his cheek. "Get out of my head."

Bitiir coughed, gasping for air. He vomited something and could not turn his head. He was suffocating.

"Not long now," Wilson said, clenching his fists. *No, not long at all.*

Images of Gomez distracting the Venusian were as clear as the scene before him, her deep eyes looking at Wilson desperately.

Marshall, the voice from the celestial stone called.

"No," Wilson said, backing away from Bitiir. "Not now."

Marshall, the voice imitated her perfectly, Justine's voice. And there he was again, not at Bitiir's side, but at her bedside, her hand too weak to move as it lay there open for him to grasp. He squeezed it, not knowing for the last time.

"Marshall," Justine's lips barely parted as they spoke. "Don't let me be the end your life."

He looked into her face but it faded. He wasn't at the hospice, he was on Venus, in this hellish world of rock and ruin. In place of her face was Bitiir's, lying helpless, unconscious.

"No," Wilson's voice trembled. He touched Bitiir's neck, feeling for a pulse. "No-no-no!"

He waved his recognition coin, the holopanel floating right above Bitiir. Wilson dialed it rapidly.

The sound of depressurization hissed and the bindings around Bitiir snapped up, pulling away all the wires and cords. Wilson shoved Bitiir off of the table, his body hitting the floor with a thud.

Wilson knelt over him, holding Bitiir sideways. Wilson made his finger a hook, then shoved it into Bitiir's mouth, clearing away excess vomit. He rolled him onto his back, doing compressions rhythmically on his chest.

"Come on," Wilson yelled at him. "You are such a stubborn bastard, come on!"

Wilson tilted Bitiir's head back, pinched his nose and breathed into his airway twice.

"I said come on!" Wilson started another round of compressions, losing all feeling in his arms. "Come on! For Ari!"

Bitiir's eyes watered furiously as his body went rigid, hacking-out the bodily fluids from his lungs. Wilson rolled him to his side to finish coughing it all out.

Bitiir wiped his mouth with his sleeve, his hands shaking uncontrollably. He tried to sit-up.

"Slow," Wilson took his shoulders and steadied him.

Bitiir's eyes flitted back and forth. "Where am I?" his mouth quivered.

"We're on Venus," Wilson said.

"I know that you dolt," Bitiir said. "I want to know where."

And there it was; the annoyingly condescending Bitiir Wilson was not looking forward to facing.

Bitiir steadied himself, then glared at Wilson. "You!" he said as though he noticed for the first time who was with him.

"Um, me?"

"Get your hands off me!" Bitiir shoved Wilson away. He pulled himself up, using the operating table for support.

"If you can stand we got to move," Wilson said. "I can explain on the way."

Bitiir didn't move.

"Here, let me," Wilson made a move to help support, but Bitiir put his hand-up.

"Why?" Bitiir breathed heavily.

"We don't have time for this," Wilson put a support arm under Bitiir.

He dragged Bitiir to the front room. All was still.

"Still clear," Wilson said. "Thanks to Dr. Gomez."

"Gomez? What's she got to do with this?" Bitiir said. "What's that ridiculous thing around your head? And—my god, what is that thing!"

Bitiir's eyes locked onto the dead Venusian on the floor.

"*Quiet!*" It felt good to order Bitiir, to have some amount of control over him for once.

"Dr. Wilson, I want to know what that thing is and what is going on!"

"If you value your life, you will stay quiet and move fast," Wilson said. "We don't have much time."

"You said you'd explain on the way."

"I lied," Wilson said. "Can you walk on your own?"

Bitiir stood straight, but his knees buckled and he held his head.

"Ugh," Wilson said annoyed. "Lean on me. But I'm not as strong as Cocteau; you'll need to help support yourself."

Wilson held out his recognition and pulled up the holomap of their level.

"What are you doing?" Bitiir said wide eyed at the holomap.

"Just a refresher," Wilson said as he closed-out the map. Reading into the map and its language too long meant he might fall into one of his episodes and not have the energy to get to the lift. "Our objective is the lift. Cocteau and Gomez are holding-off the Venusians—the monsters who took us—so we can make it."

"So *you* can make it," Bitiir sneered. "They don't care a lick what happens to me."

"*We*," Wilson said. "They expect us both."

Bitiir raised an eyebrow, cracking his cheap toothy smile. "Really?"

Wilson shook his head. "Just come on, and stay quiet."

He thought about Gomez and Cocteau, just outside the door fighting off the Venusian. Did they take it down? Or were they leading it in confusing paths through the level like the original plan? He would know as soon as he opened the door.

Wilson pulled up the holopanel. *Here it goes.*

He opened the door and they entered the corridor.

He half expected to still see Gomez still distracting the Venusian, but all was clear.

To the lift then, Wilson thought. He memorized his route, he knew exactly where to go.

Then he thought of them, running alone.

Cocteau has an energy emitter, something in his head told him. His conscience? *She said to trust her. Go to the lift.*

But she can't work it, he told himself. *And trust hasn't helped us this far.*

He envisioned the map in his head and it all played-out before him. He could intercept their path. Gomez, standing helpless before the Venusian, and he would be there to shoot it down. He could do it, as long as he paced himself.

He decided to take the detour and find Gomez before going to the lift.

They moved swiftly. Wilson kept his arm with the energy emitter free, pointing in the direction they needed to move.

He expected Bitiir to look scared, or at least confused, but he didn't. He moved wherever Wilson dragged him to move, just giving Wilson a completely unimpressed frown.

Right before they approached a turn, Wilson paused them, pointing his fist to aim the energy emitter down the corridor before entering it. Bitiir furrowed his brow and curled his lip, as though he silently laughed at the sight of Wilson.

Arrogant piece of work, Wilson thought infuriated. I should leave *him* *where he is the next time he does that.*

If not for him, then for yourself, Gomez's words repeated.

"You know, those things, they aren't smarter than us," Bitiir said.

"What?" Wilson said. "Stay quiet."

"By that perturbed expression on your face," Bitiir whispered, "I thought it would do you good to know they're not smarter than us, these, um—"

"Venusians."

"Yes, Venusians," Bitiir said. "Think, if someone like you or Cocteau can manage to escape their grasp, and they're distracted by whatever crazy plan you concocted-up, they are certainly not smarter than us."

Wilson glared.

Bitiir shook his head. "Why?"

"Why what?"

"Why didn't you let me die back there, it would've been easy. I would've been out of your hair, and dare I say, out of the way for Ari?"

"It's Dr. Gomez to you," Wilson said. "She's the only good person on this mission and doesn't deserve any of this.

"Be careful Dr. Wilson," Bitiir grinned. "I can guarantee I've known her a lot longer than you; she's not what she seems."

"It's not like that with her," Wilson said. "I could never, not with anyone ever again. She just reminds me of—"

Wilson stopped himself. Why was he telling Bitiir all this? It was only ammunition Bitiir could use against him later.

He looked at Bitiir's face, a starved expression for more of Wilson's words. He indulged.

"I've seen enough of death that I've ever wanted to see," Wilson said. "That's why I didn't let you die; I didn't want to see it again."

Bitiir sneered. "You romanticize everything, which is why you're so insufferable."

"I can still leave you behind."

Bitiir seemed to take the hint and stopped talking.

They continued down the maze of corridors, hoping with a slim chance they would find Gomez and Cocteau alive.

*　*　*

Idiot! Cocteau thought as she ran through the maze of blackened glass corridors. *Gomez you idiot. When I find you, if the Venusian hasn't killed you, I'll kill you myself.*

After Wilson locked himself in the room, the Venusian became enraged, out of control. In its strength it almost shot Cocteau's head clean off.

In the confusion, she could never tell what Gomez did. Somehow, the Venusian stopped attacking her, and went for Gomez instead. Gomez bolted and the Venusian followed in its provoked state.

How could she do this? Cocteau tried to remember the path they decided on to lead the Venusian away.

Was she going the right way? She was turned around in this labyrinth. As long as she and Gomez made it to the lift, they could count on Wilson being there with his working energy emitter. Their distraction would give him the time he needed to make it with Bitiir.

She clenched her right hand, her energy emitter clinging to it. *If I could get this thing to work. And damn Gomez! Where did she go?*

In reality, Cocteau was impressed with Gomez. Even in her state-of-mind, Gomez had the guts to take on the Venusian herself. She saved Cocteau's life more than once on this mission. She stuck with her, even when she abused and tried to push her away.

Gomez was right, Cocteau thought back to her words back in the lift. She was still her, even if her communication and control was taken away. *She said she would follow through on her end. She can be counted on.*

She trusted her.

There was no use in running through this maze. They agreed to meet at the lift, no matter what happened. Gomez held up her end of the deal, and whether she was there to meet them or not, Cocteau respected her enough to follow through with her part. Gomez knew what it took to complete the mission and what she was doing. Cocteau had to do the same.

She changed course and headed for the lift, just as Gomez expected her to do.

In the time it took to run, her mind cleared of everything. No matter what happened, she would get her team out alive, no matter what it took.

She skidded to a stop.

"Gomez!"

There she was, next to the lift and cornered by the Venusian standing over.

Where the hell is Wilson!

Cocteau knew what she had to do. She always acted on instinct, putting her all into it and that made her a survivor. It was what she trained her team to do.

I will do it, she raised her arm. *Now or never.*

And it was never.

There was a blast from an energy emitter, but not from Cocteau.

She'd seen good men and women, people with personalities and individual minds, gunned down for no reason other than they were in the way. To become lifeless husks that once held something dear and beautiful. There was never a reason when things like this happened.

Just as there was no reason for all the intelligence that made Arianna Gomez who she was, to suddenly be gone.

Gomez fell back, her eyes emotionless as the fabric of her suit burned away and melted into the charred skin that once covered her abdomen. Right where the Venusian shot her.

Cocteau froze, unable to make a single shot.

"No!" A desperate screech overwhelmed Cocteau as she looked behind. Wilson and Bitiir found them.

Wilson threw Bitiir to the ground and pointed his energy emitter.

Chapter 21: Radiant Energy

They say that energy travels in the form of waves. Different from sound waves that travel through the vibration of particles in the air (hence no sound in space), radiant energy travels through electromagnetic waves. All things emit a form of radiant energy or radiation.

The main source of this energy ultimately comes from the sun, traveling through space to be absorbed by its surrounding celestial objects.

Living objects consume the sun's radiant energy one way or another, be it directly absorbed or consumed from other sources. Energy is never destroyed, only transferred. Once that energy is consumed it can be emitted and transferred out in various ways and forms.

The energy emitter of the Venusian race did just that; it could artificially emit the radiant energy naturally consumed by a living being, transferring it through a condensed focal point, and could be amplified by the mind and will of the wielder. One would deduce that this would create limitations for the wielder, but in reality, made possibilities of the energy emitter limitless.

And Marshall Wilson was only beginning to understand this.

Rage. That was what he felt as he watched Gomez's body curl, like an insect shot with poison. The day Justine passed he felt nothing; a sickening emptiness that haunted for years after. This was different.

His head hot, he could feel the fire building within him. He stared at the monster that stood over her, unfazed by the life it just ended. Such a being should not be allowed to exist.

And he did it. All his rageful emotion focused on the energy emitter in his hand and he released it, right in the path of the Venusian.

Cocteau dove out of the way, the heat of it scorching her arm as it passed. The Venusian didn't even turn as energy hit the back of its head, tearing it into thousands of pieces from the pedestal of its body and splattering red blood like an uncontrollable hailstorm.

Its lifeless exoskeleton fell to the ground, a crimson pool forming on the smooth black glass.

Wilson dropped his arms and shook. He felt the Venusians warm blood smear across his face. Did he just murder? Not self-defense, but actual murder? Cocteau and Bitiir were on the ground, also covered in splotches of its blood. He dared not think that this was his doing, that his rage did this.

He ran and knelt beside Gomez. Her eyes were still wide open, expressionless as death always made them. He couldn't bear to see them drained of their liveliness, and so he held her in his arms, pulling her close. Searing tears ran down his face, mixing with the Venusian blood and dripping onto Gomez's perfectly white bodysuit, staining it.

He waited for her to speak, to give her last words before going beyond his reach, just as Justine did. But last words rarely happen, if ever, and Gomez was gone. Truly and undoubtedly gone.

Bitiir stumbled over to them. "N-no," he said kneeling over her. "She can't be, not Ari." He looked at himself, at the blood spatter. "Red, their blood is red!"

Wilson turned his head. "You—this is your fault!"

"What?" Bitiir's face was sullen. "I never wanted this to happen. I—"

"You did this!" Wilson not letting Gomez go. If they arrived moments sooner, maybe he could've stopped this. If he hadn't detoured looking for her—if he just went straight to the lift and hadn't tried to prevent her death in the first place—

And he wasn't about to let Bitiir put the blame on him, not after all Bitiir did to cause this. "Look at her—this is your doing! If you hadn't organized this mission—if she hadn't insisted we go back for you—she'd still be—"

"She's the one who came back for me?" Bitiir looked surprised. He bowed his head into his hands. "My god, she came back for me."

"For you," Wilson said. "A sniveling little—"

"That's enough!" Cocteau stood over them. She closed her eyes. "We all know who couldn't make the shot." She looked down, remorseful. "Dr. Wilson, you must lay her down; it's her time to rest. She did the right thing and we need to do the right thing."

"Lay her down?" Wilson refused to look at Cocteau. "You mean leave her behind."

"We cannot take her with us," she knelt next to him. Her face silently said she'd seen this before. "She must be left behind. Let her go Dr. Wilson."

"For once I agree with our admirable captain," Bitiir's voice shook. "It's what Ari would've wanted." He stood. "She wouldn't want to hinder our endeavors. That's not her."

"I can't," Wilson clenched tighter. "I can't let go."

Cocteau put a hand on his shoulder. "You must let go, or you'll die down here too. She knew what taking on that Venusian meant. She asked us to tell them something, remember?"

" 'For once I wasn't selfish,' " Wilson repeated.

"She said that?" Bitiir's eyes wide.

"We need to find who 'them' are," Cocteau said. "And tell them; that's our new mission. She has a mother on Earth, others close to her."

"She's with her mother," Bitiir hung his head and shook it. "No one else is close to her. Oh Ari, why would you say that!"

"How do you know?" Cocteau looked curiously.

Bitiir lifted his head, his eyes like bullets. "Because I do."

Cocteau bit her bottom lip. She stood straight, a flame coming alive in her eyes as all emotion melted away, like wax off a candle. "Let's go Mr. Space Archeologist. Let her go."

When Cocteau said, 'Mr. Space Archeologist', it wasn't mocking like she usually did. It was soft, enduring, as though she'd known him by that for many years.

He kissed the top of Gomez's head, and laid her gently onto the warm volcanic glass. He pressed his fingers on her eyelids, closing them to sleep. He wiped the stream of blood that slipped from the corner of her mouth.

Marshall, the voice that only he heard echoed. He stood, looking down at a peaceful Arianna Gomez.

"We are all soldiers," Cocteau patted his back. "And this a part of it." She pulled away. "We are not out of the woods. We still have to fight through that upper level to get our gear and leave this place. Bitiir, take this," she tossed an energy emitter to him. "Large ring goes around your head, box thing on your upper wrist. I still haven't figured it out yet, but you might be able to."

"You trust me with this?" Bitiir eyed the emitter in his hands.

"Just don't shoot any of us in the back, okay," Cocteau said. "We are all soldiers, including you."

He nodded, placing the ring around his head.

"Come on soldiers," Cocteau beckoned. "The lift, before any of them discover what's happened here."

"Yes, the lift," Wilson kept starting at Gomez, perfectly still. He took one of the small golden blades she'd been given to defend herself. Useless to her. He slipped it under the cuff of his sleeve. "But we can't just escape."

"Pardon?" Bitiir finished strapping the emitter to his hand.

"Don't you see?" Wilson wiped the sweat and blood that dripped from his face, blemishing the back of his hand. "What happened here with Gomez? This is only the beginning. When we escape, if we escape, it's not over. We need to ensure they cannot pursue us. Ensure that they cannot hurt us again. To end this fight so there are no others. And there's only one way to do that."

Bitiir looked nervous, but Cocteau cracked half a grin. "What do you propose, soldier?"

Wilson turned away from Gomez to look up Cocteau and Bitiir. "We end them, forever."

Chapter 22: Control

The lift moved fast.

Not fast enough, Cocteau thought while watching Bitiir and Wilson. Both looked different from who she knew. Bitiir, always confident, now unassured—the same look she saw in soldiers during their first deployment.

Wilson on the other hand was resolute, his brows curved in determination.

Who were these people?

Bitiir found his legs shortly after they left Gomez, though he was still not light on his feet as he should've been.

I'm losing them, she thought. Flashes of her emitter not firing, Gomez taking the hit.

I can't think of that right now, she continued. If they were going to live she had to move on, even if it meant suppressing all emotion, feeling nothing.

The lift slowed. "Are you ready?"

Her team nodded. They recognized the fight that would meet them once that lift door opened; Wilson warned them.

All that was left of the Venusians were on the final level, waiting for them to come, like a mouse to a trap. But all escape paths were here, and they were left with little choice.

She hoped no more awakened as Wilson foresaw. Even a few were more than her party could handle. She would fight through, but could Wilson and Bitiir?.

The image of Wilson's face, wild and bloodshot as he killed that Venusian made her skin crawl. She was aware of what it meant to kill to survive. But the way he did it, she didn't understand. The only people she ever saw with that expression were the ones who joined the military for the gore and not for the glory.

There's no doubt he could do it, she thought. *But Bitiir, for all he is, I don't know.*

The lift stopped.

Wilson stepped to the front, armed and ready, Bitiir and Cocteau behind him. She still couldn't shoot the energy emitter and Bitiir had yet to try. She kept the curved blade she found in the hall of dead Venusians on hand.

The lift door parted slowly, light flooding in, blinding them.

She squinted, focusing her eyes. "Be ready for anything."

They jumpedout.

No one was there.

"What the hell?" Cocteau looked around; she didn't recognize that they were even in the Venusian compound anymore.

This level was all white, and shined like polished marble. The ceiling emitted a white light, everything around them glowing in the clearest purity. Walls met floors and ceilings at sharp angles, and the same pattern of elongated humanoids continued, etched in gold.

"Where are they?" She said frustrated.

"They know we're coming," Bitiir said, lowering his arm. "At least that's what *you* said." His 'you' sounded bitter, directed at Wilson.

"I wouldn't lower that if I were you," Wilson said. "And yes, they are expecting us, which is precisely why we can't see them. They're here alright, watching us; no point in hiding from them. Stay on your guard."

Cocteau studied her surroundings. Were they really being watched? If so, was there any point to stealth? They needed to focus, and if she didn't do something, Wilson and Bitiir were likely to argue. She needed to distract them, refocus them on the objective.

"This hall shouldn't exist," she said. "Just like that obsidian level shouldn't have. What's your hypothesis Mr. Space Archeologist?"

"I would deduce," Wilson said keeping his eyes ahead and his arm aimed, "that the Venusians have done some experimenting with both the rock that is here naturally, and rock that must've come in through meteorites. They somehow are able to produce enough oxygen to change and manipulate it. Or," he glanced behind, "there's a big part of Venus's history we don't know about."

"Will you blokes stop," Bitiir shivered. "I don't like this waiting to be trapped. This was foolish—they could kill us any moment—"

A piece of wall beside them blasted away.

Cocteau didn't wait. She grabbed Bitiir and Wilson and pulled them down as another energy blast shot at them.

Two Venusian appeared from around the corner at the end of hall, both pointing energy emitters.

Cocteau and the others dove ahead, into a side corridor for coverage. Cocteau poked her arm around and tried to shoot. Nothing happened.

"Damn it!" she yelled.

Wilson took a deep breath and gulped. He jumped from behind the corner and shot.

Miss.

He dove back right as an energy blast scraped his arm, burning away a piece of his sleeve.

"Ahh, that hurts!" he clenched through his teeth.

"Go!" Cocteau ordered. "Do your thing, we'll hold them off and get the gear."

"How?" Wilson yelled to them as another blast shot into the wall behind them. "I can't get past them."

"We'll manage," Cocteau said. She glanced at Bitiir, cowering below her. "How are your legs?"

"Better," he said coolly.

"Get off your lazy ass and start shooting."

"I don't know how," he said.

Cocteau grabbed Bitiir's ear and yanked him up. "Figure it out." She shoved him in front of her.

Bitiir pointed his arm around the corner, his head low.

Nothing happened.

Another blast and he pulled his arm back.

"I told you, I don't know how," he said. "Which is not something I often say."

"I have to get by," Wilson said.

"We got this," Cocteau nudged Bitiir's shoulder. "We'll running across to that corridor there," she pointed across the way. "Got that? That's the way to our gear. Wilson, stay low and wait."

She stepped into the line of fire, pulling Bitiir with her.

"Are you crazy?" Bitiir tried to shove her grip.

She grinned. "Just a little." She cocked her chin in the direction of the Venusians. "Hey, turds. Can't hit nothin' can you?"

Another shot and she ducked, pulling Bitiir down with her.

"You're going to have the run of your life," she muttered in Bitiir's ear. "Evasive maneuvers."

"Evasive what—"

Cocteau ran diagonally toward the Venusians, turning down the corridor across from them just before they could hit her.

"I hate you!" Bitiir screamed from behind.

Good, keep screaming, she thought. *Keep their attention away from Wilson. Let him do his thing—let him save us.*

Her thoughts blinked in and out of their many training sessions on Venus station. How she insisted on teaching them to move evasively on the Venus surface if anything were to happen, be it from natural elements or from one of their own. And the Bitiir's sneering face as he criticized the wastefulness of such time in the VR room.

And now he ran with her.

Survive, she told herself. *Survive.*

* * *

Wilson moved quickly after Cocteau and Bitiir distracted the Venusians. There was no telling when he'd run into another one or how many. He assured Cocteau and Bitiir there weren't many, but in truth, he had no idea how many there were, not after his vision of the reawakening. Maybe they'd be overwhelmed by numbers, he didn't know. He didn't care. He had a mission and it wasn't to escape; it was to end the Venusians no matter the cost.

He couldn't tell the others. They would've never gone along with his plan if he had. Their hope is what drove them and he didn't want to take that away. He wanted them to have it, even in the final moments of their lives. Have the hope he couldn't bring himself to have.

They're not smarter than us, Bitiir's words repeated in his mind

Was it true? He was the first to know that technology did not equal intelligence, and were these Venusians truly not any more clever than him, or Earth people?

He stopped.

Venusians.

Two of them, taking a corner at the end of the hall.

Two and two, he thought. *That makes four on this level. Unless*— his chest stiffened, thinking of Cocteau's and Bitiir's possible fate—*those are the same two.*

He approached the end of the hall carefully, peeking around the corner at them.

No, couldn't be the same two, he thought relieved. He pictured the map of the level in his mind. The ones Cocteau and Bitiir distracted wouldn't have been able to make it to here, not with the path they took. *They always travel in twos, in even numbers.*

The next hall he needed to turn down was a few feet before them.

They aren't looking this way, he thought. *I might be able to make it.*

But they were moving, pacing. Once they reached the end they would turn and see him.

He breathed and readied his emitter.

I cannot do a kill blast, he thought. *I won't have enough in me to shoot twice if I do that, not with their thick skins.*

He felt it, the emitter already pulling energy from him.

No, he told it. *Not like before. I need to control myself. I must control my emotions. It will be fatal if I don't.*

He pictured *her*. Justine's flaxen hair, waving in tangles, catching the salty air. It was the anniversary of their meeting on Cape Canaveral and they returned to the beach to celebrate. But it was more than that. He wanted it to be special, for that moment to be perfect.

"The launch will be any minute," he told her. He watched her shift on the towel, the mumbling of other voices and conversations from beach goers blurring from his vision as he saw only her.

"Shouldn't you be there?" Justine said. "I thought you worked this launch?"

"Ah, they don't need me," he shrugged. "I'm just the space archeologist. My part comes after the probe launches, when it gathers enough data."

"Where to this time?" she asked.

"Over South America," he said. "They want aerial views of ruins in Chile. To study the road systems of the Incas and gather data on the plant, wild-life, and rock composition—"

She kissed him.

"You're my favorite person," she said as she pulled away, "you know that?"

He smirked. "You're my favorite."

He took a deep breath. It was time. "There's another reason I wanted to be here today."

"Oh, why's that?"

"I've done a lot of thinking," he said. "I always thought my work at NASA would be the most important thing in my life. They promised that one day I could even make it up there, study ancient civilizations from one of the stations. Even be the first one to study civilization beyond Earth if we ever make it that far. And I thought being a part of that was the most important thing in my life. But you know, it isn't anymore. It's a shallow life to live only for yourself. And I've decided I want to live for someone else."

He kept it hidden under his beach towel. He pulled out the little black box and presented the ring to her.

She beamed.

"Yes," her voice with that slight airiness when she was excited. "Oh, yes-yes!"

A perfect moment. He embraced her, feeling her warmth as the rocket with his probe launched; all he ever hoped for coming to fruition.

The memory flooded in his mind in less than a second, but it was enough to make him feel the peace he felt that day.

He aimed the emitter.

Two pulses of energy left the emitter, the first hitting one Venusian in the back, the other at the base of the neck. It was enough to knock them down, but there was no visible damage.

He ran forward. Cocteau said they had a hard time getting up after falling, but he wasn't sure how much time that was. He ran not slowing for even a moment.

He heard their screeches, their cries from behind. *Kill the Earthchild—Kill the murderer!*

Chapter 23: A Fleeting Moment

Cocteau and Bitiir continued to run, but the Venusians drew nearer. They turned down a hall and another blast flew past them. Cocteau smelled burning hair.

She quickly patted the back of her head, chunks of hair falling from her ponytail. *Damn!*

"I can't keep doing this," Bitiir fell against the wall. "I can't."

"We're close," she pulled out her recognition coin. "Our gear should be right this way."

"Why?" Bitiir said. "Because Dr. Wilson said it was there? Do you seriously believe a thing that man says?"

"He needs the gear too," Cocteau said. "We all need it to get out alive.

"I don't think he cares," Bitiir said. "Convenient to get us out of the way for whatever stupid thing he's planning."

"He's the only one who can read the map." Cocteau knew there was a chance of truth in his words. But they agreed to stick to the plan, and they would. "And this the way to our gear."

"Like I said," Bitiir continued. "Convenient."

They hurried further down the hall. She waved her coin until the outline of a door glowed. She pulled up the holopanel and opened it.

Bitiir slipped in, Cocteau following, closing the door behind them.

Humidity hit her face, like a brick to the ground.

A wall of vegetation stood inches before them. The air was warm and moist, not hot and dry like the rest of the compound.

They were in a massive greenroom, a jungle filled to the brim with stems and leaves. Green tubes, wide and tall, filled with condensation stood out among the dense foliage. Vines crept up and around them, carrying twisted fruit and long thorns that begged those that looked upon it to heed the warning of its sharp talons.

Bright colors painted the plants, colors Cocteau didn't realize plants could ever be. Flowers burst open, spiraling in brilliant reds, yellows, and blues from their oversized petals. Fern-like greenery grew above their waists and blocked the view of the cool spongy material Cocteau felt below her feet. Circles of purple UV light glowed around individual plants, casting an artificial glimmer to the room and turning their white suits to a shining fluorescent green.

There was no ceiling in sight, just fog rolling like clouds on a gray day. She saw no end, only the infinite growth of life.

"I guess this solves our oxygen mystery," Bitiir panted, his hands on his knees. He took one of the water pouches, gulping the entirety of his contents.

"Careful!" Cocteau cringed. "We don't have much left."

Bitiir rolled his eyes. "We can get more." He gestured to the whole room.

Cocteau said nothing. She learned long ago that leaders shouldn't react to criticism in high stress environments, especially when the other party was right. She just hated that it was Bitiir who was always right.

"Damn," she said as she pulled up the holomap. The map gleamed a phosphorescent orange against the dim purple light of the room. "We're one hall off!"

Wilson previously showed her how to pull up the map and navigate it before they left the lift. A sudden image of him came to the forefront of her mind: Wilson buckling over in pain, holding his head every time he delved into the holomap's resources. She couldn't understand the language like he could. In a way, she was relieved as his newfound abilities from the Venusian memories affected him so adversely. She was weary looking into the map, seeing a pulsing power surge through the holographic diagram.

"They've probably figured we're going for the gear," Cocteau closed the map. "We need to cut them off before we can't get—"

"Pfft," Bitiir gave a disdainful snort, with a look that was half sneer, half annoyance. "Typical."

"We really don't have time for your shit," Cocteau said.

"And we don't have time for yours." The glow of the UV light made the dark circles under his eyes more disdainful. "You're so impulsive! There's no way we can cut them off, there's just no way. If they know where we're going, there's probably somebody already there to kill us on sight. This is what happens when people like you and Wilson play leader. Nothing's done right, nothing's thought through. This is exactly why Gomez is dead!"

It was worse than a gut punch. Worse than shooting herself in the foot. Worse than if she admitted it to herself. It was her fault; if she was a better leader—if she wasn't so impulsive and let her anger get to her so easily—she could've worked the emitter and saved Gomez. If she wasn't those things she wouldn't even be here in the first place.

Bitiir brushed aside some ferns, walking away.

"Where in hell do you think you're going?" Cocteau reached to grab him.

"Don't!" he turned and batted her arm away. "I've had enough!"

"Enough of what?" Cocteau's voice cracked slightly. She tried to keep it steady, but it was slipping. He'd gotten to her. "Enough of seeing how things are done below your little corporate micromanaging? How things happen in the real world?"

He continued pushing plants aside, trying to walk away from her.

Cocteau grabbed Bitiir up by the arm. "You want to die, soldier?"

Bitiir glowered at her. "I am not a soldier!" His voice was steady, precise with every word. "I don't want this—I don't! This wasn't supposed to happen, none of this! This is not my mission, not the mission I organized! Everything is out of control."

"Bitiir—"

"Let go!" Bitiir reached back and smashed one of the water pouches right into Cocteau's face.

She dropped the grip on his arm. The burning on her cheek where it hit her, like slaps from long ago as warm water dripped down her neck. Bitiir's face, hysterical, like the paternal face she knew from the past, also hysterical with anger. Her hands clenched tight, shaking with resentment of years holding back.

And her right hook hit Bitiir in the jaw.

Bitiir fell sideways from the power of the punch, ferns pushing aside like waters parting the red sea for his fall.

"Enough!" Cocteau stood over him as he wiped blood from the corner of his mouth. "Like it or not mister, you can't control everything and this mission was out of our hands even before we landed on Venus."

He looked up, his glaring eyes like darts. "You don't get it, do you? None of this will ever be over, even if we do make it out by some miracle. You have no idea what's waiting for us if we make it out alive. We're better off dead."

Cocteau pulled him back to his feet. "You can have your little adolescent breakdown when we get back to Venus station. Right now we need—"

The greenroom door flew up.

Without looking they dove into the jungle of plants, fruits, and vines. They didn't need to see to know what was coming for them. They tarried too long.

She knelt into the ground, the spongy, wet unnatural black soil drank into her limbs as she leaned close. She hoped against all hope that the ferns were enough to cover the glow of their suits.

She expected an energy blast to go over their heads, but nothing happened.

"Why aren't they shooting at us?" Bitiir's voice whispered. She couldn't see him, but he was close, hidden like her.

Cocteau eyed the plant life.

Rare and essential, she thought. That's what these plants were to the Venusians. Random facts about biospheres and planets sustaining life flooded Cocteau's mind, memories from her unfinished time at university.

They don't want to damage the plants.

And now we have an advantage.

The absence of energy emitters didn't even the playing field, but it bought them time. If only she could get hers to work.

The cautious rustling of plants being pushed aside neared them.

She didn't risk whispering, she just started crawling. Hopefully, Bitiir was smart enough to catch-on.

I'm distracted, she thought as she swam through the ocean of vegetation. *Why am I so distracted?* The artificial soil was nothing like she experienced before. Instead of caking her with mud and wet earth as she half expected, it dried her out, making movement all the more difficult. It sucked all moisture from the surface of her body, harvesting it away to the precious plants that struggled to survive.

I'm a soldier, a leader, she held her breath. *No matter what Bitiir says or thinks. Even if Gomez is dead, I still need to be a leader, a better one.*

Everything was quiet; no rustling leaves or bending of stems. She couldn't even hear herself. *It's dangerous to be distracted.*

Cocteau's head yanked upwards, a Venusian hand wrapped around it in an instant. The two that pursued them stood on either side of her, beads of moisture clinging to their heads.

One forced a foot on the back her legs, pinning Cocteau to her knees while it restrained her arms behind. They figured it out, how she fights drawing strength from her legs and core. This position made her powerless. She could take on one Venusian, barely; but these two were more than she could handle, especially under exhaustion.

The other Venusian holding her head jerked it back and she felt the pinpricks of hair being ripped from their follicles. Its long fingers on the other arm formed a fist in front of her face, an energy emitter pointed at her forehead.

Execution. She squirmed, but couldn't move. *Execution to pay back for what happened to their comrades.*

An energy emitter fired.

And the Venusian in front of her fell from the blast.

Before the other Venusian could react it too fell away, blasted aside from another shot.

"I'm alive?" Cocteau touched her face.

Bitiir stood no more than ten feet away, arm up with his energy emitter pointed, the foliage around him simmering in embers that burned a path of his shots.

"Bitiir, I—I don't know—"

He still had his emitter pointed.

Cocteau's heart thumped.

"Bitiir no," she put her hands up. "We're a team, *we need each other!*"

Bitiir took a deep breath.

He lowered it.

"Relax," he smirked. "I just saved your sorry ass. You really think I'd kill you now?"

Cocteau glared as she stood. "You looked like you were going to."

Bitiir eyed the emitter and fingered the gold cord on it. "Funny thing is maybe I would've; but I didn't. This is a curious weapon good captain, very curious. Once you start, it's hard to stop, where your mind has to be for it to work. Dr. Wilson was right, you must surrender for it to work. Surrender to that part of yourself that most try to suppress. It's dangerous, very dangerous indeed."

He took the emitter off and tossed it to Cocteau. "It was a fleeting thought captain and I don't think I shall be able to do it again. You saw how I was, losing it back there. I can't allow my mind to go there anymore. I will surely die if I do so."

Cocteau put the emitter on. Was Bitiir right about what it meant to surrender?

"Let's get out of here," she said. "Dr. Wilson is depending on us."

"Don't need to tell me twice," Bitiir marched through the plants, toward the entrance.

My god Wilson, Cocteau realized the emitter would never work for her, no matter how hard she tried. *Why does it work so easily for you?*

Chapter 24: The Monolith

Wilson's heart raced.

He dialed into the holopanel before him. The invisible door illuminated, the one no one was supposed to find.

But he did, all thanks to his stolen pass sequence. It slid away, disappearing into the surrounding wall, revealing the opening to the operations unit.

He remembered operations on the Venus station; lively, full of mechanical and computer wonders, people bustling to facilitate different functions of the station. Inaudible voices floating with orders, memos, and gossip. They kept the heart of the station pumping, veins of information constantly transferring, keeping the station from plunging into the planet below, or worse, flinging-off to the abyss.

But the room he entered was empty of all life.

He quickly used his holopanel and pass sequence to seal the door behind him.

Here goes nothing, he thought.

The operations unit for the Venusian compound was covered in white marble like the rest of the level. Rows upon rows of marble slabs stood upright like headstones, no more than a couple feet high. Smooth and clean of all imperfections, they were empty of any markings. Wilson walked down the rows, hoping to see something, anything, to indicate how the compound was run.

A ten foot monolith stood at the center and forefront. Wilson approached it, feeling its energy field. He felt static cling to him and hairs began to stood on end as he approached it closer. A familiar tendril of thought touched his mind.

"The celestial stone."

Somehow the monolith before him was channeling its energy, emitting it to the other stone slabs in the room.

Marshall, it whispered to him. There was no question that it was directly connected to the stone. He cringed. He hated how it continued to mimic *her* voice.

"You're not real," he said. "I know you're using my memories against me, what I remember of her voice. It's not going to work this time."

He waved his recognition coin.

Like dominos falling, the operations room came alive. The stone monolith lit with hundreds of holographic symbols glowing in yellow, orange, green, and red, layers of information forming as symbols sequenced themselves into discernible codes. The rows of stone slabs all too began to glow with symbols and maps of the compound, each seeming to take on a designated function.

I don't need to self-destruct, he thought. Like any civilization with advanced tech, it took two or more individuals to activate a self-destruct. He was the only one. *I only need to corrupt different living functions.*

He reached and scrolled through the compound's codes. "They're like DNA sequences." He didn't know why he spoke aloud. But the energy from the celestial stone made it feel like there was another living presence near him, and he felt the need to speak.

Each sequence he looked through used the Venusian symbols to form a function for the station. He ignored the growing pressure in his head as he read through them, trying to find the right one to manipulate.

Then the familiar ringing came, like tires scraping on the road.

A force slammed him against the marble, his vision blurring as he slid against it.

The coding around him dissipated as his vision came too.

"W-who," he couldn't think straight. He had locked down the doors; who had the rank to override it?

Venusian memories flashed across his mind like a deck of cards, shuffling so fast he couldn't make out details. But he could feel; he felt the exhilaration and fear that entered their hearts every time this Venusian's presence came into a room. Larger than life in both mind and way, he felt the compulsion to obey, a thousand eras of conditioning all groomed into this being that demanded assimilation and subjugation to its command. Chosen to lead their people to survival and dominion over the Sun's solar system, few were ever higher in authority. And none were alive anymore that were.

The Venusian high general.

He turned over, and his view of the room was immediately blocked by the outline of an energy emitter between his eyes.

Chapter 25: Suffocate

uffocation.

There was a time when Wilson felt the crushing of his lungs, desperate to breath anything.

It was when he was chosen to go to the space station, to directly handle the incoming data from an archeological probe that NASA collaborated with the university to create. He engaged in a series of training sessions to prepare for the mission, one of which included water training.

It was exciting that someone like him, with his knowledge of ancient peoples was chosen to undergo such a task. He was the first in a new initiative to study the possibility of life beyond and develop a system of discovering evidence of intelligent civilization. His papers on patterns of existence and civilization going beyond our world caught their attention. And his program became the hope against NASA's corporate competition.

But much like that day in water training, those hopes were drowned, suffocated out of existence. During water training something went wrong.

No one could tell him exactly what happened but his suit failed him. Under the water, he first he heard the snips, the sound that comes right before glass cracks. Veins bleed across the visor of his helmet and burst, like the divine sending the floods. Cool, stiff liquid spilled into his helmet and he choked. He tried to hold his breath, but only so much could be done in panic. He found himself unable to control his body as he inhaled gulp after gulp of pool water, chlorine stinging as it entered.

Even though it happened in a matter of seconds, each gulp of water that entered his lungs felt like a weight of a thousand years as he sank, unable to take in life giving oxygen. Assertive hands pulled him from the pool and out of the suit. The pain that came with forcing water out of his chest was a relief as he felt the lightness of breath again. The medic assured him he'd be alright.

That was also the same day Justine gave him her grave news.

And Marshall Wilson felt the weight of suffocation again as the Venusian General wrapped its fingers around his neck.

The general raised him off the ground, holding him against the monolith. Its other arm pulled the energy emitter ring from his head and crushed it, rendering the emitter useless.

He gripped its arm, desperately trying to breathe, his legs twitching.

A low growl emanated from the high general, an inaudible language. Then the piercing ring filled Wilson's ears, making him cry out. He squeezed his eyes shut, the pain becoming unbearable as he felt warm fluid drip from his ears. Blood?

The piercing ring continued, blocking all sound. Wilson's shortness of breath made him weak, and he felt his body going limp as he used what little strength he had left to hold himself up within the Venusian grip. If he let go, his airways would close and it would mean the end.

Then a voice.

The ringing deadened as Wilson felt the familiar pressure in his head. A clear, ethereal voice spoke:

"Child of the Earth, you shall pay for your sins this day," the Venusian General's head tilted slightly. "You are no descendent of the Sun!"

Why wasn't the general shooting him? The energy emitter was right in his face, and the general just held him, letting him writhe in agony. He opened his eyes.

He looked down the Venusian General's arm, the gold chord of an energy emitter woven into its exoskeleton, all the way to its head.

It stared at him, with its deep dark eyes, as though reading him. Even from the emotionless face, Wilson knew it was relishing in this moment, seeing him struggle to breathe. The general could've killed him, but it didn't. It just watched him suffer. The general knew what he'd done to its people, and already figured out what he was going to do next.

"All Earth children shall burn before we're through," the Venusian General said with its mouthless voice. "And we shall rise again as the dominant race of this system. And you shall give me what I want while you beg for death."

Something familiar in this Venusian's domineering voice struck through him, like a knife through wet tissue. This was no ordinary Venusian. It alone commanded itself like no other. The pressure of a memory seeped into Wilson's consciousness as he sought the general's identity.

A former past of one of the Venusian memories he possessed witnessed the naming of the one that held him, a ceremony that gave them their authority and power. The ironic part was that the naming ceremony stripped them of their name as it gave power. This Venusian before him had no name; it had forsaken it long ago as all Venusian do when they take on a role of authority. General was it's only identity and the only association it wanted when it agreed to command this compound and weld the celestial stone.

And the Venusian General gave no quarter to those in the role of rival.

"We know of the alien station that orbits our world," the Venusian General said. "And the uncalled invasion and stealing of our resources. My comrades are awakening and your numbers will be no match. You shall give me access to that station's coding and the identity of the celestial being that commands it. You will not fail to do so."

Wilson suddenly saw the rows of Venusians in his mind, memories of the first awakening. They were asleep until the general commanded them to arise, to take back what was theirs. But it was more than that. It wasn't about taking back Venus or the unlawful colonization of their planet; no—this was much bigger. This was about the Sun, the entire solar system. The emergence of Earth beings was an atrocity, a rivalry for the birthright of the Sun and all its resources. He saw arms and limbs were cauterized together, reanimating and filling the empty husks of the awakened and filling them with purpose.

And Wilson saw the true nature and face of the Venusian race.

They're not smarter than us, Bitiir's voice echoed.

Something burned in Wilson's chest as his mind came back to the present, resolute in what he needed to do. He gasped, but he needed no air for this. The burning in his chest increased and spilled into his arms.

And Justine's face flashed across his mind.

It only took moments, milliseconds even. His arm was already in position, gripping the Venusian General's arm. He stretched his wrist and Gomez's knife shot into his hand as he swiped, tearing the cord of the energy emitter on the Venusian General's arm.

It screeched, throwing Wilson aside. He rolled over, coughing and sucking in as much air as he could at the same time.

"Foolish Earthchild," the Venusian General hunched, widening its arms and barring it's fingers like teeth at him "You think cutting my emitter will save you? I always get what I want and you are no exception."

Wilson coughed, glaring at the oversized creature before him. He would give this general nothing, even if it invaded his mind. He would fight it, fight the impulse to give in, or die trying.

An immovable wall appeared between Wilson and the Venusian General.

Captain Cocteau stood between them.

Chapter 26: The Captain's Bane

"Cocteau!" Wilson gasped.

She stood in her fighting stance, the curved blade she stole from the lower level held in her front hand, her arms a shield across the vitals of her body. She wore the energy emitter even though she thought it useless, but hoped it would give a look of intimidation to her foes.

"Go," she said. "This one's mine."

Wilson's eyes widened. "But—you don't understand—this is the Venusian General."

"You heard me!" She spat, not taking her eyes off the Venusian General. This one was bigger, bulkier than the others. And she had no patience for Wilson's sentiments. "As soon as he moves, get out of here with Bitiir."

Wilson stood and backed away. The Venusian General made a move for him, but Cocteau swiped her knife at it, like a claw from her fist.

The general made another move on him, and this time Cocteau stepped forward, with a curved swipe meant to gut a human.

The Venusian General straightened its back, as though offended by Cocteau's gesture.

Cocteau shook her head.

The Venusian's head locked on Cocteau, its bottomless eyes pulling her in. It crouched in an offensive stance, challenging her.

The corner of Cocteau's mouth came-up. "I've fought tougher."

The Venusian General put its arm up and Cocteau's knife glided across the forearm of the exoskeleton. It backhanded her face and punched her gut all in one move.

She almost lost footing as she shuffled backward.

"Cocteau!" Wilson shouted.

Cocteau started laughing, wiping blood from her split lip. The general's strength should've knocked her right over. But it was playing, testing her before giving the final blow.

Cocteau made a move again, this time going for the legs. The Venusian General must've anticipated the move as it dodged.

"Go!" she ordered.

Wilson hesitated.

"Cocteau—"

"Go smart ass" she yelled. "*That's an order!*"

She lunged at the Venusian General again as Wilson ran from them, her curved knife reflecting gold as she fought to keep the Venusian away from him. Whatever alloy it was made of, it was sharp enough to pierce Venusian exoskeleton. She felt an animalistic urge as she prepared to slice again

Her head heated with bloodlust as the Venusian General suddenly became more. It was no longer the horrifying creature as her eyes locked into the deep emptiness of its eyes. It was a fair-haired man that she slashed at.

And she was there again. With every slash, every punch, every kick, she was no longer on Venus, but in the shower locker room on base, fighting off that fair-haired man and the two others that decided to jump her after a late night shower.

"Just another crazy bitch-face trying to be a man," the fair-haired man laughed as he shoved her onto one of the locker room benches. "Look at her, she doesn't even look like much of woman.

Cocteau's hair was still down and dripping. She had barely put on her underwear when they showed up.

Three of the other men nodded in agreement.

"Felix, she's a captain," his friend cautioned.

"Yeah, I can think of how she got that," Felix made a rude gesture with his hand. "I'd be made captain pretty quick too. Let's see if she'll do that again for us."

The men erupted in roaring laughs. Cocteau tried to stand but the fair-haired Felix kicked her face.

"Just try that again you slutty little bitch," Felix said. "We're going to show you what happens to bitches like you who try to do a man's job."

Their grins made her sick, but she had known the pain men could cause as she felt the childhood pain of her father's slaps.

Make her act like a young lady, will you, her father's voice echoed. *She was fighting again. For god's sake—just look at her—at least make her look like a girl!"*

Then Cocteau did it; what she had always wanted to do, and now she could as a full trained military captain. As the men put their hands on her, she was still just wet enough to slip from their grip, and sliced the forearm of the one closest to her.

"Oh my god, my arm, *my arm!"* the man she sliced cradled his arm, blood spewing everywhere. "She cut it down to the bone! *My arm!"*

"Where did she even pull that knife from?" another asked.

"Wouldn't you like to know," Cocteau smirked, taking a defensive stance, holding her claw in front of her, ready to gut any that came near here. Blood from the knife mixed with the condensation of the bathroom ran down her arm. The smell of it made her nostrils flare. "No man will put his hands on me again."

"You're dead bitch," Felix shook. "Hear me, dead. Don't hold back boys, just do it!"

The two uninjured lunged at her as she slashed her claw at them, catching one in the stomach and shoving him away. Someone tried to grab her from behind and she threw him over. Everything happened fast and her instinct took over. A head smashed into the corner of a locker, another knocked-out cold with blood draining from his nose. She broke out of a bear hug and sliced the hands of whoever it was. Before she knew it, she had Felix in a sleeper hold on the floor, his friends either dead or knocked-out, bleeding around them.

Cocteau loosened her sleeper hold, careful not to kill him as he struggled. She wrapped her legs around him so he couldn't escape.

"Thought I was weak, didn't you," Cocteau said, tasting the blood that dripped into her mouth, relishing in her victory. "Bet no one told you I was always freakishly strong in school; bigger and stronger than any of the boys. Got into a lot of fights back then, lost a lot of them until I figured out how to win; hold *nothing* back."

"Die bitch!" Felix gasped, trying to break free of her hold.

"Shut up!" Cocteau ordered, pressing her knife into his throat. "You don't speak unless I say so. Now, I have the inkling that this isn't the first time you've pulled this stunt," she whispered into his ear, stroking her claw gently along his neck. "I've got news for you. This isn't the first time I've held someone in this hold. I can keep this up all night if I have to. In one move, I will end you." She motioned like she was going to break his neck, then pushed the knife into his skin, just enough to let blood drip. "You're going to answer my questions. One blink for yes, two for no."

He made a move to escape, to break her hold, but she was stronger. She pushed him right down.

"I wouldn't do that if I were you," she snarled. "One for yes, two for no! Tell me, this is not the first time you've done this."

He blinked twice.

"Now we're getting somewhere," she said. "How many, one?"

He blinked twice.

"Two?"

He blinked once.

"Ah, two," she said. "And you thought I would be just like them. Unable to defend myself against you big strong men." She pulled her grip tight. "Are they still alive?"

He blinked twice.

Cocteau felt sick inside. "Because of you?"

He blinked once.

She had enough of him. "Listen, and listen closely my little bird. You are going to sing your song to your commander and authorities. You're going to name names, give locations, make those bodies found."

She loosened her grip enough for him to talk.

"W-why would I do that?" his voice was raspy. "You bitch!"

"Because it will be the only way for you to explain why I ensured you could never do this again." She pulled her knife away. "This knife is good for more than one thing."

And it was that moment, her action, her choice that made Marie Cocteau the lone wolf of space. Felix lost all that gave him his manhood that day, Cocteau made sure of that. The claw of the lone wolf got him, neutering his masculine pride and ensuring that he could never harm another in the way he attempted with her. He sang loud and clear to the location of desecrated bodies, and families were finally reunited with the deceased of their loved ones.

She should've been court marshaled, but feminist lobbyist and lawyers would plaster this all over the media and create indefinite lawsuits that the military could not afford. So they did something worse to her.

They told Cocteau she had gone too far, had used cruel and unusual punishment among those who were supposed to be her comrades. She was strong, true, but too dangerous to be kept among troops. She was ordered into solitude, banished from this world. They shipped her off to SIC, as a 'formal representative' out of safety procedure and protocol. Cocteau was out of the hair of the military but did not officially work for SIC. She belonged nowhere, had no loyalties, and was isolated from the world, trapped in the abyss of space. And that was how they liked it.

And she remembered it all as the Venusian General grabbed her arm, the feelings of weakness, of humiliation, the loss of identity as she was banished from her world. Using all that was left of her brutish strength she tried to strike, but the Venusian grabbed her other arm and shook the blade from her hand.

I am going to die, she thought.

And she surrendered to the acceptance of her lot.

Warmth from her chest made its way down her arm and she felt it, building up in the energy emitter.

Let go, she told herself. *Let go to survive.*

She was thrown back as the blast of her energy emitter hit the Venusian General, knocking it into one of the monumental stone slabs.

"Wake-up!" Someone shook her. "Captain, wake-up!"

Cocteau opened her eyes. Was she knocked-out? Wilson stood over her, mouth hanging open.

"You're breath stinks," she barked. "What the hell are you doing back here?

"You came back for me," Wilson's voice was raspy, clearly injured from whatever the general did to him. "I came back for you."

"Of course I came back," Cocteau said sitting-up. "It's my job, but not yours. You shouldn't have come."

Wilson helped pull her to her feet. They both glanced at the still body of the Venusian general.

"Dead?" Wilson asked.

"I think so," Cocteau said. "That was a pretty strong blast. But just to make sure—"

She pointed the emitter at the head of the general. Nothing happened.

"I don't think it's going to work," Wilson pulled the broken cord on Cocteau's arm.

"Of course," she huffed. *Right when I start getting it to work.* Her curved blade was nowhere in sight. She was weaponless again.

Wilson ran up to the monolith and pulled up a holopanel.

"What are you doing?" Cocteau asked.

"Unfinished business," Wilson said. He dialed into colored codes that appeared on the monolith.

Lights around them flickered.

Wilson turned and started running. "We don't have much time"

Cocteau ran after him. "Time?"

They ran, not looking behind. Corridors blurred in Cocteau's vision as she followed Wilson. Lights flickered and the floor rumbled and the air around them warmed, heating and scorching their skin.

"There you are!" Bitiir was in full Venus gear, waiting by an empty wall and a pile of their gear. "What the hell is going on? The floor, the walls—"

"No time to explain," Wilson said, grabbing his suit and putting it on. "Is the gear okay? Is everything working?"

"The gear works alright," Bitiir said. "Whatever they did on the surface seems to have worn off, as if it never happened."

Cocteau also started pulling on her gear, the urgency of their task quickening as a loud crack sounded from the wall, and it rattled. She pulled her oxygen pack onto her back.

Wilson slipped on his EC, then paused. "Where's Gomez's gear? Her EC?"

"We took only our gear," Bitiir said. "We couldn't take anything else."

"I got her EC," Cocteau said bitterly, attaching Gomez's EC next to her own. "Only thing we can use. I know it's hard, but leaving her behind means leaving unnecessary gear behind." She wasn't going to let guilt slow her down. She suppressed it, a mental wall building as she put on each remaining part of her suit.

Wilson didn't move. His eyes fixated on his helmet.

"You're supposed to put that on your head," Bitiir said smugly.

Wilson stared at the glass of his helmet.

"It was a helmet," Wilson said. "It was a helmet—*it was a helmet!*"

"Whoa, Wilson," Cocteau put her glove free hand on Wilson. She couldn't lose him, not so close to finally escaping this place. "I just powered on my EC. It's the following dawn according to Venus station and Earth time. The Infinite should have enough solar energy by the time we reach it to take-off. To stay in orbit, I don't know, but that's the least of our problems right now."

There was a stirring and rustling down the halls. All the lights went out.

"Time to go." Cocteau locked on her helmet, the emergency lighting in her suit powering on with the signature SIC trill. Wilson and Bitiir did the same

The three of them were a light in the darkness.

"Wilson, do your thing," Cocteau said through the suit's intercom.

Wilson waved his recognition coin and typed in his access codes.

Red lights started blinking around them, strobing between darkness and a crimson glow.

"What's supposed to be happening here?" Bitiir asked. "Have you thought any of this through? Are we even at the right—"

"Shut up," Wilson snapped.

They agreed to meet here for the final stage of escape, if they made it that far. He'd explained to them that this was where the antechamber for the entrance was located. Though Cocteau started to feel doubtful as darkness stretched longer between each flash of red.

"The way out is supposed to be right here!" he yelled in panic, shadows cast across his face. "I didn't think my shut-down and overpowering of essential systems would affect entryways like this. This place will go up any moment."

"*You what?*" Bitiir said desperately. "Our survival depends on leaving through this entryway and you did *what?* You said you'd take care of them, not blow the entire compound and us with it!"

"What did you think I meant?" Wilson whipped around. "We can't let them follow us. And you agreed to let me do what I needed to do."

"I didn't think— "

"Damn it you two," Cocteau had enough. The floor shook and another crack like thunder echoed. "Wilson, think of something fast —is there another way out?"

Wilson shook his head. "No, this is the only way."

Another thunder crack. Cocteau squinted down the corridor as something moved at the other end. The outline of a Venusian— then two—*then three*—coming closer with each flash of the lights.

"Shit!" She turned to her team. "Shit-shit-shit!"

Another rumble shook the entire corridor, knocking them to the floor. Then, like a whip snapping against the wall, a thin white glowing line appeared and it began parting.

"That's it!" Wilson yelled. "That's the way!"

"Get in there," Cocteau pushed herself to her feet. "As soon as you're in, start closing. I'll hold them off." She kept her eyes on the Venusians, struggling to stand with their awkward legs against the rumbling floors.

The entryway parted slowly, Wilson and Bitiir slipping their fingers into the opening and pulling against either side of it.

"It's no use," Bitiir said. "It's not going to dislodge."

"It's the system," Wilson panted. "Everything's going to get slower until it fails."

Cocteau said nothing. What was the point? They were stuck and the Venusians found their footing. It would be moments before they reached them.

"There," Wilson exclaimed as it parted another few inches. "Get in!"

Cocteau twisted around just as Wilson barely squeezed through the thin opening. Bitiir pushed himself through, disappearing into the dark antechamber behind it.

She instinctively reached for a weapon and pulled nothing. *Damn, I don't have anything!*

She made for the entryway. She pushed herself into the opening and stopped.

She was stuck.

Cocteau was bigger than Wilson and Bitiir, both who were thin and wiry compared to her. She flexed and relaxed muscles, wriggling like a hooked worm. She couldn't move.

"Come on," Wilson's voice sounded in the intercom. She couldn't turn to see him.

"I can't," she said. Her head locked in the direction of the Venusians. They were almost upon them.

She felt a tug, someone pulling on her arm.

"Start closing it," Cocteau ordered.

"No," Wilson said.

Another hard tug on her arm.

"Do it!" Cocteau knew it would take too long with all the systems shutting down. When the Venusians reached her they would surely pull her from the opening; they were strong enough to get her out and rip her to shreds in the process. But the entry would close, and her team would be safe.

"Move it soldier!" Bitiir yelled.

Cocteau felt a kick on the side of her back and suddenly space. Just enough for her to slip through.

"*Warning,*" a soothing female voice blared in Cocteau's helmet. "*Oxygen source removed. Please reattach*"

She fell in, landing against a hard, jagged floor of black volcanic rock.

Bitiir had kicked her oxygen system off, making room for her to enter. Her suit would filter any sulfuric gasses, and they were still in an oxygen filled environment so she would not suffocate, at least for now.

Then she was grabbed, Wilson and Bitiir pulling her away from the opening. The antechamber was dark with no visible light of its own. She turned to thin opening, the only light that caught her eye.

Through the opening Venusian arms reached through, the red glow behind them reflecting like fire against their exoskeletons.

Wilson waved his arm and pulled up a holopanel, rapidly typing into it.

"They're trying to open it," Wilson said.

"Then do something," Bitiir said, exasperated.

"I am," Wilson gritted his teeth. "You're so infuriating! My pass sequence might be able to override them—*I don't know!*"

"Move!" Cocteau shoved them aside just as energy emitters appeared in the opening. Rapid blasts of light energy shot at them, blasting pieces of the walls around them, rocks splitting and raining down.

"I thought this was the way out," Bitiir yelled over the energy blasts.

"It is," Wilson answered, bracing for another blast. "The antechamber is for pressurization. We have to pressurize our suits before we can go on the surface or—"

"Or we'll be crushed," Cocteau said.

"Can't pressurize until the opening is shut," Wilson ducked under another blast.

"Keep moving," Cocteau panted as she dodged. The energy blasts lit the room just enough for her to get her bearings. It was small, square with a low ceiling.

"*Warning,*" her suit's SIC voice said. The light in her helmet shut-off. "*Suit on low power mode.*"

"We need sun," Cocteau said. "My suit is draining."

Wilson hunched in a corner typing into the holopanel.

"Look out!" Cocteau ran for Wilson, but tripped on something hard and fell.

Wilson ducked as another blast went over his head.

This isn't working, Cocteau thought. She looked down at her feet and saw a lump sticking out of the floor. The red light from the opening illuminated it.

It was her oxygen tank.

"Take this!" Cocteau threw her tank at the opening just as a Venusian shot another energy blast.

A mix of concentrated oxygen against the fire-power of the energy emitter was enough. It exploded in the opening, a deafening resonance. The force of heat and pressure threw them across the room, and the Venusians away from the opening.

Blackness. That was all Cocteau saw.

Am I knocked out? She thought.

"It's closed," Wilson's voice said solemnly in the intercom.

Cocteau sat up. She wasn't knocked out. She looked around in the pitch-black room, so dark she could no longer orient direction. The kind of darkness to where she forgot if her eyes were open or closed. She felt it swallow her, invading every part of her being to the point that her disorientation made her question her very being and existence.

"What if they open it?" Bitiir's intercom voice asked.

The glow of a holopanel appeared, like a beacon, and Cocteau saw Wilson's helmet floating above it. "I'll lock it down," he said. "Only the general's authority can open it."

"General?" Bitiir said bewildered. "What general?"

"General's dead," Cocteau said. "We'll be safe."

She stood up, and walked over to the holopanel. She couldn't see Wilson's face from the holopanel's light reflecting off the glass. She only saw a mirror of herself staring back.

"We'll need to share oxygen," she said to him. "I lost mine back there."

"Yeah," Wilson laughed. "I could tell."

Using the light of the holopanel she attached her oxygen system to the emergency oxygen system on his suit.

"What now?" she asked.

"We wait," Wilson said. "It will take time. The room has to pressurize to match the surface. That is if the system failure doesn't take it down first. But the holopanel's still in order, so it must still be working to some degree."

"My suit's almost out of power," Bitiir scooted close to the light of the holopanel. "I don't know if it will work."

"It will," Cocteau said, her reflection also staring back from the glass of his helmet.

"How do you know?" Bitiir said soberly. "It might not."

"And it also might," Cocteau said. "We won't know till we try."

And so they waited.

Even with the destruction of the compound behind them, the antechamber stayed still. Occasional beeps from the suits warned them of pressure and temperature changes.

The holopanel suddenly shut-off and they were left in darkness with only themselves.

END PART II

Part III:
In Regeneratione

Chapter 27: Where is Home?

His sharp grin was unsettling.

"Tell us again please," the man in the suit feigned patience all too well with his smile. "That we may better understand, hearing your own words."

He looked at perfect ease at the end of the oversized conference table surrounded by his board members. A board filled with his supporters, allies, and enemies. All wore the signature SIC insignia on their collars and their eyes all bore down on Abdul Bitiir, who stood at the other end of the table.

Interference was minimal today. The broadcast of SIC's emergency board meeting within the VR room of Venus station was perfect. Bitiir had very little adjustment to do on his headpiece, camouflaged by his avatar within the VIP conference room on Earth. In a flawlessly tailored virtual suit and oversized gold watch on his wrist, they saw what he wanted them to see, and visa-versa.

He knew their gaze was meant to intimidate, but he was not easily intimidated by the likes of them. He couldn't be sure if the board was actually there or if that was what his boss wanted him to see. The AI's of SIC were smart enough to mimic any human in a virtual world, and his boss knew ways around the AI ban.

"You've read the reports," Bitiir said. "I do not wish to re-live such a menacing time of my life."

Although he spoke the words, they could not be further from the truth. Bitiir re-lived every moment and couldn't stop reliving it.

Before the board meeting he rested and saw every second of it again when he closed his eyes. He dreamt of the moment when he was trapped within the confines of the Venusian compound's antechamber. In utter darkness with Cocteau and Wilson, just waiting to see if they would live or die. They came so far to escape the Venusians, and Wilson's ill-conceived plan to destroy the compound clearly backfired. They were trapped, buried within SICs artificial mountain.

On the edge of nothing, and with Arianna gone, he held no notion of something as silly as escaping.

And then it happened.

The room shook and the darkness ended. The ceiling above parted and revealed a circle of light. A light at the end of a long tunnel.

"The mountain," Wilson said into the intercom. Bitiir could see no faces behind the glass. "This verifies it. The compound was the natural mountain before SIC built on top of it. The Venusians must've created the tunnel through the artificial layer to reach the surface and blown away the section with the surface colony."

The official SIC trill sounded in their suits and Bitiir looked down at his EC. The small bit of light that came down started charging their suits, even if minimally. He knew he could depend on SIC's technology, he always could.

They were going to be alright.

He glanced at the time; had it really only been one night Earth time? He felt as though he'd spent an entire night in Venus time. Venus's slow rotation made a single day stretch for one hundred sixteen Earth days. And was also why Venus lacked a strong magnetic field.

"We'll need to climb it," Cocteau said. "It looks like it's at an angle, so it shouldn't be too bad. They had to get us down here using it."

Good, Bitiir thought. He didn't know if he had the strength to climb even a ladder.

They made their way through the tunnel. On hands and knees they gripped the rough wall, the circle of light growing ever so slightly with each step closer.

Bitiir no longer tracked the time; with his eye on light, time felt endless.

And the moment finally happened. Hands reaching through the ring of light, grabbing at its intangible refractions. They pulled themselves to the open surface, light blinding them. On a cloud covered planet, everything was bright compared to the darkness that engulfed them below.

They laid as best they could with their gear on, panting and heaving for the precious oxygen in their suits. The weight of the surface pressure fought against their will, the Venus haze around them making everything feel all the more heavy.

Bitiir watched the swirling atmosphere above him; so alive and so volatile. Sprinkles of acid rain spattered across his helmet. He imagined himself on Earth, on a cloudy London morning, chilled misty rain hitting his face as he held a warm hand, a mother's smile looking down at him.

"Up and at 'em," Cocteau's irritatingly brusk voice sounded and he felt himself pulled to his feet. Must she always take away his moments of peace?

"Can you get a signal?" Wilson asked.

"Doesn't matter," Bitiir said coolly. "This was a one team mission. The admiral won't risk sending a rescue party or sacrificing anymore equipment, not after missing as many check-ins as we did. We are already marked MIA."

"Typical," Cocteau sneered.

Why? Bitiir thought. *I'm only speaking the truth.*

"I can see the anchored lines," Cocteau pointed into the distance, on the other side of the mountain where they were. "We'll ride them up. I know we're tired folks, but it's what we gotta do to survive. We'll take a rest before going up. You can make it soldiers." She typed into her EC. "I'm sending a check-in signal right now. Even if we can't do verbal communication, this should go through. I'll send another when we reach Cerberus City. That should give them time to prepare for our return."

She looked Bitiir.

"Can you handle that?" she asked.

He smiled. "Of course." His charismatic smile hid anything he did not want to show.

And he smiled that charismatic smile at his boss, the man in the suit across the conference table.

"But your spoken words are one thing compared to a written report," the man in the suit said. "Abdul, come-on. What are you playing at?" His smile mirrored Bitiir's. "We're friends."

Hardly, Bitiir thought. They had a relationship but it was not something he would call friendship. More of an understanding.

"Ladies, gentleman," Bitiir began with his most charming charade, eyes warm and welcoming to both human and AI around him. "I cannot express how much I appreciate your concern for my well-being connected to the events on the surface of Venus. But I can assure you, those reports you read are as real and horrific as they appear to be. You wanted evidence, surety that our patrons could safely sign a liability waiver and explore the planet below. But I can tell you this: there is no liability waiver they can sign that won't backfire on us when they discover what's down there."

The man in the suit's smile disappeared. Board members around the table smirked.

"How much are they paying you?" He asked.

"What?"

"The UN? US government? NASA? Some fanatic environmental terrorist?" The man in the suit's face stayed stoic. "You really think that we're going to take any of this science fiction bull-shit? What do you take us for Abdul? This was your project. And it's clear you failed the objective. You promised payout and all we see are losses."

"This isn't about losses," Bitiir said.

"When is it not about losses?" The man in the suit shook his head. "I'm sorry Abdul, but if this is real to you, it's clear that the psychology report we received is correct: you are too mentally unstable to continue working in the fragile environment that is the Venus Station."

"What, no—that's not—"

"The board already decided when we read the reports," the man in the suit said. "Our purpose was to inform you that you're on indefinite disability."

"You needed the entire board together to tell me that?"

The man in the suit did not change expression. "We're sorry Abdul. We are only concerned for your well being. You will have full disability benefits, don't worry. SIC takes care of their own."

Bitiir gulped. *Bullshit.*

"And looking at the reports," the man in the suit continued. "if you and the other team members continue in a way that puts you and others at risk, you will need to be confined to your quarters until the station's psychologist deems you no longer a danger to yourself or others."

"Humor me, if you will," Bitiir continued to smile in his most charmed way. "Is that before or after I sign your liability waiver and silence agreement? Before or after the next transport to Earth passes us?"

The man in the suit didn't blink. "If you must be confined for your safety and the safety of others you will not be able to enter a transport. That would only endanger you and anyone taking that transport. It is not my decision Abdul, that is up to your psychologist and what's best for you."

Prisoner, Bitiir thought. *Just like that insufferable Cocteau. And on my own station!*

There was no choice—he had to sign all of SIC's waivers and agreements if he was to ever leave this station. But he wasn't going to give them the satisfaction just yet. He wanted to give them cold feet first.

"Then we shall see what my psychologist deems necessary for my safety," he grinned. "I thank you all for your concern. It warms my heart knowing my SIC family is looking out for me. Truly warms it." *I would murder you all on the spot if I could. Wait till I return to Earth and I will bury you so deep that no one will know you ever existed.*

"Of course," the man in the suit nodded. "Sorry Abdul, but being on disability, there really is no need for you to report to the board anymore and we have some other matters to attend to."

"I understand," Bitiir said. *Oh, I understand perfectly.*

"Great," the man in the suit clapped his hands. "Goodbye Abdul."

The VR broadcast cut-out.

* * *

Bitiir sat on the end of his bed, an empty bottle in his hand. He didn't bother using a glass. No point if there was no one to impress.

The window in his suite was pulled shut, closing out any reminder of the planet's surface.

He didn't want to believe what had happened. It seemed no one wanted to believe it either. Hallucinations from an unknown gas anomaly is what they told him. That was what they chose to believe. Hallucination or not, what he felt was real. And now he was a prisoner in his own quarters. Why couldn't he get this right?

That fact was, he'd never done anything right his entire life, at least not by what his father called God's standard. He had done right by himself, or at least he thought he did. It had been a long time since he thought of his father, thought of God. And maybe some of the 'supposed' gas anomaly was still in his system, because all these thoughts struck his mind.

You leave this house you will be nothing. You hear me Abdul? By God, you are no longer my son if you choose this godless life!

His father's words dripped with poison. It had been almost ten years since he heard them. A bead of sweat rolled down his face.

"I can't do this." Bitiir stood and went into the washroom chambers. He stood over the sink and switched on the faucet, turning the dial to as cold as he could possibly get. He cupped his hands, letting the cool water flow into a pool in his palms, numbing them. He splashed his face repeatedly, not caring how much water landed on the floor and trying to wash away the heat that tarnished it.

Arianna Gomez's face kept appearing, along with his father's words: *You leave this house you will be nothing. . . you are no longer my son if you choose this godless life!*

The sink was full of water and he dipped his face into it. The burning behind his skin slowly dissipating as he drowned out all thoughts of Arianna, his father, and God.

Relief. The cold water finally cooled his face and he pulled it out. With his eyes closed, he reached for a hand towel. He wiped his face, taking deep breaths as he did. He opened his eyes.

Ari!

There she was, standing behind him, in the mirror.

"No," Bitiir yelled, scuffling backward away from her judgmental gaze.

Then his foot caught water.

The room spun and his vision turned red as the back of his head hit the wall behind him. He slid down, the room fading.

"Baba, baba, look at me!"

Abdul Bitiir was seven again. He was doing cartwheels in the courtyard of their summer home in India. His father always worked, and it was one of the rare occasions that the family could spend time with him.

His family sat on a blanket, eating all the treats they could never have when they were in London, the place his parents met. They rarely visited Egypt, where his father was born. If anything, his father avoided it.

Suddenly a call sounded around them; the adhan. Abdul stopped in his tracks. A sweet, melodic voice, the muezzin, sung phrases of God.

"Abdul, come," his Indian mother beckoned him. "With your brothers and sisters."

His older siblings—three brothers and two sisters—rolled-out individual prayer rugs in the covered part of the courtyard. They began reciting their responses to the adhan.

"Abdul?" His mother beckoned again.

"But mama, I almost got it right," Abdul said, doing another cartwheel. "Just a few more times and I'll—"

"And disrespect God for some circus tricks?" His mother gave that look, the one where disappointment ripped out your soul.

Abdul slouched. "But I didn't have to before."

His father stepped next to his wife. "Abdul, we pray as a family."

Abdul sighed. His father's tone meant more than what was said. He ran ahead to grab his prayer rug and begin.

The family knelt together, reciting the melodic prayers and giving praises, thanks, and recognizing God as the only god. Abdul kept thinking of how he was going to perfect his cartwheels.

Bitiir blinked back into the present, away from his summer home memory. Looking up at the washroom ceiling, it spun. Concussion? Drunk? He tried to stand, but the pounding in the back of his head forced his eyes shut again.

His mind wandered to cold memories of a wintery Europe.

"School will be good for him," he overheard his father saying one night to his mother, in the parlor of their London home. Twelve-year-old Abdul hid, looking through the crack under the door.

"He's my last baby," his mother argued. "Can't we wait another year? Or send him to public school?"

"To that trash heap they call education?" Abdul couldn't see his parents faces, but he saw the shadow of their feet. His father's voice was stern, decisive, the shadow of his feet unmoving.

"There are plenty of fine educators there," his mother sounded desperate. Her feet scuffled closer to his father, her shadow moving frantically. "He can stay home."

"No," his father's feet stepped away from his mother's, toward the fireplace, the light of it making his shadow disappear. "I didn't leave Egypt to have my extraordinary son attend an ordinary public school. I know his gifts and they will not appreciate him. He's the only one smart enough to take the business when I'm gone. He's going to boarding school."

"But—"

"He's going!"

Nausea brought Bitiir back to the present. He rolled on the washroom floor and tried to force his eyes open, but they refused and he drifted again.

Abdul, we love you, and we've given you everything! the echo of his father ten years prior echoed in his memory *Why would you do this?*

"Everything?" Bitiir laughed. They were sitting in his new office at SIC headquarters, London. He passed the bar exam the day before and was immediately given a contract. One he already agreed to before applying to law school.

"How did you—" his graying, bearded father seemed lost at words to say as he gestured around the room. "You were supposed to come home. What did I pay for? All that time you spent, with me, wasted for what?"

"Dad, how do you think I spend my nights and weekends?" Bitiir shook his head. His father was oblivious, but by the look on his face, he was beginning to piece it together. His father had given him the money to pay for law school, but had no idea SIC was sponsoring him as well. Double payments, more money to play with. "I never wanted the business, you did."

"What is wrong with a father wanting the best for his son?"

Bitiir smirked. He wasn't going to be drawn into the empty 'I wanted the best for you' argument. He knew better. "You should've asked Ammon, he would've wanted it. Or better yet, Mariam. But god forbid you should have a woman take over for you."

"Don't you dare," his father pointed a finger at him. He was mad. To most, pointing a finger was just a gesture, but for Bitiir and his family, it was an insult, something the British and Americans never understood. "I am not the villain here and don't you use any of that jargon you learned from school to make me into one."

"Maybe you should've been more careful what schools you sent me to." Bitiir put his feet up on his desk, a completely relaxed position. He wasn't going to let any of his father's bigotry or closed-minded ideals get to him. He knew who he was; Bitiir was finally free, and there was nothing his father could say that would change it. "Why are you here dad? I've got a lot to do. I'm a busy person."

"Yes, you look so very busy Abdul."

Bitiir was ready for his father to shove his feet off the desk, but he just stood there, unmoving.

"Something wrong dad?" Bitiir reached over and started drinking an amber SIC concoction he poured right before his father arrived.

"We still expect you over later," his father said. "Be a real man and tell this to your mother's face."

"Oh, I'll be over," Bitiir said. "I would never disrespect mother that way. She's not you."

And there it was, the face he had been waiting for: defeat. For once his father didn't look disappointed or angry, but defeated, a loss of words. For all that he was, none of it showed. He looked at Bitiir, then at the door.

"You don't need my permission," Bitiir said sitting up. "You can leave, but you're welcome to stay, I won't force you to do anything."

His father's gaze turned to its usual decisiveness. "You had better come to your senses when you come to see your mother. I'll have no more of this nonsense. You have till tonight to make things right."

And Bitiir did make things right, at least for himself when he went to his parents at his childhood home. First, there was silence, then yelling. Mother's tears couldn't even sway him as he went for the door to never return.

"You leave this house, you will be nothing. You hear me Abdul?" His father tried to sound strong, but his voice shook, broken. "By God, you are no longer my son if you choose this godless life!"

Bitiir's eyes flew open to the present and the past faded before him. He sat-up leaning against the wall. He wanted to stand, but couldn't.

Abdul? Abdul? Is something wrong? he remembered a soft feminine voice whispering comforts in his ear. The smooth hand that stroked his chest.

He was back in the hotel room, the one they liked to meet at. He stepped out of bed, pulling on underwear and carefully taking his shirt off the hanger. He would stand for no wrinkles.

"Abdul, what's wrong?" The woman in his bed switched on the light. Arianna Gomez looked at him unblinking. "Everything alright?"

He continued to button his shirt, avoiding her penetrating gaze.

"Everything is fine," he reassured her, turning with his grin. He smiled his toothy smile, the one that always seemed to drive people off topic, distract them into doing what he wanted.

Gomez didn't look convinced.

"Really, you think that's going to work on me?" she said amused. "I'm the one who taught you how to utilize that smile of yours."

Bitiir shrugged. There was no use hiding things from her; she was too smart, even for him.

"I saw my father yesterday," he said nonchalantly as he pulled on pants.

"And?" Gomez gestured for him to continue.

"That's all," he said.

"That's all my ass," Gomez threw a pillow at him. "What happened? You're acting too weird not to tell me."

Bitiir sighed as he buckled his belt. "Fine, I saw my father. Well, more like he came to see me. Wants me to come home, take over the business, that sort of thing, very cliché. I told him I was completely content where I was."

"Did he support you?"

"Not exactly," Bitiir sat on the foot of the bed. "You see, I promised a long time ago that if he paid for my college and let me go to law school, I would come back and use it for the business. Accused me of betraying the family, betraying God." Bitiir chuckled, trying to make it all seem less intense than it really was. It wasn't really any of Gomez's business to know about his personal life.

"Betraying God and family," Gomez whistled. "That's a little harsh for choosing to work somewhere else."

"Um, it's more than that," Bitiir stared at Gomez, his Ari. He couldn't take his eyes off her. She was so different, unlike anyone he had ever been with, and the opposite of what his parents would approve of.

"What?" Gomez pulled the sheet tighter over herself.

"It's—" Abdul wasn't sure how to say it; he didn't want her to get the wrong idea of what this relationship was. "Working for SIC—*being with you.*"

"He knows about me?" Gomez sounded too excited.

Great, Bitiir thought. "He knows I'm with someone. That I've been with *people.* He thinks it's only since I've started working for SIC, but really, this is me."

"Oh," Gomez said. "He thinks since I've gotten you involved with SIC that I must be—"

"The temptress snake that has stolen my boyhood," Bitiir's laugh rang musically. "His words not mine. So he gave me the family ultimatum," Abdul mimicked his father's Egyptian accent, "apparently the same one his father gave him." Mimicking his father made him feel vindicated in his thinking, especially since he trained himself to speak in a perfect oxford accent.

"And I told him I never wanted to see him again." He patted her leg. "So that's that. Sit with me at the banquet tonight?"

Gomez's jaw dropped. "You what?"

Did he really think changing the subject would work on her? It had at one time, but she was getting to know him too well. That wasn't good.

"Come on," Bitiir said. "He was holding me back. Our father-son relationship is far from picture perfect. In fact, he's always been toxic to me and I don't need that in my life."

"What about your brothers? Your sisters?" Gomez sat up. "Your mother?"

"I thought you'd be proud of me, I did what you said," Bitiir defended. "I stood up for myself, cut out the toxic things in my life."

"Yes, but I didn't mean cut out your family," Gomez said. "You need your family—you need your father—believe me, I know."

Bitiir sighed. "Ari, I know what you must think of me, but my family is not who you think they are. They don't know me, they don't understand me, never have" He put a hand on her face. "Thanks to you I found a family and I can finally be who I am."

Gomez put her hand over his, smiling. "Abdul," she whispered. "Abdul—I think I love you."

Abdul froze. That was not what he meant; because of Gomez he found SIC and through her he made a new corporate family. She was a part of SIC and a big part of his life, but not in the way she thought. The last thing he wanted was to do was hurt her, but he couldn't lie either, that wasn't him. He hated lying more than anything, even if he was good at it.

"You don't have to say it back," Gomez said calmly, looking him in the eye. "I know that people can be in different places at different times, but I just wanted you to know how I felt, and now you know. I love you."

"Ari, I-uh," he still didn't know what to say.

"Go get ready for your big banquet," she said, hitting him with a pillow. "You got to look good for those big execs. I hear they've got a big project lined up, top-secret, off-Earth and very serious."

He put his face level with hers. "Good thing I've got someone on the inside to help me with my homework." He kissed her, long and passionately. Her arms wrapped around him.

"They're only looking for the best," her lips traveled down his neck as she spoke. "Afterall, it doesn't take just anyone to push a project like Venus forward."

"I'll see if I can't put on my best charm," he said, releasing himself from her sultry arms. He posed himself in the way that always got him what he wanted: shoulders rolled back confidently, toothy grin, laid back casual eyes. "For the both of us."

"Perfect," Gomez said. "Get going, I'll see you there. Wouldn't look good for us to show up together."

Suddenly, the memory faded and all the years flashed forward for Abdul Bitiir. Hands he shook and the smiles he gave as he accepted the role of making the Venus project happen. He saw distant stares from Gomez as he ghosted her. She'd gotten too close and that was dangerous to him. He distanced himself under the guise of protection. Other opportunities presented themselves, as well as other beautiful people.

Then he met someone, someone different. Someone that reminded him of the gentleness of his mother growing up. A woman somewhat naive to his charms, but treated him with a kindness he rarely knew. He felt an affection he had not felt in a long time, and he bought a ring to seal that affection.

But before he could present the symbol of his emotions, she tore out his heart. Told him he was not good for her, and she was going to seek opportunity elsewhere on the recommendation of a close friend; the recommendation of a planetary geologist she worked with.

"Why, why would you do this to me?" Bitiir could feel his eyes swell. He could cry, but he will not allow it, not in front of Gomez.

"She should know who you are," Gomez said to him. They were in her New York lab, her research scattered all around them. "She had to know exactly the kind of man you would be to her."

"You don't know anything!"

"I know first-hand!" She whipped around to face him. "You are the kind of man who doesn't love anyone except himself. The kind who can't commit to anything truly important. Who will always choose his career, his ambition over people."

"Don't lie to me," Bitiir said. "You didn't do this for her. You were jealous and *selfish*. I had a real relationship with her, and you just couldn't stand to see it, *could you?* I was honest—I didn't love you —you knew what kind of relationship we had. And you're the one who pressured me to head the Venus project. You knew what that meant for us and it was over the moment I accepted. And be honest my dear, we both know why you wanted me—I was the only one who could make Venus happen for you."

"I've always known what I've wanted," Gomez's lips were tight, "And I know how to get it. But you still can't admit it, can you? You can't ever admit what you really want. If your mother could see you now."

Bitiir felt rage; not anger, but ferocious rage. "And you will never admit how selfish you really are."

"Then we have nothing more to say."

The look on her face was one Bitiir never hoped to see. It was empty, not a hint of anything of who he thought she was. It faded into another, one he did not recognize. It was her expression at the time of death, looking into his eyes once more.

"Tell them," her motionless body somehow speaking to him. "Tell them I wasn't selfish. For once, I was not—"

And then she was gone.

Bitiir's current nausea became too much. He leaned over the rim of the toilet, retching up the bottle he drank away, her image still ingrained into mind.

Tell them. . . I wasn't selfish. . .

"Ari," he said, flushing away all the vileness he rid himself of. "You were right. But I was right too. I forgive you. Please, forgive me, *forgive me!*"

And the words haunted him through the rest of his sleepless night.

Chapter 28: What the Girl told Him

Marshall," the voice that mimicked his late wife whispered to him. "Marshall—*Marshall!*"

He shot up, his entire body soaked in a cold sweat.

His bedding was thrown on the floor and he himself was on the edge of the bed. He stood and gathered his blanket, wrapping it tight around his shivering body.

He turned on his imaging screen to watch the live feed of Venus. Like a burnt sunrise it floated, filling his room with its warm glow. Venus station was so cold and unmoving compared to the planet he watched.

He couldn't think back to what happened, he refused to. He wanted only to think of the present, to exist only in the current.

But the visions haunted him. If not consciously then in the back of his mind. The voice of the celestial stone still lingered, calling his name repeatedly. And flashes of the true nature of the Venusians he discovered made him shiver beyond the chill in the air.

Confined to quarters, he tried to fill his time with research, to return to the basics of his long drawn-out education. He found himself writing about things he already knew, but wanted to reiterate. And before he knew it, he was no longer writing in English, but in the language of the Venusians.

He hid his journals from the station's psychologist, not wanting to give SIC more reason to keep him prisoner. They forced pills down his throat when he lashed-out, pills that made the doctors and psychologists whisper 'liar' out of earshot.

That was why he slept so much. No one called him delusional to his face, but he knew they thought it. And they denied him the satisfaction of validating his suspicions.

I can only imagine what they've done to Cocteau, he thought. *Knowing how she is. Bet Bitiir talked his way out this one and is sitting pretty right now.*

He heard the entry to his quarters open.

Great, he turned his back to the entry, *more pills to knock me out.*

"I'm feeling fine," he said, refusing to turn around. "I don't need any more mind killing drugs." He knew it was useless as they forced the last set on him, but he was not going to let them think he was okay with any of this.

"I'm not here to give you drugs Marshall Wilson."

The voice that spoke, it was nothing like he had ever heard before. Deep and feminine like the aged wise, yet containing the innocence of a young child. He whipped around.

Then dropped his blanket.

The girl, the same one he saw that day in Gomez's lab, stood in the center of his quarters. The girl that no one else acknowledged and yet followed the admiral observing his every move. She wore the same black dress he saw her in before, and had her dark hair swept up in a sophisticated twist. She held her hands gently in front of her, just below her star pendant that reflected a familiarity.

Wilson, rendered speechless, stared at her pendant. Surely it couldn't be?

"Ah, my pendent?" the girl's hand brushed against it nonchalantly as she smiled slightly, perfect white teeth peeking out. "You've seen something like this before, haven't you?"

He looked into her pendent, mesmerized that he'd not made the connection before. When on the surface, the stress of survival made him forget everything nonessential in his life. The star pendent she wore contained a small stone in the center, no bigger than a chip from a pebble, and resembled the celestial stone on Venus.

Wilson noticed how awkwardly he was staring. He nodded, taking composure.

"On the planet?"

He nodded again.

She sighed. "That explains a lot, answers many of my hypotheses." Eyelashes fanned over sparkling eyes, deep and dark. "You didn't mention seeing a stone like this in your report. Neither did Captain Cocteau or the lawyer Bitiir. Why?"

"What?" Wilson's words fumbled within his mind. No introductions and right to the point. The girls spoke strangely; the way she enunciated was better than many grown adults he knew, as though she were an adult trapped in a child's body. Who was this girl? Was she really here, or was she just another part of one of his supposed hallucinations?

"Your reports," the girl's eyebrows narrowed. "None of you mentioned seeing a stone like this. Why?"

"Bitiir never saw it," Wilson said.

"And the captain?"

"Probably thought the same thing I did," he said. "That stone we saw, it's extremely powerful." Why was he answering her? Something in her voice, her demeanor relaxed him to the point he felt no inhibition to speak. "Who knows what SIC would do if they knew about it."

The girl's smile twitched as she raised her nose proudly. "Right you are."

She held her pendant in her hand, approaching Wilson. He made no motion as her short self stood beside him and held her pendant out, gesturing for him to take a closer look.

"This is truly something special," she said. "And you are truly something special. You've been touched by time infinite. Touched by a celestial stone. I myself am a product of the power these stones hold. A very powerful, very rare item. Mined outside of time itself, within what you perceive as the fifth dimension. I may look like a child in your eyes and that is the power of the stone. My celestial stone is small, just enough for me to maintain myself. But larger ones can spread their influence beyond a single individual."

Wilson looked at her stone, just as grand as the one he saw on Venus, even for its small size. This one also pulsed like the other, just fainter. "Who—who are you?"

The girl let her pendant fall to dangle gently against her black dress. "I am the one who runs this station and all your Earthly space programs, though most don't know or realize it. You may call me Persephone."

"Persephone—like the Greek goddess of spring?"

"Or queen of the underworld," she smirked. "But it's only a name for me. My foremost name is not of your world or system, and cannot be uttered at this time."

Wilson took a step back. "Those pills were strong, but I didn't think that strong."

"I am not a hallucination."

"Then why are you here, now?" Wilson said "Why did no one else notice you before in the lab? How do I know you're real?"

"I know, I know," she put her hands up non-threateningly. "How very deus-ex-machina of me to appear when you're stuck with no way out. But I can assure you, I am as real as the very air you're breathing, and as real as the events you experienced on the surface of Venus. And as real as the celestial stone you saw and the one you see me wearing. I have a talent for making myself inconspicuous. Why am I here? I am here because I need your help and you need mine. I know you desire freedom. Listen carefully and you will know all you need to gain that which you seek."

Wilson thought for a moment. "What the hell, why not?" He sat on the edge of the bed. "I have nothing better to do." He decided it didn't matter if she was real or not, or if she was one of SICs tricks. He was trapped with no other options. "So what are you? A goddess or something?"

Persephone laughed. "Some of us would like to think so, but no. We possess no extraordinary power, only knowledge. I am one of countless overseers from another system, far beyond the current capabilities of your Earth race. Overseers are charged to maintain one objective: the survival of a planet race in this beautiful and harsh reality we all exist within. The Earth race is my charge, and why I came to investigate the planet you call Venus."

"Why aren't more of your kind here?" Wilson said. "If you're charged with the survival of the Earth race, why did you allow this to happen to my team?"

"I may only influence and direct at fingertip's length to protect a planet race from extinction," Persephone spoke carefully, but not condescending. "I cannot tell you or the other Earth children what they must do; it is their choice. I can have no direct hand in any of your matters—it is forbidden—or we shall end up with a product like the children of Venus."

"You know about the Venusians," Wilson said. "Does SIC?"

"I do," she said. "They don't. And they would deny it if they did."

"Of course," Wilson huffed. "I was supposed to give them the okay to begin development on Venus. Now I'm being punished for what they think is opposing them. And you—you said you run this station—why are you keeping me prisoner?"

"At fingertip's length," Persephone chided, reminding him. "I didn't confine you here. Your superiors have done so and I cannot take away their agency, their decisions. But be not too harsh on them —I can promise you that SIC is merely a means to an end."

Wilson shook his head. This was too much. "You said I'm touched by time infinite. What does that even mean? What did that celestial stone do to me? To Arianna Gomez? Who are these Venusians?"

Persephone bowed her head compassionately, her voice still and steady. "Celestial stones are peculiar things; not good, not evil, just peculiar. They do not play by the rules of this existence as they are mined outside of it. Because of this, these stones are able to influence and manipulate reality. They cannot, however, change reality. Your theories on relativity only touch a small part of what these stones are capable of."

"They destroyed Arianna's mind with it," Wilson said. "The Venusians down there, they tried to invade mine and it backfired."

"I take it that was not their intention."

"No." Wilson said. "I—I killed them and ended up with their knowledge instead; their thoughts, memories, and emotions.

The girl looked up at him, pleased. "You did that? Well, I can say they certainly did not expect that at all. What were you thinking of at the time?"

"What does that have to do with anything?"

"Why, everything," the girl said. "It is what makes you powerful, makes you human."

Wilson sighed. "I thought of *her*—my late wife. Justine."

"Marshall," Persephone stood in front of him. She touched the top of his hand, warm and delicate, her head level with his. "You know of true sorrow, and that is what makes you strong—stronger than that of your teammates. Whenever a celestial stone is used for the purpose of seeing and feeling another's thoughts, it is not a one way road. The Venusians gave up their humanity long ago. All that you were thinking and feeling when the stone touched your mind was as human as human can be. Whatever you felt, they felt it too and it was too much for them to handle after denying themselves such a human thing for so many generations. In that moment you thought of Justine, it backfired and in exchange you gained something from them. *All things must come to a balance or be consumed by the other, this rule is true on all planes of existence.* I cannot explain it, for it is beyond the science of this dimension. But it happened, and that's all that can be said."

She paused, closing her eyes as though thinking. Wilson didn't mind the silence with her. It gave him a comfort he never knew he yearned for.

"I empathize with you Marshall Wilson," she said, her eyes still closed and her hand still on his. "Know that you are not alone."

Wilson put his other hand over hers. He believed her.

She released the embrace of hands and opened her wide eyes. "As for the race you call Venusians, there is much for you to know before you can gain what you desire." She held up her celestial stone. "Close your eyes Marshall Wilson, you already contain the memories of what you need to know. Let my stone guide you."

He swallowed, cringing at the thought of diving into the Venusian memories again. "Yeah, looking into their memories does something to me. It overloads my head. If I go too deep it will kill me."

She smiled. "Please, let my stone guide you. With its assistance, you will have nothing to fear for it will support you where your mind cannot."

Weary of her request, he closed his eyes. The familiar tendril of thought brushed against his consciousness. This one was light and warm, kind in nature. He felt no pressure in his head as he did in the compound, thinking of the Venusians and accessing their memories.

Persephone's voice spoke in his mind. "The Venusians are an ancient race, prehistoric to the appearance of life on Earth, and the first dwellers to emerge in this system."

He saw creation. Elements coming together from a mother sun. When he saw them, the plants all formed at once. Clouds of material organizing and becoming. He saw a young Earth, alive with volcanic activity as elements continued to organize and create. Venus came to view, also living with activity as it formed to a young planet, blue with water against brown land, beginning to burst with primitive life.

"Venus is the twin to your Earth in almost all ways," Persephone's voice spoke over the visions. He saw the evolution of life on Venus, so similar to Earth, yet unique in its own way. Life came to being, then passed away, growing and dying in a forever cycle. "Like Earth in every way, except in its evolutionary path. The Venusians understood many things your people have yet to discover. And the one thing they understood more than anything was the inevitability of their end. Nothing lasts forever and the Venusians came to fear it. Thus started their journey to immortality. If they could harness the power to overcome death, they would become the most powerful beings not only in this system, but others they desired to compete with."

Then he saw through their eyes, Venusians viewing their solar system. They watched a young Earth, evolving more slowly and not yet teeming with advanced life like Venus. But they saw it, all the ingredients of evolution ready to create life as soon as Earth was ready. He felt their curiosity, but also their fear. Then their anger grew to a jealousy of another that could take what was theirs.

"Those Venusians you experienced are all that's left of the once-thriving planet race that succeeded in the impossible: cheating death," Persephone continued. "Now that I know they have a celestial stone, it is evident how they came to the present."

"You said a celestial stone is powerful enough to influence and manipulate reality, but not change it," Wilson's mind spoke to Persephone "That means it could manipulate time, or how we perceive time."

"Yes."

"That's how they're doing it," his mind said as more visions passed him. "They're manipulating time."

"It would seem so," Persephone's voice said.

Another vision came to view. The celestial stone from the Venusian compound, but this time it was being given, from the hands of being like Persephone clad in white, to the leaders of Venus. He couldn't make out distinct features, but he could feel it, the understanding of what was happening. The Venusians found a way to their survival, and made empty promises to obtain what they needed to succeed.

"No one can time travel—but you can draw it out," Persephone's voice continued. "They are using a very dangerous technology that even we, the overseers from celestial society, shun. Time loop technology.

"For the Venusian compound to be undetected, to technically not exist on this plane of existence, they have to be harnessing time loop technology with the power of that celestial stone—it's the only answer I can think of. It's dangerous technology Marshall Wilson, I cannot emphasize that enough. Time loop technology, if not precise, has the most dangerous of consequences."

He suddenly felt the elation of the Venusian race, more memories pulled from his subconscious. They had found a way, they were saved. No more death, no more fear. They were immortal. They would be the rulers of this system forever.

"Time loop technology can enable its wielders to exist in a way that they do not deteriorate, age, or come to death. But it can also trap them, reliving a moment indefinitely. Because celestial stones do not play by our rules of physics, in all their power they can cause great destruction and even redirect an evolutionary path, just as it did for Venus. The Venusians know this, and will do the same to Earth if given the chance."

He saw visions of days passing, a world dying around him. Venus, once teaming with life was deteriorating. Water boiled and dissipated, oceans disappeared.

"They've existed within a time loop," Wilson tried to wrap his head around all she explained, "where they've rested for an epoch, asleep until they could reawaken. SIC building the artificial mountain on top of their compound must've disturbed the time loop somehow."

"An epoch for us, but only an instant for them," Persephone said. "Time loop technology would manipulate their perception and the moment they appeared to you, would've only been moments to them. I had heard rumors from other overseers that the Venusians had a contingency plan when they realized they doomed their world. That hidden compound powered by the celestial stone must be part of that plan."

"If you knew about this," Wilson said. "Why act now?"

"I thought it was just that—a rumor," she said.

Wilson gulped. Something she said disturbed him. Redirecting evolutionary paths and doing the same to Earth. "How did they doom their world? I must know."

"You already know."

He dug deeper, the power of Persephone's stone bringing Venusian memories to life without pain or pressure. He saw the stone connected to various devices, Venusian hands directing its power with their minds. Then the Venusian atmosphere changed, turning a sickly yellow as he heard the cries of pain and death overcome all else. The celestial stone kept few alive, but they were despairing, knowing that their immortality plan had failed.

He saw it happen. The time loop technology damaged the planet's rotation and evolutionary path. Damage beyond anything the Venusians understood. Their planet began to die.

"The ancient Venusians abused time loop technology trying to overcome death. In doing so they destroyed their world," her voice was full of solace. "They unintentionally slowed the rotation of their planet, causing a chain of events that could not be unbroken. Including the evaporation of their water, the most precious of substances. Whatever is done with time loop technology cannot be undone."

And the idea came to him just as it came to the Venusians so long ago. They saw no way to repair the damage to their world. He saw the compound and the hopes it held. He saw them eye young Earth, so alive and untouched, with their envy for it. Why should a Venusian perish and give way to such a naive world, still in its embryonic state, unaware of the workings of celestial society and unaware of the universe around them.

But Earth was more; it was a second chance to recreate what was theirs, now destroyed. They would sleep until the right moment, then recreate their heritage, and exterminate any Earth race that would emerge. Earth would be the new Venus and they would live on. No more death, no more hunger, no more struggle to survive. They would be the immortal overlords of the solar system.

The Venusian memories closed with this promise, and the soft tendrils of thought dissipated. He opened his eyes.

Persephone no longer held the stone. She simply stood, looking at him, waiting.

"Were you there" Wilson asked curiously. "When the Venusians did that to their world?"

She blinked slowly, her eyes softening. "I'm afraid not. There are many more ancient beings that oversaw Venus. What you saw was all from within you, a remnant of the minds that died down there. I've been around for as long as your homeworld has existed, but was not yet ready to take charge or come to your system until life developed, long after the Venusians went to sleep. To the other overseers I am young. I only know what I've learned from them, and hope not to make the same mistakes—or take the same shortcuts—as they did with Venus."

"Um yeah," Wilson said. "Best not to."

Persephone nodded. "I must show you something that has confounded the rest of the crew members on this vessel. Allow me?" She made a nod to the remote on his bedside.

"Oh yes," he reached over and gave it to her. "Not sure how much good it will do here. My viewing screen can only get minimal broadcasts from—"

She popped open the remote and tore out pieces and replaced them with some of her own.

Where was she hiding those?

She pointed the remote at the viewing screen. Images of diagrams, photos of Cerberus City, and fluctuations of the same nature he saw in the documents he first received at the moon orbiter.

"Those readings," Wilson gasped. "They're coming from Cerberus City. Just like—"

He stopped.

Persephone frowned. "Keep going."

He shook his head. "Just like the ones we investigated on the surface, right above the compound."

"Take a look at this." She scrolled through interior images of the city. Empty.

"Nothing," Wilson said. "It looks the same as when we went through. Or," he thought about the celestial stone and its capabilities to manipulate perception, "it just appears that way."

The corners of Persephone's mouth smirked. "Correct."

"Which means," Wilson sunk his head into his hands. It made sense why visions of Venusians still haunted him, why he could still hear the voice of the celestial stone calling to him. "Their celestial stone is in Cerberus City."

"Someone had to bring it there," Persephone said. "It cannot move on its own."

"I made sure they could not come after us." Wilson stood, frustrated. "I destroyed their compound!"

"They are clever Marshall Wilson," Persephone said. "You know this. And with the power of the stone they can use time loop technology to manipulate whatever they want to survive."

Wilson didn't want to believe it. "What I did can't be reversed, but it can be paused indefinitely, couldn't it? The celestial stone can give all the time in the world. They had more than enough time to do what they needed; to escape, to awaken the rest of their race, and fortify themselves elsewhere, even in our own city."

"The Earth race is a threat to the birthright they gave-up long ago," Persephone said. "In exchange for the celestial stone they now hold, they denounced their birthright to the Sun, to your system. And that birthright has passed to you, to the Earth race. You are the true heirs of this system. Like them you are descendants of the Sun, but you have claim to it. They would see you and your world burn to reclaim that birthright, rather than see it fall to a planet race they deem inferior. And with their celestial stone, they are unstoppable. And with this knowledge, what shall you do?"

Wilson fell back onto his bed. He folded his arms over his stomach.

Persephone peered over him. "What do you fear, Marshall Wilson?"

Why did she have to keep saying his full name like that? It made him feel like he was the child in the room, not her.

"I'm afraid, " he closed his eyes, "of never setting foot on Earth again." His thoughts were drawn to the visions the stone invoked, the voice of his beloved speaking his name. A voice young and strong, deteriorated to a frailty that should've been of old-age, but was caused by malicious disease. He opened his eyes. "Of dying before my time." *Just as she did.*

"And that was what they feared too," Persephone said. "And look at what they've become."

"I know what I must do," he said solemnly. He knew what Persephone was asking of him. "I've seen them, I know their true nature, who they really are. They're not as invincible as they would have us believe. They share more similarities with Earth people than they like to think, or reconcile with. I know how to stop them."

An unspoken idea was also on his mind: what if he saw their celestial stone again? It still called to him—*she* called him, his Justine. He had come across the stars and for what? Seeing into the celestial stone made it clear. It was to find her, to see his Justine again.

Marshall. He heard the whispers.

"You, against all of them?" Persephone said, the side of her lip curling so that Wilson couldn't tell whether it was disbelief or encouragement. Did she hear the whispers too?

"The Venusians are an invading race," Wilson sat up. "If history has taught me anything about invasion and annihilation, it's swift. Their strike will not wait. I cannot wait." He couldn't wait to see her.

Persephone opened up the remote again and pulled one of the chips she inserted. She put it in his hand and folded his fingers shut.

"This will get you where you need to go," she said. "I wish you well, I sincerely do for I know what you are undertaking. You are the only one who can face them and face their celestial stone. You've already done so and succeeded. You are the only one who knows the face of the Venusian race, I can see it in your eyes. I give you a word of warning: do not be consumed by the stone. The Venusians are under the illusion that they control it, but they don't." She eyed him, an unfooled expression. "Do not look back into the shadows the stone holds or you shall be consumed. Keep your back to the stone and you will be free of its grasp. Come into its power, and you will be forever trapped."

Wilson gripped the chip in his hand. "I am free to choose how I use this?"

Persephone gave a nod.

"I understand." He looked down at the chip. She was right that he would gain what he sought if he listened, but it came with a price. She said she needed his help and he knew what that help meant. And why she couldn't intervene any further than she already had. This was his fight, the fight of the Earth race. For justice's sake the Earth race has to stand for their birthright; for their right to exist.

He knew what his newfound freedom was intended for.

He decided without a doubt to go.

Back to Venus.

Chapter 29: The One Who Returned

Wilson ran down the sleek SIC hall. Did he really need to run? No one chased or followed him. They didn't even suspect he left quarters with Persephone's almighty chip. He was finally free and it felt good.

Persephone warned him that her chip would give him passage and access, but was tied to Venus station. It was useless once it left the proximity of the station

I'll get my suit, he made a mental checklist of what he needed. *Hopefully my EC is still attached to it with all of Cocteau's command codes.*

He felt like he was creeping through the Venusian compound again when he ducked behind an alcove, hiding from SIC staff members. All oblivious to the eminent danger that lurked below on the planet.

Better that way, he thought. *Don't want to draw attention.*

He found his way to the maintenance department. Using Persephone's chip he broke into the locker room and stole one of the navy blue maintenance uniforms. Fortunately, most of the SIC employees in upper positions took no notice of the maintenance staff, so his face would blend away just like all the others that passed through.

Rolling a trash bin and toolkit in hand, he made his way to inventory. There was a room he knew of from Gomez, one tied directly to her lab, where they stored all planet materials, or materials that came in contact with the planet. That was where his Venus gear would be. He took a side hall that led straight there and entered.

Inventory consisted of a low ceiling, walls filled with clear glass doors that served as passage to different storage units. All he had to do was locate the right one.

He found it quicker than expected. He entered a storage unit labeled: 'Quarantine and Dangerous—Keep Out Unless Authorized.'

Inside were bins upon bins filled with tools and probes that touched Venus. Various rock samples—all of Gomez's work—were separated into different bins depending on weight and size. He came upon recent entries of toxic items. Given that those who cataloged his gear believed it was filled with the strange gas anomaly, they would've deemed it toxic.

Using his maintenance tools, he cracked open the bins and found his and his teammates Venusian gear.

He wrapped everything in plastic and wheeled his gear away without a second thought.

He cut through Venus Station command nonchalantly, no one taking notice as he trolleyed his gear within the trash bin. He remembered when he first saw command, when he was introduced to Admiral Jones. How he marveled at the wide view of Venus filling the entire room with its golden beauty, and the complexity of a bustling staff. Though nothing changed, all seemed quiet now. Venus no longer held his eye, and staff were merely cogs, pieces of SIC. The marvel was gone.

Command was directly connected to the employee launching bay, where the Infinite was stored. A small red door to launch lay on the far side of the room. Staff could pass freely during the launch sessions. All other times it was locked.

As Wilson crossed the command room, the wide window no longer faced Venus. The station rotated and faced the great abyss, pinpricks of stars spread like a blanket across the window. Wilson thought of Persephone, those like her and who watched them from afar.

Stay focused, he told himself he approached the red door. He put the thought from his mind.

He waited outside the door, feigning the clean-up of a spill. He heard something break and everyone looked away as a yelling match ensued on the other side of the room. He slid Persephone's chip across the access panel and slipped into launch.

It was uncanny being in launch alone. He'd only seen it brimming with steam, bright lights, and SIC employees. Now it was dark and empty.

Dim motion lights snapped-on and the Infinite filled his view. His footsteps echoed as he walked to the transport. It looked bigger, more intimidating than before.

"Now or never," he told himself and he stripped down from his maintenance disguise. He unwrapped his Venus gear, pulling on each piece one by one. It still smelled like Venus.

He had two ECs; his own and Gomez's.

He powered on his EC and inserted Persephone's chip. He scrolled through it and to his relief found that it hadn't been wiped; all the data from the planet was still on it. He powered on Gomez's and found all the access codes he needed for Cerberus city.

You cannot hold command codes, plus all the access codes, Cocteau's memory repeated to him when she downloaded her command codes to his EC. *It's dangerous to put them all in one place.*

He synced Gomez's access codes to his own EC. He threw it aside when finished, then pulled up Cocteau's command codes on his own.

This chip can do anything while on this station, he thought.

He froze, his hands shook. A memory from Venus suddenly entered his mind, but it was his own. He pictured himself, crazed as he altered the coding to the Venusian compound to collapse on itself, his thrill at the thought. The look on Cocteau's face when she realized what he'd done, and almost destroyed their lives in the process.

He shook his head. *Stay focused!*

He knew what to use for the chip for next. It was key to stopping the Venusians forever.

He continued to dial into her command codes, using Persephone's chip to alter and change commands.

"That's some fancy disguise you got there."

Wilson jumped, startled. Who knew he was in here? He turned around.

It was Cocteau. "I think I like the maintenance one better. Better matched your stupor."

He almost didn't recognize her; she stood still, serene.

"How did you get out of your quarters?" he accused.

She looked at him. "Why?" Her tone was soft, nothing Wilson knew she could do. Was this the same woman he saw take down a Venusian single handedly? Was this the same person that hated his guts, that cussed him out on a regular basis and everyone around her? His hotheaded captain who had a permanent stress line across her forehead. The one who saved their lives and made escaping the compound possible with her brute strength alone.

"Don't try to stop me," he said. Was he really saying this to her? She could snap his neck with the flick of a finger.

She cracked a slight smile. "I wasn't," she said calmly as she walked past him, right to the Infinite. "I just need to know why? You know SIC deemed all this nonsense. Is what you're doing worth it?"

He bit his bottom lip. "I don't know."

"Hmm." Cocteau leaned against the transport. "With the press of a button, I could alert the entire station. But I won't; this is your decision, and you will need to be the one who lives with the consequences. Are you ready for that Wilson? I know I wasn't when I did what I did. I just did it, and now I'm here, forever banished to this station without a planet to call home. Are you ready to risk everything?"

Wilson took a deep breath. "It's not about me."

Cocteau laughed. "Ha—that's what they all say—the heroes, the martyrs. I warn you most fail. Or chicken-out, doesn't really matter. I've seen enough deaths to know how things like this end. Unless you are completely committed, do not set foot off this station."

They stood, the silence between them screaming louder than words.

Wilson rolled his shoulders back. "I know what I saw. I know what they are. And I know what will happen if I let SIC convince me otherwise. I'm afraid, but what the Venusians are scares me more. That's why I must go."

Cocteau said nothing. Instead she approached Wilson, grabbing his arm.

He flinched, trying to pull away. Her grip was too strong.

"Calm down, I already said I'm not going to stop you," she said, pulling his arm to her. She dialed into his EC. "I saw what you were trying to do with the command codes I gave you. Let someone who knows how, work it for you. Didn't tell SIC I was planning on passing them to someone else and it looks like Bitiir has the good sense to keep his mouth shut on this one; otherwise you'd be stuck here. I refused to sign those asinine waivers, but it makes no difference if I sign my life away; I still serve this station. My situation doesn't change. Something big has to happen for them to change their minds. They told me if I kept an eye on you and Bitiir I'd be given freedom to roam."

She paused, her eyes locked onto his. "I've always been a prisoner Wilson, and not one person seems to understand that. Maybe one day I'll be free. You have a way out. Take it, before it's too late. And maybe, just maybe, save us too if you can." She finished dialing into his EC and set his arm free. "There, that should do it. Don't do anything I wouldn't do."

Wilson straightened his posture. "Goodbye."

"No goodbyes," she said. "Or you'll back out at the last second. Go soldier, and good luck."

Wilson found his opportunity and ran. He went into the Infinite, using Persephone's chip to power it up. He sat in the pilot's chair, barely knowing how to operate it, but he didn't need much experience. Autopilot from the last mission would bring him to the coordinates.

Then risk it. . . Is it worth your soul Wilson? Is it worth his? Theirs? Going back is the only way to make things right, to save us all. The memory of Gomez's words made Wilson wish for that 'moment.' The moment when you look back and feel that tinge of nostalgic confidence. He knew that moment was not real no matter how he wished it so. This was all him and whatever strength he could muster came from within himself. No one could give it to him.

He didn't look back.

Wilson's elation only heightened when he finished powering the Infinite. His intercom tuned into the station's radio, confused conversation flitting between SIC staff as to why the launch bay was activated.

Alarms sounded, and he got a signal that Cocteau cleared the bay.

"Cease and desist," Admiral Jones' voice ordered through numerous speakers and intercoms. Red and blue warning lights came on. Wilson ignored it all, Persephone's chip overriding any electronic initiative they took to stop him.

"We are arming to use force," Admiral Jones warned. "This is your last warning!"

The admiral's warnings became empty threats as soon as Wilson opened the launch doors. No one would be able to enter without being pulled into the vacuum of space.

And there it was, the swirling yellow planet below him once more.

Marshall, he heard it call to him.

"I'm coming," Wilson smirked. "You'd better believe I'm coming."

The signal of override blinked again, Persephone's chip holding the launch doors firmly open.

And he launched.

Persephone's chip played one last chord for his escape. It locked in the autopilot so that no one could override it, even from a distance. But from here on out, he knew the chip would no longer play a part; he'd be too far from the station.

He was on his own.

There was no telling how long it took from launch to penetrate the atmosphere of Venus. Minutes? Hours? He no longer kept track of time. He shut down all communications so he wouldn't have to listen to their ranting.

Eventually fire rolled across the windows, and the hull shook, the pressure of the g-force pinning him back. Although nauseated, he didn't pass out like he did before.

He hoped Cocteau was safe. Maybe his escape would show SIC that it was useless to keep them holed up on Venus Station and they would send her back to Earth. He hoped.

He floated aimlessly through clouds, their sulfuric yellow gasses golden in the speckled reflections of sunlight that peeked through randomly. Although Earth days passed on the station, it was still the same extended Venus day he arrived and left the planet.

The deadly precipitation covered the windshield, glittering as stars across the sky. Then it came into view, the pride of Earthkind and humanity: Cerberus City.

It felt like he never left as the Infinite took the same flight to dock. Just as before, the dock lifted the transport into the city, but this time no lights came on to greet him. Instead, he was enveloped in darkness as he passed the bay doors.

And he felt it. The Infinite stopped as did everything around him. Although he could not see it, he could feel it. He crossed a barrier of time and was completely shielded from anything SIC could send down to find him. The celestial stone was here, he could feel it's power distorting perception, and what was truly present on the station.

He shut everything down and all became still.

He switched on the emergency lights. He didn't bother looking out through the windshield; he knew what was waiting for him.

He walked down to the hatch remembering remnants of his childhood. Nothing significant, just pieces. The excitement of a swing, the sweet taste of ice cream in the summer, sitting in a classroom, friends that came and went, his days at NASA, Justine's smile and their hopes and dreams together; it all passed by. And he wished there was someone he could've passed those experiences onto.

And he thought of how much Justine wanted to pass those experiences on. Ovulation and pregnancy tests never seemed to work right with her. It was her want of such things that became her downfall, how they found the malicious cancer. And why she was no longer with him.

He opened the hatch.

He was greeted by a stab in the back, electric shocks penetrating his suit and forcing him to his knees. He did not fight as his helmet was torn off.

Venusian fingers wrapped around his face blocking his view.

He could hear the murmurs of the crowd around him, the ones that came to witness his undoing.

Chapter 30: The Children of Venus

All was black.

Wilson saw nothing around him. He wished the darkness was space so he could float into the abyss. At least then he could die peacefully.

It will be over soon, Justine's voice echoed in his mind. It still hurt to think of her name.

"I know," Wilson said. "I just didn't think it would be so soon."

Always break expectations, don't I? She laughed.

His mind was in the room where it happened. The hospice was warm, the morning sun shining through lace curtains and lighting her face. It was sullen, losing color from the treatments, but he saw through it; it still held joy. The same joy that he saw that first time on the beach at Cape Canaveral, when she first intertwined her hand with his, the first time he touched her lips with his, when he asked her to marry him. And when she told him he would be a father.

But promises of fatherhood never happened. Tests after a violent miscarriage told them that something more sinister was at work within her. And that she would not survive it.

He stroked her golden hair. "I don't want you to leave."

"I know," she said. The cancer had taken its toll.

"Without you I have nothing."

"You have so much, Marshall," she said, stroking his face. "Don't let me be the end of your life."

He continued to stare at her, not wanting to lose a single moment.

She sighed. "You will see me again. Once again when you least expect it."

Comforting, but empty words. He wouldn't see her again.

Soon after, in the moment of drifting to sleep, she was gone. He held her hand so she would not be afraid. She was never afraid.

He was.

And still is.

His suit was ripped to shreds as Venusians bound his face so he couldn't see. There were high-pitched screeches all around, as though a mob had formed around him. The piercing ring of their language sounded in his ears. He no longer flinched at the sound. The ringing cleared and he heard the words they chanted: *Kill the Earthchild! Gut him—rip him—tear him—we will have blood!*

"You shall pay for what you've done, Earthchild," a high, raspy voice said in his ear. "Then all Earth children will know who the true heirs of this system are, those who are most deserving."

Wilsons jaw was stiff. "G-go ahead bastard," Wilson was able to push through the pain. He hardly ever swore. It felt good. "Just try. We'll see who's deserving."

He felt the long fingers of his Venusian captor wrap around his upper arms and yank him. Did they just understand what he said? Like blood seeping through wounds, pain erupted through his body as he felt an electric rod shove into his back again. He refused to cry-out. He would not give them the satisfaction this time.

The Venusian gurgled something inaudible. Wilson buckled over from a punch to the stomach.

"Move," another one yelled, and Wilson was pushed back to his feet and shoved forward. The pain from the rod still ran up his spine and made every move as difficult as though he were carrying the weight of stones throughout his body.

He was thrown onto his knees, hitting something warm and smooth with his knees. The Venusians removed the bindings from his eyes and he squinted at the sudden light.

He was kneeling over the planet, looking through the glass floor of the Grand Courtyard. They were beside the ledge of the ceiling fountain.

A horde of Venusians surrounded him, at least five hundred, all screaming and cursing him: *pitiful, foolish, revolting, weak!* Their awkward bodies clashed against the simplistic beauty of the room. Now he knew their numbers. Wilson saw a beam of sunlight peak through the fast moving sulfuric clouds.

A warped energy field filled the center of the ceiling fountain, blocking any view of what created it, though Wilson had an inkling of what it was.

The crowd quieted.

Larger and grander than all the others, the Venusian General stepped through the crowd before him.

Alive! Wilson thought. Cocteau's blast didn't kill.

All was silent as the Venusian General stared him down with its empty eyes. Wilson knew what they were all thinking deep behind their expressionlessness. The thoughts and memories of those he killed with the celestial stone still lingered. A scornful hate and disgust at his very existence.

"Brothers, sisters, comrades," the Venusian General's voice sounded, echoing throughout the entire courtyard with its indignant mechanical voice. "We have passed judgment upon this creature. Let us hear his words before we sentence."

"Earthchild," the Venusian General's head tilted. "Why return to us knowing that we mean your doom?"

"You can understand me?" Wilson said. "How?"

"We do not need to explain our translation technology to the likes of you," the Venusian General's voice spat. "We have understood you all along."

"So that's the ringing I hear?" Wilson said. "Your translation tech? Am I able to access it because of the memories I hold—"

"You will only answer what you are asked!"

Wilson sneered. "You killed someone dear to me. My teammate —my friend. I want retribution."

The general gave a low rumble, a mock of a laugh. "And you killed many of my own. An eye for an eye as they would say."

"As we *Earth* people say," Wilson said smugly. "Hammurabi, sixth ruler of the Amorite Dynasty, Babylonian Empire. First recorded laws."

"I've seen your libraries in this facility," the Venusian General said smoothly. "I am well aware of your Earth's history, or what you claim to be history. Are you really so conceited to think that you are the first and last to have such a saying? Earth children are more arrogant than we thought. All the more satisfying when we end you and your wretched race."

Excited murmuring sounded all around.

"Earthchild," the Venusian General said. "Face the fate of your comrade."

A ripped left sleeve of a SIC Venus bodysuit, blood-stained and filled with flesh, was thrown before Wilson. It landed with a thud, blotting the flawless glass with its crimson contents.

Wilson wanted to look away, but he had already decided he would stay strong. He held his composure at the sacrilegious sight. *She did not feel pain*, he told himself. *She was already dead when they did this to her. I will not let them take me!*

"We've taken the access codes from your comrade," the Venusian General said. "When we saw her mind she gave us all we wanted and more with the knowledge of your Earth race."

"Take what you want," Wilson said. "But her access codes will do you no good without the command codes."

"We shall see Earthchild," the general said. "No Earthchild shall live to take the inheritance of the Venusians. Brothers, sisters, comrades, let the retribution ritual begin."

In one swift move, the Venusian General wrapped its fingers around its head, finally revealing the secret that made Wilson return.

Chapter 31: Fall from Grace

One word: human.

The Venusian General removed its head, that is to say, it's helmet.

Beneath it was a face too hauntingly familiar. One that could've belonged to anyone, but it didn't. It was Venusian and human. Female, she had wild white hair, tangled from wearing the exoskeleton head. And the eyes were no longer bottomless pits as the helmet gave the illusion to, but bright and determined beneath a strong brow. The color was aflame, a swirling yellow amber as if Venus herself were alive in them.

These things, he had told Cocteau. *Only monsters can be that cruel.*

He remembered the hall of Venusian carcasses. He finally understood. They weren't carcasses, but biomechanical armor suits. And the gruesome surgical tools that lined the walls were meant to mold them to the human Venusian that played host.

Monsters? Cocteau's voice echoed. *It's clear that you've never fought a war—you don't know.*

And now he knew. Humans could be monsters and the Venusians were as monstrous as humans could be. The Venusians were as close to human as one could be that has rejected humanity. That was the true nature of the Venusian race, to be a human that forsakes humanity.

The Venusian General stood before him, fiercer and more terrifying in that her true human nature.

"Tell me Earthchild," she said smoothly in a deep feminine voice no longer hidden within the confines of the helmet, "was it easier to murder us before you knew who we were?"

She lifted her head high, raising her arms to welcome Venusian onlookers. "Look into the face of your enemy," she ordered the Venusians, "so that he may see the fire in your eyes and know that justice shall be ours in the presence of his evil."

All the Venusians removed their helmets and revealed a race of beings, as diverse as the people on Earth. Their eyes, even among their unique features, were unified with the same yellow-amber, connecting them all to their hellish world.

"We see your sin and condemn you," they said perfectly unified. "Dispense justice."

The Venusian General approached Wilson, looking down on him. "You have trespassed upon a world that is not your own and killed those superior to yourself, the most serious of sins. Justice must be satisfied and we will not be starved thus. Let your execution mark the beginning of a new reign in this system, the rightful heirs to the Sun. Your Earth shall pay the debt of our world as we take what is ours. We will be eternal."

They destroyed their world, Persephone's words sang in Wilson's memory. *Changed the evolutionary path. . . They will do the same to yours. . .*

"You had your chance and blew it," Wilson said. "You destroyed your mother world, the very world that gave you life." He gave a small laugh. "Plus there are billions of us against you. Do you really think you can win?"

The Venusian General smirked. "We shall see." She held out a recognition coin, minted with an exotic caricature of her face and body. "Immortal object, reveal yourself."

The warped energy surrounding the fountain suddenly dissipated, revealing the celestial stone floating beneath the tip of the ceiling fountain

"Fear not, Earthchild," the Venusian General waved the coin and a holographic panel appeared in front of her. "I saw what you did to my people within the stone's central hold." She dialed into the panel and the stone glowed brighter. "That mistake is rectified and shall not be made again. Don't even try to meld your mind with it again. If you do, a penalty worse than death will take you."

Do not look back into the shadows the stone holds, Persephone warned him. *Or you shall be consumed. Was this what the Venusian General referred to?*

The general continued to dial, all other Venusians standing at perfect attention, unnaturally silent. One pulled off Wilson's EC and handed it to the general.

"I thank you for returning to us," she turned the EC in her long, golden exoskeleton fingers. "For you have provided us the means to take full control of this vessel, and thus given us the means to take your precious toy of a station that floats in our orbit. See the beginning of the end Earthchild, and die knowing you made all possible."

She held the EC within the holographic panel. Orange and green holographics appeared, ones and zeros dancing around one another as command codes uploaded and intertwined with stolen access codes. The Venusian General leered over it, mouth parted slightly. "My brothers and sisters, witness the rebirth of our race, our civilization—*our world!*"

The lights went out.

Confused mutters reverberated. The light from the planet beneath cast a sickly yellow glow under their faces and the celestial stone quivered.

"What is this?" the mutters asked. "Is the system restarting? Have we full control of the vessel?"

The room shook and red warning lights flashed.

A sudden jolt sideways told them their answer.

Wilson's captors let go from the force of the jolt. He took the opportunity and jumped over the ceiling fountain ledge, pinning himself to the inner side of it.

The floor tilted as the gravity of the planet took grasp and vertigo became the norm. Venusians slid across the glass floor, screaming and panicking as a sound system repeated error messages:

Life support systems failing.
Pressure systems failing.
Hover systems failing.
Evacuate immediately.

Cerberus city was falling, crashing to the world below.

The world beneath swirled and spun. A horrid and hollow screech sounded, a wailing banshee warning them of the oncoming collision.

The rumble of the air outside shook the city, and the frail ceiling fountain sculpture shattered into thousands of pieces. Iridescent glass particles dusted the open faces and shards tore through flesh, revealing the crimson contents beneath Venusian skin. Unstable Venusians flung in a torrent around the courtyard, skulls smacking against the ceiling and floor like bloody sponges against concrete.

Wilson clutched the ledge, desperate not to meet the same fate. He couldn't see through the clouds, but he knew the surface beneath fast approached as the city plummeted down. A number of Venusians tumbled lifeless, spreading their gore across the glass.

The Venusian General also clutched the ledge of the fountain, helmet gone and ripped flesh across her face. She desperately dialed into her holopanel, the celestial stone glowing brighter and brighter.

Wilson laughed.

"Won't work," he yelled at the general. "Didn't learn the first time, did you?" It didn't matter if she heard him, he wanted to say it. He wanted his retribution. "I've coded the city to lock down when the solar balloons depressurize. You are all trapped, *trapped!*"

The glass floor cracked, chasms of lines spreading from the heat and pressure of the planet. The moment it opened, Wilson knew what would happen.

The Venusian General seemed to realize what he'd done and stopped dialing.

She looked up. Wilson looked too.

The celestial stone.

The Venusian General tried to dial again, but another jolt sideways sent the general's recognition coin flying and shut off the holopanel.

"You!" she bellowed.

Like a spider to its prey, she dug her exoskeleton fingers into the edge of the fountain, ripping herself toward him.

Wilson had no strength to move. The general reached him, holding the fountain with one arm, grabbed Wilson around the neck with the other.

"I don't need an interface to use the stone," her crazed eyes bore into his. "And I shall destroy you as I save my race!"

No interface with the stone was dangerous. Wilson knew its power and no safeguards meant the Venusian General could do anything she wanted, no matter the cost.

Dead and unconsciousness Venusians tousled helplessly around them, while those still living and awake continued to scream in terror.

They should've hit the ground by now, but everything moved slower for Wilson. He knew all was happening in a matter of seconds, but each second stretched longer than a minute.

The Venusian General closed her eyes. Everything around him continued to slow as he felt a sprout of consciousness reach out, like the tap of a finger against skin. He suddenly felt the minds of all those still alive around him, horrified by their fate. The Venusian General called on the power of the celestial stone and forced it on him, exerting its power. The pressure in his head pulsed warm blood from his nose, down his chin and onto his neck. The presence of all the Venusian consciousnesses together was exorbitant, their collective dominated by the general as she dominated Wilson's mind and body too. He could see the pain of their race, the apathy they had for the despicable being he was. She drowned him in the regret of their dead world and the cold-hearted vengeance they sought. The emptiness of their souls kept them strong and hard like the very armor they wore.

A warp sound emanated from the stone, getting louder as each light pulse slowed.

The time loop, Wilson thought in agony. *She's making a time loop and I can't stop it. She's taken my mind and I can't stop it!*

The city was spinning out of control, and Wilson didn't know how much longer he could hold on or if time mattered anymore.

A fate worse than death the general promised. And she cared not about her own warning as she melded her consciousness to the celestial stone, destroying his very essence, while simultaneously freezing time to save her race.

You know of true sorrow, he remembered Persephone's words. *It is not a one way road. . . All things must come to a balance or be consumed by the other, this rule is true on all planes of existence.*

Then a whisper: *Marshall.*

He felt something soft touch his cheek; a tendril of thought, familiar and tender.

He glanced up. The celestial stone's light was stretching toward him like it did in the central chamber of the compound. It was glowing bright, almost blinding.

And he thought of *her.*

Not of her death.

Of her. His Justine.

The joy he felt when she said yes on the beach, the tenderness and intimacy of their wedding, the overflow of adoration he felt for her when they talked, the careful caress of her smile that lifted his spirits when he was down. He remembered all the things that made her life beautiful and how they touched him, the memories to cherish. A joy that made all pain and suffering fade away, and the sorrow he felt for losing it. And how happy he was for his sorrow, for he knew he had felt true joy with his Justine.

He finally understood sorrow is the price humanity pays for joy, and it's worth it.

The Venusian General's eyes grew wide as Wilson's memories were forced to the forefront, taking control of the celestial stone's power. She no longer controlled him or the stone.

And it was too much for her.

The Venusian General released her grip. Wilson could feel it— she no longer had the strength to hold him, even with the advanced power of her suit. He could see her memory; all semblance of humanity conditioned out from an early age, trained to reject any and all sentiment. She never knew of joy or sorrow and never would. And he pitied her.

She was ill prepared. She could not handle the depth of his emotions. Her mind became lost to his will.

You will see me again, the voice of Justine emanated from the stone.

Don't look back, Persephone had warned him. *I give you a word of warning: Do not look back into the shadows the stone holds.*

Wilson gripped the edge of the fountain and closed his eyes.

Don't look back.

The floor was getting ready to rupture. And if the sulfuric gasses didn't kill him, then the impact of the ground would.

Don't look back.

Her voice called him. *You will see me again. . .*

He looked back.

And there she was, Justine as clear as day. Her shining, golden hair full and healthy, her crystal eyes glimmering beneath fine lashes, and a smile so full that all imperfections ceased. She wore her white sun dress, the same one she favored that day on the beach when she agreed to be his companion. It draped delicately over her curved body, flowing in the gentle sea air. But she was no longer a memory, not to him. The celestial stone made her memory—her shadow— real.

Wilson wept.

This was her at her best and brightest, how he wanted to remember her. The light of the stone one with his mind as she held a hand out to him, smiling her usual smile.

Marshall, she breathed.

She said he would see her, once again when he least expected it. He forced himself to believe her words; it was the only thing that kept him going all these years without her. He decided to believe it was this moment she spoke of, using the stones' power to be with her across time.

The pulse from the stone stopped and everything in the Grand Courtyard froze. The light increased, turning the Venusians into shadows as the room turned to white, bleaching out Wilson's sight to anything else.

Marshall Wilson continued to stare into the celestial stone, at the shade of the woman who had once been his wife. The light blinded him, but he could not tear his eyes from her. He had waited so long to see her again, to truly hear her voice and finally let go of his mourning. He could feel time stopping around him, embracing him to this space.

One phrase slipped from his mouth as he succumbed: "I see you, *Justine*."

And in a moment all was perfect. And in that moment the entire city flashed out of existence, into a realm that only theories of relativity could explain. His perfect moment looping for eternity.

A last whisper of a name echoed across the planet of love and beauty. Wilson's voice giving a final farewell to the hell he left behind. *Justine.*

Chapter 32: Savior of the Earth, Descendent of the Sun

I am quite interested in that captain of yours," Persephone said.

"Captain Marie Cocteau?" Admiral Jones scoffed.

"Yes," she said. "She's an extraordinary individual."

They were in his SIC conference quarters, a room covered by a dome of glass on the Venus station. It was a perfect view of space, Venus, and the surrounding moons.

Jones shifted uneasy in his seat. He sat at the end of the black table while she stood. He hated consulting with this girl that wasn't a girl. His superiors forced him to entertain and work with her, for her influence was great among Earth organizations. How she persuaded and made her way with little conflict was unknown to him.

"Be interested for the next six hours because she's getting ready to return to Earth," Jones said. "Out of here on the next transport. Along with that lawyer scumbag. Good riddance."

"Returning to Earth?" Persephone said, sitting with perfect posture. "Is that so? I can't imagine why SIC would want to send them back."

"Dangerous," he said, lighting a cigarette. "Too dangerous to even be kept confined to quarters. You saw what that maniac space archeologist did. Stole the Infinite and destroyed the whole damn city down there. Still can't figure out how he did it. I can't find anything after that implosion he created. Even took the rest of the artificial mountain with him. Nothing more than an asshole terrorist if you ask me. Probably sent by one of those anti-SIC, anti-corporate groups."

"I see," Persephone said. "Well, with Cerberus City gone, no trace of artificial material left on Venus, and the return of the indisposed crew members, it seems my concerns are alleviated. I too shall be returning to Earth."

"Why?" The admiral looked sincerely perplexed. She had insisted on being involved with the Venus project, and she wanted to leave it behind. "There's a lot more to do here."

"I have many other matters I must attend to," Persephone said. She watched out the window, looking at something the admiral could not figure out and stroking the stone in her necklace. "There are responsibilities to your Earth I cannot overlook."

"Good luck," Jones said. *And good riddance.*

"I shall be keeping a close eye on her indeed," Persephone said to herself. "On Cocteau and her posterity. She truly is something special. They all are."

* * *

Many weeks later...

Cocteau and Bitiir sat, strapped in the transport taking them from the moon orbiter to Earth.

They did not speak of what happened. Cocteau actively avoided Bitiir the entire journey from Venus to the moon orbiter. She wanted to hate him, for everything he did—the mission, Gomez's fate, dragging Wilson into it—she wanted to hate him for all of it.

And now she was trapped with him alone in the tourist side of the transport. She was no longer allowed access to anything beyond what SICs tourists received.

"Hmm," Bitiir hummed to himself.

"What?" Cocteau spat. He'd been sighing since they entered the transport, trying to passively get her attention.

"Just—" Bitiir shrugged his shoulders. He shook his head when she glared, refusing to look her in the eye. "Please, captain, hear me out."

"I'm not a captain anymore."

"Cocteau, please, there is something I must tell you."

"Keep it to yourself," she said. Her gaze became indifferent, warning him not to test her. "I was done with you a long time ago."

"It's about Gomez," Bitiir said.

All the more she didn't want to talk to him. She turned her indifferent gaze away from him.

"I know it eats at you," Bitiir said. "I know because it's eating away at me too. But it shouldn't for you. What happened to Gomez and Wilson wasn't your fault. It was mine."

Cocteau glanced at him. He folded his hands neatly, looking at them as he spoke. "The fault lies with both her and me. I know I said this mission, the station, everything was my doing, but really it was her project all along. She was the one who was going to change science, be immortalized by her discoveries and innovations. I promised her that. By all means none of us should've been there. Gomez, she's the one who got me into SIC, and I made Venus my project. But it never really was mine. It was hers all along, a dream she desperately wanted me to make a reality and I failed her. But even though I failed her, there is one thing that gives me solace; she passed in peace. Her final words—I know who they were for—and she was at peace with herself if she said them."

I'm afraid, the memory of Wilson's voice spoke to Cocteau. *But what the Venusians are, scares me more. That's why I have to go."*

A wave of emotional exhaustion swept through her.

Numb. That's how she felt. She had no more room to hate. She didn't have the energy to hate. She especially didn't have the energy to hate someone like Bitiir anymore.

And her face softened at Bitiir.

Cocteau did not mind the silence like he did. Somehow, she felt the need to break it for him. "You going home Bitiir?"

He looked at her quizzically. "You're asking me?"

"No one else is around," Cocteau gestured to the empty cabin.

"Yes," Bitiir said. "I'm going home."

"Where's home?"

"A small town in India," said with a far-off look. "My real home."

"Oh," Cocteau said. "I didn't realize you were Indian."

"Yes," he said, giving her an obvious expression. "Why?"

"I just thought you were British," she said. "You sound British, you act British. And you brag all the time that you're from London."

"I know," Bitiir said, his voice calm and level. "But I've always considered India my home; it was where I was happiest. You know, you're the first person from SIC I've told that I'm really from India. I never cared to let anyone know." He paused. "I didn't want them to know, if you get my meaning."

"I can understand that." Cocteau nodded. "Good thing I'm technically not from SIC." She sighed. "I'm guessing you have family there?"

"I do." Bitiir didn't smile. "They're coming to pick me up. At the bullet train station."

His face became stoic.

"Well don't go jumping head over heels to see them," Cocteau said, making light of the situation. She felt awkward.

"It's not that," Bitiir said. "I am happy to see them. I just don't know if they'll be happy to see me."

"Why wouldn't they?" Cocteau knew she was asking a loaded question. "They did come all the way from India for this."

Bitiir took a deep breath. "It's complicated."

Cocteau knew complicated.

"What about you?" Bitiir said.

"What about me?"

"What about *you?*" Bitiir emphasized. "Are you going back to any family?"

Cocteau noticed how chapped her lips were. She rolled them back.

"Come now," Bitiir said. "It can't be that bad."

"I have no family."

Bitiir raised an eyebrow. "Oh?"

Cocteau shook her head. "It's complicated."

It truly was. . .

He's dying you know, her mother's voice chided her years ago.

"And why should I care?" a younger Cocteau said to the transmission screen. She'd just spent a year on SICs moon orbiter. She was about to be transferred to Venus when news came about her father. "That man caused us nothing but misery."

Lucinda Cocteau's face hardened. Even with the delay of video transmissions, her reaction was quick.

"Really Marie, this is your father," Lucinda furrowed her brow like she always did when she disapproved. "He loved—"

"Don't," Cocteau fumed at being called Marie again. "You know as well as I do how he felt about me. This is your first transmission since I was exiled, and it's to tell me he's dying."

"You're so cold," Lucinda said. "That man provided for us, raised you."

"He made me miserable!" Cocteau said.

"You made him miserable," Lucinda scoffed. "So miserable that he can't even tell you himself—"

"Can't what?" Cocteau fumed. "Can't tell me himself that he's dying? Fat chance in hell at that! You know the real reason why he won't talk to me. And he won't. I humiliated him, Lucinda. It's what I am he's ashamed of, don't you understand? I didn't look or act enough like a girl, I didn't care about boys and that stuff that girls should—everything I am humiliates him."

Lucinda's face broke. "I just thought you should know, in case you wanted to come say goodbye."

Cocteau smiled, suppressing a laugh. Why? None of this was funny. "You know I can't leave without their consent."

"You can appeal for bereavement."

"No, I can't." Cocteau didn't know how to make her understand. She never could. "I am not allowed on Earth unless it's absolutely necessary for SIC. Even then, I am under strict observation when I go. Apparently I'm too dangerous."

"Cut that nonsense." Lucinda leaned forward. "You know as well as I do what this is really about. If you really wanted to come back, you'd find a way; you always have."

Cocteau knew there was truth in that, but it didn't change anything. "Lucinda—"

"Still won't call me mother?"

"Why should I?" Cocteau looked at the ceiling. "You never acted like one."

She could tell that one hurt. Lucinda looked away.

"Then I guess he's right not to call you daughter," Lucinda said. "He disowned you years ago anyway."

The screen cut-out.

"Cocteau?" Bitiir waved for her attention. "Are you alright?"

"Sorry," she said, adjusting her mind to the present. "I was just—ugh, it doesn't matter."

"Listen," Bitiir pursed his lips. Not in a frustrated or angry way, but sympathetically. "We've known one another for a while now, albeit, not on the best terms. I'm sure you resent me and I don't blame you. I can assure you I resent myself more. Besides that, I think we know each other well enough that I can ask you this: when are you going to love yourself enough to finally be happy?"

Cocteau was taken aback. She opened her mouth to snap at him, yell obscenities. But no sound came out.

"It's okay," he smiled gently, genuine unlike his usual forced one. "Who am I to ask? I promise, I know a thing or two about loving yourself. I loved myself a little too much to see how I hurt those around me. But Cocteau, you don't seem to love yourself at all, to the point you cannot see how it hurts you and others. After today, I don't think we will ever see one another again, but I hope I can leave you with more than what I did on Venus."

"Bitiir—"

"Please," he said raising a hand.

Cocteau looked at his eyes. For once they did not dodge her gaze, but looked deep, his facade finally gone. This was the real Bitiir.

"Abdul," he said. "Call me Abdul."

Cocteau nodded.

She remembered flashes of Gomez's face smiling, heard Wilson's laugh. That was how she wanted to remember them. Maybe she could do Bitiir one better and tell him the one thing she could never tell them. "Thank you."

Chapter 33:
Reconciliation and Hope

There wasn't much to say as Cocteau and Bitiir parted ways at the bullet train station. They weren't close to begin with, so there was nothing in their farewells.

Cocteau stepped through the crowd, wearing civilian clothes for the first time since she liked to remember. She only donned her dog tags, a keepsake of the life she was forced to leave behind.

It wasn't as though she hadn't been back to Earth since her banishment; she led plenty of teams through the SIC transport system. But this time was different. She was alone, stripped of all titles, honors, and authority. She always had a directive, an objective to fill, a mission to complete. Presently, she only had obscurity.

Wilson did the members of his landing team a favor when he defied SIC. SIC wanted no connection with them or the incident on Venus. They were free.

She was free.

The sign above her directed guests to ticket purchases. She glanced to the side.

"Abdul?"

He was maybe twenty feet away. He didn't see or take notice of her. He didn't need to. He was surrounded by something more intriguing.

An old woman, dressed in traditional Indian clothes and a hijab, sat in a wheelchair and held his hand. Two adult women, feminine versions of Bitiir, were gleefully hugging him. They stepped aside as a tall man stepped in front.

He was identical to Bitiir, except in the eyes; the eyes were old, sorrowful to his years. He smiled, talking Bitiir in his arms, kissing him atop his head.

Cocteau couldn't see his face as it was buried into the tall man's chest. She walked away.

When are you going to love yourself enough to finally be happy?

Is that what you were talking about Abdul? She shook her head. *Because I can't, I just can't!"*

She continued toward ticket sales. The final threshold, she could choose any bullet train, any direction. She saved enough money from her time serving SIC. She could run away from this life as far as she wanted—just like she had always done—and start over fresh, with no connections and with no one.

This is your decision, her final words to Wilson. *And you will need to be the one who lives with the consequences. Are you ready for that Wilson. . . Are you ready to risk everything?*

She stopped in her tracks.

"What am I doing?"

Cocteau was not perfect and never would be.

She thought, Does it matter?

She sighed, falling onto a bench, setting her duffle bag next to her. There wasn't much in it; light enough to lift with one hand. She leaned her head back.

I want to be happy, she thought. *Like Abdul back there, like Gomez when she talked about her mother, like Wilson when he thought about whoever it was he left behind on Earth. I want joy, even if there's a cost.*

Someone coughed and she felt her duffle bag move.

"What the hell?" She sat up. Someone touched her bag. A thief? She looked for the culprit.

A man, in his mid-thirties, had taken a seat beside her on the bench, looking through a brochure. Her bag was still on the bench, creating a barrier between them.

Who does he think he is, touching my bag to make room for his ass? I'll show him!

Gomez's face suddenly appeared. *You know what your problem is— you keep saying 'I'. You always try to do things on your own, you never need anyone else's help. And you don't care who you hurt in the process.*

Cocteau took a deep breath.

She threw her duffle bag on the ground, stuffing it under the bench.

The man looked up from his brochure. "Um, hello?"

Cocteau smiled. "Hi."

"Can I help you?"

"I'm sorry," she said. "I just realized my bag was taking up a lot of room, and this is a very crowded station."

"It's okay," he laughed. "I should've been more careful when I sat down not to bump it. You probably thought I was trying to steal it or something, which judging by your dog tags, I would've regretted doing so."

Cocteau shook her head, laughing. *Finally, someone with some sense.* She noticed the brochure he was reading: military recruitment. "Are you interested in the military?"

"Ah, this?" he stuffed it into his jacket. "Just a hobby of mine. I'm too old to join, but I still like to read about it."

"Oh," Cocteau said. "Well I definitely know a thing or two."

"Really?" he said. "Could I ask you some questions? It's not everyday you meet someone with military experience."

"You know what?" Cocteau didn't recognize her own voice. Was she saying all this? "This may be a little forward, but I can tell you all about my military career over dinner. That is, if you like, and you don't have any travel plans—even though you're in a train station." Cocteau hated looking weak. *This is a mistake.*

The man looked up considering it. "I don't mind forward," he smiled. "It's actually refreshing. I just arrived back in town and my ride isn't going to be here for a while. Lunch?"

Cocteau felt a tightness in her chest lessen. Had it been there this entire time?

"Yes," she said. "That sounds great."

"I'm Sean." He held out his hand. What's your name?

Cocteau smiled, taking it. "Marie."

The End

Afterword

Hell is not a world of fire and brimstone as described by Dante. It is a cold mindset. The complete halt of progression.

There is no doubt that William Shakespeare created some of the most memorable and fascinating characters. Why were they so memorable, and why do we still enjoy them today? It's because, for the most part, they had flaws. Of all the characters he created, the ones furthest from perfection are the one ones we relate to the most.

During his time as a playwright, the medical world believed in the four humors: black bile, red bile, green bile, and yellow bile. An imbalance in any of these biles meant that you were sick, either physically or mentally.

Shakespeare's imperfect characters had flaws attributed to the imbalance in one or more of these biles. An imbalance of black bile meant that you were depressed, mourning, and unable to let go. An imbalance of red bile meant that you were angry, chaotic, and out of control. An imbalance of green bile meant that you were envious, selfish, and easily jealous of those around you. And finally, an imbalance of yellow bile meant you were too ambitious, overzealous and overbearing.

How does knowing character flaws of classic literature and humans help us understand humanity and its role within our lives?

In Greek legend Orpheus fell to the temptation to look back at the shadow of his dead lover, even when Persephone warned him not to. Marshall Wilson did the same. Why was this so? Because they were human and it's believable that they would look back. The four humors create real, imperfect humans. We're all real, imperfect humans.

The Venusians were far from the immortal perfection they hoped for. Their downfall was not embracing their own humanity.

Marie Cocteau decides to finally embrace her imperfections and asks us 'Does it matter?'. When we reflect on the imperfect nature of humanity, and see the joy given us in overcoming our weaknesses, we can answer her question: Yes, it does matter and it's okay.

We are human after all.

About the Author

H.B. Nuttall is a writer and educator, working professionally for over a decade. She's written and presented entire course curriculums on writing. She currently teaches secondary level writing classes. She completed her graduate studies at *Grand Canyon University.*

Raised in the Finger Lakes region of New York, she now resides in central Arizona with her husband and children. She is a member of the *American Night Writers Association.*

Connect:
Website: www.hbnuttallwriting.com
Instagram: hb_nuttall_writer
Twitter: @HBnuttallwriter
Facebook: @H.B. Nuttall